Also by Kathleen O'Reilly

The Diva's Guide to Selling Your Soul

Looking for
Mr. Goodbunny

KATHLEEN O'REILLY

doWn tOwn press

New York   London   Toronto   Sydney

An *Original* Publication of POCKET BOOKS

DOWNTOWN PRESS, published by Pocket Books
1230 Avenue of the Americas
New York, NY 10020

Library of Congress Cataloging-in-Publication Data

O'Reilly, Kathleen.
    Looking for Mr. Goodbunny / Kathleen O'Reilly.
       p. cm.
    "An original publication of Pocket Books"—T.p. verso.
    ISBN-13: 978-0-7434-9941-5
    ISBN-10:   0-7434-9941-7
       1. Single women—New York (State)—New York—Fiction. 2. Man-woman
relationships—Fiction. 3. Personal coaching—Fiction. 4. Mate selection—
    Fiction. I. Title: Looking for Mister Goodbunny. II. Title.

    PS3615.R454L66 2006
    813'.6—dc22   2006040249

This Downtown Press trade paperback edition July 2006

10 9 8 7 6 5 4 3 2 1

DOWNTOWN PRESS and colophon are
trademarks of Simon & Schuster, Inc.

Designed by Jaime Putorti

Manufactured in the United States of America

For information regarding special discounts for bulk purchases,
please contact Simon & Schuster Special Sales at 1-800-456-6798
or business@simonandschuster.com.

Acknowledgments

I would like to express my appreciation to Carla Birnberg, who answered lots of questions regarding life coaches. And many thanks to Lauren Lipton for her patience and help with all my journalism questions. And also to Erin at Babeland for her patience and help with all my female toy questions . . . and mainly for never laughing.

Looking for
Mr. Goodbunny

Prologue

I live in a one-bedroom apartment on the Upper East Side. A quiet place, with off-white walls, a galley kitchen that doubles as storage for my reference books, and a view of the East River, which sounds more picturesque than it is. The water's not too murky, but the dismembered bodies that get fished out on a quarterly basis ruin the ambience.

Anyway, I like my place, because it's my castle. At night, it's just me, my television, and the pink pearl bunny that makes me smile. As I was growing up, I found various methods of pleasuring myself, some creative, some adventurous, and some not completely sanitary. But one fine spring day, via an anonymous mail-order site on the Web, I took back my orgasms from all the black-hearted cads who were determined to leave me either bro-kenhearted or celibate—or both. It had taken the best part of my adult years to find the key to my own sensual nature, the so-lution being a motor-powered rocket launcher that didn't care if my hips were too wide. When the stress of my solitary existence got to me, I'd take out my frisky friend and let him have his way with me.

I settled myself down on the couch for my nightly ritual, *The Late Show with David Letterman* and my vibrator.

Over the years, I've learned the value of a good vibrator. It's there when you need it, never insults you, never tells you it had a good time, blah, blah, blah. And best of all, me and Mr. Bunny have been together ten long years. That's more than most marriages I know of.

So as the Top Ten List counted down, so did I.

I turned on Mr. Bunny's controller, and he buzzed just as he's supposed to.

High . . .

Higher . . .

Highest . . .

Click.

No, that wasn't me. Mr. Bunny wasn't turning anything on.

I spent a few quality minutes cursing the undependable nature of batteries and then padded over to where I kept the spares. I padded back to the couch, took an extra sip of wine, and flicked the switch on the controller, ready for liftoff.

Silence.

Okay, maybe those batteries were bad, too.

I tried one pair after another, my fingers working frantically, until I had emptied my battery drawer, and the painful truth began to settle in: my bunny had died.

It seemed like only yesterday that he arrived in a brown-paper package, discreetly addressed from M&L Manufacturing, and my love life had never looked back.

I took Mr. Bunny and his wire-attached controller in my hands, thinking that maybe the batteries were overrated. After a few fumbling attempts at manual maneuvering, I discovered they weren't.

My stress levels were still heart-attack high, the wine bottle was empty, and even *Letterman* was a rerun.

You ever had one of those days? When the best part of the day turned to crap?

Mr. Bunny had been a faithful companion for ten years. He was my rebound lover, my Friday night lover, my lover when I didn't feel like shaving my legs. He was Everyman to me—in many ways, far superior.

I hated to say good-bye, mainly because with the death of Mr. Bunny, I had no excuse not to go out into the world to try to find a replacement. A real replacement that's powered with blood and passion rather than AA batteries. It had been a long time since I had a man in my life. Three long, lonely years, not that I expect your sympathy, although it'd be nice.

To be perfectly fair, men provided several things that Mr. Bunny could not. Conversation, usually centered on their life, their work, or another woman's breasts. The warmth of human touch, usually as precursor to asking for either a loan or a blow job—sometimes both at the same time. But they were human. They had a human touch, something Mr. Bunny could never acquire.

With a heavy heart, I wrapped him in the Sunday Style section and laid his translucent pink form out on a casket designed by Pyrex, offering a quiet thanks for the memories.

I placed a single finger over the on/off switch and pushed one last time. Hoping against hope for some sign of life.

Alas, it was not to be.

Eventually, I realized I could not mourn my tiny companion forever, so I removed him from the Pyrex and then buried him in my kitchen trash, right beneath the container of three-day-old Szechuan chicken.

I tried television, music, but nothing felt right. Finally, I showered and went to bed. After a couple of hours tossing and turning, I knew what I had to do.

First chance I got, I was going to find a new vibrator.

One

The first step in self-realization is looking hard in the mirror. When you hit your teens, you count pimples; your thirties, you count gray hairs; and when it's too late, Xanax works well.

—ELLE SHEFFIELD

They were sheep in dire need of a sheepherder. Three women alone on the town, and I was their guide. One of the illuminati leading the way through the highways and byways of empowerment in a male-dominated society. My name is Elle Sheffield, and I'm their life coach.

The restaurant was Town. A dark, cavernous place where the air-conditioning always runs too high and martinis cost more than most apartments, but I was there with my group to prove that if they could make it in New York, they could make it anywhere. Since we all lived in New York, this was an important concept.

Barbara McKee, who was my inaugural patient, was short, with frosted blond hair, and had the look of a gun-shy Chihuahua, complete with the ADD eyes that made it seem as if she was always in over her head. She glanced around, checking out the full lunchtime crowd. It was a happening place; I reserve only the best for my ladies.

As the hostess led us to our table, I gave them all a perky smile, full of confidence, just to give them a little upper. "We're here for dessert and drinks only. Got it?"

Tanja didn't look happy, not that Tanja ever looked happy. At twenty-four, she was the baby in my group. There were bus drivers with better people skills than Tanja. But she was improving. Slowly.

"But it's the middle of the afternoon. We're supposed to be having lunch," she said, her frown set in cement.

I quirked an eyebrow at her. "And that's the point. We're going to do something unexpected—out of the norm. Today, ladies, you need to visualize yourself standing out in the crowd. That's our assignment."

There was general unhappiness in the air. Barbara was nervous, as usual. Tanja was plucking at her nonexistent sweater lint, until I gently, yet firmly, moved her hand away. Joan looked calm and poised; however, I knew it was a sham—she gets this little tic in her cheek, it's a dead giveaway.

As often happens to the unsuspecting passive-aggressive diner, our table turned out to be near the kitchen, the pans slapping around at deafening intervals. Before the hostess could pawn off the cheap seats on us, I grabbed her arm. "Excuse me. Can you give us the table near the bar? It's too loud back here, and we have important things to talk about."

The hostess, probably an *Apprentice* castoff, stared pointedly at my hand on her arm. I had invaded her personal space. Like I cared. I wasn't giving up until I got what I wanted.

"I'm sorry, that table is reserved," she said, her mouth curved in what some might call a smile. I saw it for the gauntlet it was.

"I'm sure they'd understand," I said, smiling back. I pointed to a couple of suits who were arguing over the check. "And look, there's another one over there. It's about to break." I looked at my three ladies, letting them see how the big boys handle things.

The hostess shook free of my hand. I let her. "This is all we have currently. If you'd like to try back later when the restaurant is less crowded . . ."

And would I let such matters slide? Was I gonna let some diva wannabe spoil six months' worth of counseling and intensive therapy? I was forty-two years old, and there were some truths that I'd discovered to be self-evident: pigs only fly when thrown from a building.

"We'll take that one," I said, pointing to a table near the bar. It was the premium spot in the restaurant, and we all knew it.

"But I said—"

I held up the hand of peace. "I know what you said. Give us the table, or we'll make a scene. You know what that means? Food flying, drinks spilling, waiters tripping, and my friend has Tourette's."

Of course she was cowed. She picked up the menus with a little huff and led us to the power table. As we settled in, I gave my girls a smile.

"You see what happens when you assert yourself to people? They're used to pawns, but each one of you is a queen." It was a lesson that I'd been trying to teach them for some time, but I think I was the only one who was buying it.

"Are you sure this place is good? This food looks a little queer," Tanja said, studying the plates passing by, before falling into a black lacquer chair.

Barbara stared down, her cheeks flushed even with the thermostats running on full. It was April, the start of spring, the best time of the year to be out and about in the city. "I think I'll get a salad. And maybe some antipasto."

"Barbara, it's drinks and dessert only. Remember, we're here to assert ourselves, not suffer through the dregs of intimidation by some twenty-year-old ignoranus who wouldn't know customer service if it bit her on the butt."

"Maybe just an appetizer?" she tried.

I shook my head. "You have to stand up for what you want, Barbara."

"But I want an appetizer," she argued.

"No," I told her. "End of discussion."

When the waiter came up, I handed him all four menus.

"My name is Todd, and I'll be your waiter this afternoon," he said, one hand poised to write. "Are you ready to order?"

"Not just yet. We only need the dessert menu," I said, and gave him my queenly smile.

He was peeved that I'd upset his little apple cart of routine, and he gave me his queenly smile, too. "I'll be back."

I turned to my group and made sure each was seeing the

ritual of power being played out before them. "Look how easy. And none of you is dead from embarrassment. Isn't that nice?"

Joan coughed at that. She was a fifty-five-year-old widow who was just starting to wade back into the dating pool. Her late husband owned a chain of boutique hotels, so she was loaded, which made the wading somewhat less painful. She made a show of putting her napkin in her lap, and we all followed suit. She had more class in her little finger than all the ladies of *The View* combined. "I didn't realize the restaurant would be so dark. I would have worn something more yellow."

For anyone to understand the absurdity of this remark, you would have to meet Joan. She's very tall and chain-smoker thin, with short brandy-brown hair that she kept perfectly styled. She usually wore warmer colors that matched her coloring, but whatever she picked, it was always fabulous and always expensive. Even I, who eschewed a career in design because I chose not to starve, appreciated her refined style.

"You look lovely, Joan. The maroon is the perfect color for your complexion," I said. "Tanja, what do you think?" I asked, testing her.

Tanja glanced at Joan, back at me, then pinged back to Joan. "Don't you think yellow makes people look dead? I would've worn something with pink. Or beige," she said. I took in her black FCUK T-shirt and wiped the sweat from my brow. Still, I lived for challenges.

"What are you doing, huh? Joan's a human being. With feelings. You can't just tromp all over them."

"I didn't mind," Joan drawled, which goes to show you what a class act Joan really was.

I gave her a little smile. "But I do. Tanja has to learn how to treat people—better."

Tanja's chin dropped into her chest. "Sorry."

"Build a bridge, Tanja. The first order of business is making small talk," I said, and launched a discussion of the political implications of a Euro-Chinese trade pact on the fashion industry. We were just getting into the spirit of things, when Todd returned bearing a tray of pastries. "The chocolate beignets are the house specialty, there's a soft vanilla cake dusted in white chocolate, warm lemon madeleines covered in anise sugar, and my favorite, the passion fruit pudding, served with warm huckleberries. What about it, ladies? One of each?"

Barbara nodded.

I cut in before this turned into a full-fledged submissive fest. "No. We need four cosmopolitans, plus a bottle of sparkling water for the table. Bring the water first, and then we'll take three orders of the beignets, and I'd like a bowl of vanilla ice cream."

Todd stopped writing. "We don't have ice cream."

"But aren't the beignets served with ice cream?"

"This is not Baskin-Robbins. Our desserts are a feast for the eyes, as well as the culinary appetite."

The toady was starting to piss me off, and I could feel the blood pressure pumping through my veins, my little corpuscles going bonkers. "I know, but we can make an exception, can't we?"

"No, we can't."

By now Barbara and Tanja were shooting each other nervy looks, but this lesson needed to be taught. "Can we talk to the chef?"

"The chef is not here," Todd snapped, the pen drumming against the paper.

"Then who's cooking?" I asked, bravely fighting the urge to steal his pen.

"The sous chef."

"Can we speak to him, please?"

"No."

I patted my lips with my napkin, just so this little twit understood that I knew his game and wasn't nervous at all. "Vanilla ice cream. Two scoops. Do it."

"No."

"Do you know who I am?"

Todd rolled his eyes.

I dug through my purse and flashed him my driver's license, snapping it shut before he could get a good look. "My name is Amanda Hesser. I review for the *Times*."

Instantly his whole demeanor changed to critic-loving sycophant. "Of course. Of course. Of course. Miss Hesser."

"It's *Mrs.* Hesser to you," I said, but I gave him a wink to soften the harshness of his meager reality. "But don't blow my cover, will you? We're supposed to be anonymous."

He gave a quick nod, and then quicker than you could say, "Four stars, highly recommended," he returned with our drinks.

Barbara eyed me with a combination of admiration and fear. "You told him a lie."

"Yes, yes, I did. But I got what I wanted, didn't I?"

"But what if we get caught? We could get thrown out of here, and I need to eat. My blood sugar gets really low, and you all don't want to be around me when my sugar is low. I get really nasty."

I took a long draw on my cosmopolitan. "Do you think they want to admit that they give a restaurant critic special attention? What sort of service model is that? No, Todd'll keep a secret. Trust me," I told her, and changed the subject before she could argue further. "How's your maid?"

Barbara wouldn't meet my eyes, a bad omen.

"What'd she take this time?" I asked, heaving a heavy sigh.

"A brooch that my mother gave me."

Joan fingered the diamond brooch on her lapel. "I don't understand why you don't fire her."

"I did," Barbara answered.

I looked at her with new respect. "A win for Barbara! Way to go!"

"But she didn't understand me."

Tanja snorted. "Yeah, right."

"No, I swear, she doesn't speak enough English," Barbara answered, looking miserable.

I took pity on her but decided to use the opportunity for another lesson. "Okay, ladies, we need a plan for Barbara. Put yourself in her shoes. If you were her, how would you fire Imelda?"

Tanja spoke up first, her fingers kneading her shirtsleeve. "Change the locks."

I nodded with approval but placed her fingers back on the table where they belonged. "Nice, nice."

"I should decrease the insurance deductible, don't you think?" Barbara answered.

We all gave her the Look. She got the Message.

Just then Todd arrived with the desserts. I pulled out a notepad and paper and started jotting what I thought looked like critic notes.

"Is everything to your satisfaction, Mrs. Hesser?"

I put a finger to my lips. "Ssshhh . . ."

"Is everything to your satisfaction, Mrs. Hesser-Smythson?" he said loudly.

"It looks divine. Thank you, Todd," I said, giving him the "Go away kid, you bother me" glare.

After he scurried away, I gave the group my little pep talk, and I could see my girls bloom under my eyes. My new profession gave me a lot of personal satisfaction, but then, I've always loved telling people what to do.

Over dessert and cosmopolitans we continued to plot the future demise of Barbara's maid. Killing her was too complicated, and Barbara had issues with calling her on the carpet. Joan, who had probably fired scores of maids, had the best solution. "You merely threaten to call immigration," she said, in her husky million-dollar voice.

Barbara frowned, little feather marks forming in her pink lipstick. "What if I just had someone call my answering machine when she was cleaning? I can bribe my doorman to do it, and when she hears the message, don't you think she'd run?"

"Unless she truly doesn't understand English," I said, willing to give the petty-thief the benefit of the doubt.

"Larry is going to be so mad," she said. "He doesn't like for me to do the housework."

Larry, as if you couldn't guess, is Barbara's more dominant other half. I suspected she fetched his slippers every night, and I knew for a fact that she planned elaborate menus every day for their dinner. Now, I was a liberated woman, who had never learned to cook worth beans (blame it on the Manhattan kitchens; they're very small), and I'd never been married, either, so I was a little suspicious of the whole arrangement and suspected Larry of trying to revive the patriarchal heydays of the '50s one homemade bread loaf at a time. However, on that subject, I kept my mouth shut. I needed all the clients I could get. "What about you? What do you like?" I asked, trying to get her to stop thinking about Mr. Cro-Magnon for a minute.

Barbara stared at me, thinking for a minute. "I like housework."

Tanja didn't have my tact. "That's so Marxist."

"Maids serve a necessary function in the social environs, filling the lower levels in the labor chain. They're required simply because no one else will do it. A lady can't work. It's déclassé." Joan finished her little speech by popping a beignet elegantly into her mouth. I swear, her jaw never moved when she chewed.

"I don't care," said Barbara in a wonderful show of courage.

I held up my last bite of ice cream (divine) and toasted her.

"There's your answer. Don't tell him you fired her, then you do the cleaning. He'll never guess."

"I couldn't do that to him."

"You could, and you should," I told her. I had no respect for a woman who situated her own needs underneath those of a man, even if he was putting the bread and butter on the table.

Joan, who was much more amenable when it was someone else's life, waved a hand, which happened to sport a rock the size of Gibraltar. "You pocket the money he gives you for the maid. Go out and get a new outfit. Barneys is having their warehouse sale next week. If you're going to turn your skin to sandpaper, the least you can do is dress well."

"Really?" asked Barbara, starting to see the advantages to the arrangement.

Even Tanja nodded in agreement.

"How's the morning commute coming along?" I asked Tanja.

"I haven't met anybody," she answered, twirling her last beignet around on her plate. "There was one notice in Missed Connections that I thought could have been me, but the guy said she was 'decorative.' " She winced.

"It could have been you," I told her, trying to prop up her self-confidence. But she was right. *Decorative* wasn't the adjective for Tanja. She had never quite outgrown the goth movement and was a huge fan of black lipstick. It wasn't her best look, but I respected her need for independence and attention. The world was full of people trying to fit in, and it needed more of those who danced to their own drummer.

She rolled her eyes at me. "Reality check. Decorative: not."

15

Joan patted her hand. "You'll find your Mr. Perfect Commuter."

"He'll run away screaming when I open my mouth," she said.

"Tanja. Is that a positive or a negative projection?"

"It's a true projection."

"We all have our flaws," said Joan quietly, and got me wondering what flaw she could possibly possess.

"Don't worry, Tanja. Joan's right. You'll find him," I said.

We stopped talking shop and moved on to the latest gossip. Running down other people's lives was pretty much a highlight for us. Just as we were contemplating the supermodel Anya Koptelova getting busted for coke possession while cruising the LIE in her Ferrari, I felt the impact of drinking four glasses of spring water.

"Excuse me for a moment," I said, and then sprinted down the stairs two at a time.

The ladies' room was a tiny two-staller that had seen better days. You expect more in the nice places, I don't know why. I hung my bag up on the coat hook and then noticed the stall latch was busted. Muttering about the decline of the service economy in this country, I checked out the other stall.

Same difference.

Well, heck, heck, heck. My bladder moved to red alert, and I was trying to keep the stall door shut, but it was just out of my reach. Then I heard voices outside the door.

A cold sweat broke out on my brow, and I thought back to all my little homilies that were supposed to give confidence. Didn't work.

16

My worst nightmares occurred in open bathroom stalls. For other people, it was running naked or great white sharks. For me, it was being caught tending to my business. I'd read in one of my books that if you faced your fears head-on, you'd see how silly they were. I knew I could do it. I mean, I was a grown adult. I counted to three and told myself no one was going to break in, that everything was going to be fine. However, there are some opinions that are destined for failure.

I exited the ladies' room and ducked into the relative security of the men's restroom, which—of course—had a lock on the single stall. Chauvinism was truly alive and well and living in America. Women were second-class citizens, each and every one of us. Talk about your crappy deals. The management probably didn't even bother maintaining the ladies' facilities. I finished my business while drafting the letter to the restaurant management in my head.

Then the outer door opened, but I knew not to panic, I could wait this one out.

I checked out the shoes (scuffy loafers with a hole in the toe) and revised the letter in my head, waiting for Mr. Loafer to utilize the urinal that God intended for men. Apparently his business involved more, because his shoe began to tap on the tile floor.

Well, double heck.

There I was, stuck, but not for long. I had spent my life dodging exposure, so it only took a moment for inspiration to strike.

I put myself together, pulled my sunglasses from my bag,

and slammed open the stall door. Using my hand to guide me, I patted my way to the sink, turned on the faucet, and washed up. Then I looked in the mirror into the triumphant eyes of Todd, the waiter from hell.

"Mrs. Hesser, I presume?" he said.

I'd been in tighter spots than this, and I wasn't about to let this little peon act superior. "Your bathrooms are atrocious. The ladies' room is a disaster."

"Which would matter if you were Amanda Hesser, but you're not."

"Try me," I said, smiling, still confident.

"We've got your picture on the wall in the back. There's dart holes on it, but you can make out the dark eyes, the tiny build." His eyes raked over me. "You're busted, lady, and unless you want me to embarrass you in front of your friends . . ."

My smile wilted. I had an image to uphold in front of my group, and getting called on the carpet by Todd the waiter dude wasn't the image I wanted upheld. "What do you want?"

"Fifty bucks on the tip."

"You're nuts," I said, and started to walk out the door. It was easier than you'd think because my credit limit wouldn't support that much extortion.

"They're your friends, and they really do seem to look up to you." Todd started tapping his little black-loafered foot.

A million insults sprang to my tongue, but none of them made it out. Todd merely smiled. I closed my eyes briefly in defeat.

"Whatever you want," I lied. "And now, if you'll excuse me,

the stench in here is starting to make me ill." I slammed open the door and scurried back to the table, holding tight to my stomach, not a complete charade.

"Ladies, we have to leave. I think I'm going to be sick," I said, packing up my bag.

"We're just gonna stiff this place?" said Tanja. She thought about it for a minute. "Awesome."

I groaned with extreme pain, only partially faked. "No. I took care of it," I lied, and then spotted Todd out of the corner of my eye. "We have to leave. *Now,*" I said, and gathered up my things.

Like the good sheep they were, they followed.

Two

Failure is not an option, unless you're a born loser.

—ELLE SHEFFIELD

My home life, Mr. Bunny excluded, had never been much. My evenings, Mr. Bunny excluded, were usually quiet, introverted, and full of take-out. I had finished my left-over Chinese, when my upstairs neighbor, Maureen Murphy, called. She worked long hours as an attorney for some high-brow firm downtown. When her day was really bad, she came over for a little whine with wine.

Sadly, she had rheumatoid arthritis in her legs, so she always called before she came down to see me, just to see if I was home.

I looked at my television longingly, but it would have to wait. So I pulled out a bottle of pinot and changed from sweat pants into my good jeans. I had a successful, independent image to protect. Sweat pants wouldn't cut it.

"Can I kill her?" were the first words out of her mouth. Maureen hated her boss, Dora the Abhorra.

I handed her a glass without missing a beat. Maureen was a woman who knew what she wanted in life, but unfortunately, life didn't want the same things. That's the way it is for big people. Sometimes I wondered if I kept Maureen around just because she made me look skinny. Not many of my acquaintances possessed that particular quality. However, on days like today, when there was no one around to notice my svelteness, I knew my suspicions about a weakness in my character were unfounded. Truth be told, I liked her.

Not having an independent image to protect, she usually wore sweat pants to tramp around the building in.

"Your boss is not worth going to jail for."

"But look how good Martha Stewart's sentence turned out. Her net worth gained an extra three zeroes, and she lost twenty pounds, all while relaxing in the soothing confines of minimum security. I could do that," she said, and promptly collapsed in my favorite brown overstuffed chair. I've learned not to quibble.

You know how they always talk about chubby girls having really pretty faces? In Maureen's case, it was true. She had this long dark hair that fell to her waist and a flawless complexion that had nothing to do with Elizabeth Arden and everything to do with her Guernsey English forebears. Package all that with intelligent brown eyes, and she could've been a Lane Bryant model. Well, except for the arthritis.

21

"Legs bothering you?" I asked, mainly because she had them stretched out like a bridge in front of her.

"Like fire. I think I'm gonna sue. Can I sue? I should sue."

I took a sip of wine because I sensed this one could go on forever. "You'll get fired." As someone who had experienced the injustice of a pink slip, I got hives just thinking about it.

"They have laws to protect the disabled."

"What'd she do today?"

"The Mancusi case. She's found another sixteen file boxes for me to index, reference, cross-reference, and catalog. I could win the case if they'd just let me sink my teeth into it. I went into her office, ready to tell her off, but she just stared down at me with those little pince-nez of hers. God, I swear she thinks she's John Lennon," Maureen said, then took another sip. This looked to be a two-bottle day, but if you saw my wine cabinet (i.e., the top of my refrigerator), you'd know I was prepared.

"Sorry," I murmured, which I knew was a useless answer, because Maureen didn't need answers; she just needed someone to listen. "Maybe they'll fire her ass."

Maureen shook her head. "No. She's a lesbian. The fear of a wrongful termination lawsuit would kill any possibility of rescuing my sanity and my legs."

"So make her quit."

For the first time Maureen ignored the wine. "How?"

"I don't know. You're the lawyer," I said, because I knew the value of plausible deniability. Blaming your life coach for failure can really kill a business.

Maureen began to scheme, her formerly intelligent eyes turning into little, beady pebbles of destruction. "I have her e-mail password," she said, and then looked at me hopefully.

Now, a moment of past history here. Before I embarked on my career as a life coach, I spent fifteen years of pure drudgery doing technical support for a media database company in Brooklyn. It was a paycheck, nothing more, and they tossed me aside like a used MetroCard. I'd recovered from the trauma, or so I kept telling myself.

"Okay, let's play hypothetical. Assuming you could hack into your company's e-mail server, who would you send something to?"

Maureen's mouth twisted in a hard smile. It's always the lawyers, you know? Remind me never to get on her bad side. "L.T.—partner and loverboy to most of the perky blondes in the firm. She's all over him during the day—the big fraud—just because he thinks all the women must love him. It'd be a snap to create something lurid and embarrassing."

"And completely untraceable," I added, because in her deepest heart of hearts, Maureen was a coward. We sprouted matching grins, the manifestation of long-term injustices, both real and imagined, and less than seven minutes later, Dora the Abhorra had started an e-mail conversation with partner Loverboy.

L.T.,

I just wanted to tell you how much I appreciated the compliment you gave me on the Mancusi documents. I've been working very hard to make a case for RICO, and I'm so glad that you agree with me that documents go a long way toward establishing a colorable claim. And did I tell you, that suit you were wearing looked tres sharp. Armani? Yummy.

Doris P. Winchell

"You're sure this is untraceable?" Maureen asked, her finger poised over the SEND button.

"You're clear. Their firewall is a joke," I answered. Okay, I wasn't exactly Bill Gates, but I knew enough to be dangerous. "You think she'll do anything when she gets a reply?"

"L.T. won't reply. He doesn't put anything in writing unless he has to."

"Then you're set," I said, and waited for her to press the button, because I sure as heck wasn't gonna do it. She took a deep breath, punched the keys, and stared at the screen for a long time, as if she could see the bits floating through the air. I knew how that stuff worked and humored her with my patience.

For about another thirty seconds.

"Want to stay and watch television?" I asked, feeling charitable because without Mr. Bunny, the evenings were longer than usual.

"Nah," she said, giving me a bored shrug.

I blinked, not sure I was reading her body language correctly. "What about your mother? How's her back? Getting up and around?" I asked.

"Listen, I need to head off—" she started, and I realized that yes, I was getting the brush-off.

I feigned a yawn. "I'm gonna be a zombie if I don't get some sleep soon," I interrupted, needing to be the first to deliver the cold shoulder.

"Have you talked to your doctor about that? It could be narcolepsy. They have drugs you can take for it."

I opened the door. "Not a narcoleptic, Maureen. I'll see you tomorrow, and I'll think good Doris and L.T. thoughts."

Maureen unsettled from her chair. "Oh, fine. Leave me alone with my worries and psychosis, but someday—"

I shut the door before she could finish. I think in another life, Maureen was a pharmacist.

Every Tuesday, Frank came over so he could help me with the books. Frank's an older guy, in his late sixties, who used to work at Bear Stearns before he was forced out. He had started as my client, but when I found out he was an accountant, I hired him.

That morning he was working on the sofa, his laptop and portable desk neatly laid out, his dapper white shirtsleeves folded neatly to the elbow, just like always. However, today he kept watching the apartment building across the street. He looked so melancholy, I decided to break the silence and see what's what.

"Gloomy day, huh?" I said, gesturing toward the window where the rain was coming down in sheets.

"I'll get back to work," he said, and put his fingers back on the keyboard, making me feel like the boss from hell.

"No, no, I didn't mean that. Is something bothering you? We haven't talked in a while . . ."

He stayed silent for a minute and then removed his hands from the keyboard. "Do you ever feel like life is passing you by?"

That was a sticky question. It's important that my persona is successful, goal-oriented overachiever; however, sometimes you need to pretend that you have loser qualities so your patients can relate.

"Yeah," I answered, and settled in my chair next to him. "Everybody does. What started all this?"

"Do you think I'm attractive?" he asked.

Any other guy, and I would suspect he was hitting on me, but Frank, he was different. "Yeah."

"If you were young and handsome, would you go out with me?"

I told you he was different. "Someone you have a thing for?"

He nodded.

"Do you want this guy, Frank? If you really, really want something, you need to visualize it." He started to grin. "Okay, not like *that*. Visualize running into him. Picture yourself striking up a conversation. Picture yourself making him laugh. And most importantly, picture yourself asking him out for a drink. Where did you see him last?"

"He's an accountant at the firm, but I feel like I have a big scarlet letter painted on my chest whenever I go near him."

"Just because they let you go?"

"I'm old, Elle."

"Well, duh, but that doesn't mean you're dead. You have to deal with your failures, Frank. We all have them."

"Even you?"

"Of course," I said.

"What's your latest failure?"

"You do my books, you tell me," I said, which is not a discussion I'm overly fond of.

"I didn't want to say anything, but since you asked . . . your line of credit is overdue. The notice was dated last week. You have sixty days."

"That was the letter from the bank?" I said, fishing in my pocket for my Tums. I was awful with money; I kept telling myself it was genetic.

He nodded. "And I saw your Visa bill. Just because you throw it away doesn't mean I won't find it."

"Did I do that again?" I said, whapping myself upside the head. "It looks just like one of those credit card applications."

"You haven't paid me in two months," he said, which made me feel worse than Chase Manhattan ever could.

"Sorry," I told him, my hands clenched tighter than they should've been. I understood that pro bono work was only for the rich, or at least those who were surviving, but it had taken me too long to relax and share my financial woes with Frank. There wasn't enough time in the world for me to break in another accountant. Besides, Frank didn't judge me or act superior; he was very accepting of my less-than-success situation. And best of all, he knew how to keep it secret.

"If you need to find gainful employment, I'll understand," I lied, but I felt I needed to make the effort.

"You're just lucky that Bear Stearns has such a generous severance package, or I'd be out the door."

"I know that, and I'm just grateful to see your bright and

shining face every week," I told him, happy with the vote of confidence. I trusted Frank's judgment. If he had faith in me, then I wasn't beaten yet.

"Why don't you ever have doubts?" he asked, watching me carefully.

"Of course I do. But I can't let that get me down." Of course, the doubts also kept me up at night, unless I took the temazepam, but that was just between you, me, and my online pharmacy. So far my client base consisted of the group that met on Mondays, some individual appointments that I scheduled at Starbucks, and a few phone and e-mail queries, which were mainly telemarketers and spam.

"I'm going to make it, Frank." I had to. I was running out of options.

Apparently my feigned enthusiasm was contagious.

"I'll ask Dylan out," he said.

"You should," I told him. "Let me give you some of my relationship books. I've got a whole stack I've been meaning to throw out when I got a box for them."

"You keep 'em."

"I've got them all memorized," I said, although I suppose he saw through that one. Truth was, a relationship book was only useful when you were in a relationship. In a moment of extreme clarity, and just a little too much caffeine, I had purged my bookshelves of anything that seemed superfluous. With my group, relationships were superfluous. Right now, we were all just trying to survive.

"Do you think they'll help?"

"Can they honestly hurt?"

"Got a point. Box 'em up. I'll take them."

"I'll get them for you next week," I told him, and then gathered up my notebook, umbrella, and BlackBerry. "I've got a two o'clock with Laci, and then I need to pick up a few things from the store, so I'll be in late. Lock up before you leave, huh?"

He caught me before I could escape. "Elle, we really need to talk about your finances. You should lay out a budget, or think about finding a cheaper place."

"I'm too old for the East Village."

"Not the East Village. Too pricey. They have studios in Staten Island you could look at. And Chuck was telling me about a place he saw over in Queens."

"Queens? Do I look like I belong in Queens? Frank, you stick to the books, and let me worry about the real estate. I'm not throwing in the towel yet. I was born in this borough. I grew up in this borough. And I'm going to die in this borough."

"It was just a suggestion," he said.

"And a great one at that," I said, blowing him a kiss. "Keep thinking. Gotta run." I ran out the door, hoping to leave my financial worries in my apartment.

But they followed me, shadowing me with their glinting dark eyes, snickering and pointing. I could hear the whispers, the snide comments, all coming from inside my own head. I don't think anyone understands how difficult it is to start over at my age, unless, of course, you've done it. If it was easy for you, I don't want to hear about it, ya know?

The fact was, I had been a darn good tech support rep at my

last job. The vice president's secretary loved me because not only could I recover her mangled PowerPoint presentation, but I also taught her how to ask for a raise. I helped the manager of operations get over the split with his wife, and then there were the real customers. I solved all their problems, technical and personal alike.

But eventually, the company's pursuit of the almighty bottom line ousted me. Nobody could afford two-hour support calls, even if I did have the highest customer-satisfaction rate.

My latest fear was that if I failed at Good Vibrations, my life coach service, what was next? I had no husband to fall back on, no immediate family, and I worried that there was an empty Tenth Street box just waiting for a new homeless person—like me.

After the database company laid me off, I spent eleven months pounding the pavement, putting in résumés, talking to headhunters, but nobody wanted a middle-aged woman with high customer-sat ratings. No, they wanted cheap and fast. Yeah, I'll show you cheap and fast. Anyway, at the end of the eleven months, I had an epiphany. I was done with computers. I was done with technology. I was tired of working for the Man. I wanted to do something for Elle. What I was good at, what I had a passion for, was helping people solve their problems. And since I received this epiphany while staring at an ad for Life Coach U, I knew that this was my calling. This was my passion.

The job of a life coach was simple. You got people to tell you their goals, and when communication was a problem, you made them up. The next part was pushing people toward them. Motivational pep talks, focus refinement, the power of positive thinking. Some coaches focused on specific arenas: weight loss, job management, relationship management. I chose a more diverse path, a path I called "emotional balance," i.e., whatever makes you happy and gets me paid.

It had taken some time and creative financing, but I was on the cusp of being successful. When I was in high school, they said I was bossy. Now everyone called it being a life coach.

No, I would make this work. This was my time in the sun. As a person never having experienced a time in the sun, I felt I was due. The hard reality was that I was forty-two. *I really didn't have a choice.*

My Starbucks was over on Eighty-first Street. Close enough to walk but not close enough to my house that I might get a stalker patient. I heard the stories in my life coach classes, patients who are too needy or, even worse, patients who feel you ripped them off. CYA, that's the name of the game. The main lesson my father forgot: always protect your back.

Laci Anderson was an on-again, off-again client who believed that her married boyfriend was going to leave his wife. She had hired me as a weight-loss coach, but I quickly saw through that sham. She was a size four and modeled for the Ford agency. It took the better part of an hour to convince her that one phone call at two A.M. does not constitute a divorce decree. We had the same conversation every week. I thought it would be cheaper if she just found a good priest, but every week I took her money because (a) I wasn't a priest, (b) I had an accountant to feed, and (c) I liked being needed. Besides, every now and then, when she couldn't afford my fee, she'd pay me in clothes, usually a size six, rather than my zaftig size ten, but I liked that she was such an optimist.

Clients like Laci and Barbara, and even Tanja on her good days, made me feel as if I was a success. Maybe it wasn't straight by the rules of Life Coach U, but what did a life coach need with a rule book, anyway? Just one more constraint to jack up the stress.

After Laci left, I had an extra hour to kick around. It was either that, or go back and face Frank, and I had had enough financial woebegones for the day.

I popped the umbrella and waded through slushy sidewalks to Midtown. My destination? The Garden of Eden. I'd heard rumors about the place, but they were good sorts of rumors. Discreet, not pushy, and they don't try to sell you tons of bells and whistles that you don't need. Best of all, they put the store inside an office building, so nobody knew what you were up to.

So there I stood, outside the imitation wood-veneered door on the sixth floor, gathering my courage to go in. I could do this. I mean, how old was I, twelve? Women my age bought sex toys all the time, usually from the privacy of their own home, using a handy-dandy credit card. No, I could be brave, I could conquer my fears, and I knew just the way. I have an exercise that I do with my clients. You divide your task into baby steps and concentrate on one step at a time. For instance, my first step would be to move toward the door.

I took a step forward. Ta-da. Mission accomplished.

The next task was to put my hand on the door handle, but then, from deep from within the bowels of my darkest nightmare, I heard a voice.

"Elle?"

If my life were charmed, the voice would have been deep, husky, and male, the kind you feel down to your toes. However, this one was high-pitched, and a lot snooty. I turned around, the Garden of Eden forgotten.

Right now I had to deal with the serpent.

"Elle Shields?"

And there she was. Leah Weber. I'd spent ten years reading every self-help book my mother ever bought me, trying to forget my high school years, but it was never enough. The voices never went away, including Leah's. The memories came pouring over me like anthrax in the spring rain, my shattered nerves stretched rubber-band thin.

The door opened, and a couple stared, waiting for me to move out of their way. I *hate* it when people look at me. I croaked her name and then headed for the corner of the hallway where it was somewhat dark. It wasn't dark enough, she found me, and air-kissed me on the cheek.

Leah was that sort of person. Student council president, lead in the school musical, and class slut, or so I chose to believe. She hadn't changed much, except her hair was blonder, her breasts were bigger, and her nose was cuter.

I, on the other hand, had two strands of gray in my short,

staid brown hair, my breasts were losing out to gravity, but my nose was cute. I thought it was my best feature.

"So, you diddle yourself as well?" I said, maintaining my fighting stance.

She giggled. *Giggled.* You know people like this, don't you? There's one in every high school across America.

"Shopping. Girls and toys," she answered.

I nodded, trying to act uninhibited and unashamed. I was neither. "Isn't it a small world? I haven't seen you in, what, twenty years?"

"And you haven't changed a bit," she said, and her eyes scanned me to confirm that yes, I was still the same squat chubster I was in high school.

Skank.

I pointed to my nose. "Did you have some work done? Seems a little smaller than I remembered, but things can change," I said in a velvety voice that indicated they never did.

She nodded. "For my nineteenth birthday."

I remembered my nineteenth birthday. The lead-in on Channel 4 news that night was the verdict in Daddy's trial. "How nice."

She put her hands under her breasts. "And these were part of the divorce settlement from my husband. Love it."

"Wow," I said, trying to look anywhere but at her chest.

"So," she said.

"So," I said, ending the conversation but wanting her to be the first to leave. If I ran away, it'd be a testament to her power over me. I'd spent the last two decades convincing myself that

Leah and the others didn't have that power anymore. I didn't want to know I was wrong.

She snapped her fingers, inspiration striking. All primordial instincts cried out for me to run. "This is perfect," she said.

"What?"

"Every year there's a few of us from high school that get together. Tiff, Mimi, Alan, Paul, and Sydney. Laugh and tell stories. Oh, this is so perfect."

"What?" I said again, a gurgle of apprehension settling in my gut.

"Here's what we'll do. This year, you can come, too!" She looked at me, her mouth open, waiting for me to compliment her genius.

"A party?"

"Just us, and sig others if they're so inclined. Nothing fancy," she said, giving my wardrobe a quick once-over. "You can do it. Say you'll be there. Good times."

More than anything I wished for the courage to say okay. A mere nod of the head would have been nice. One little token gesture that could tell her that I was over it. That the past was gone, and my life was grand, not because of them but in spite of them. Yet inside me there was still a piece of teenage girl passed out on a toilet, and even the sweet promise of revenge wasn't enough to make her come out.

"Can't," I said.

"Why?"

"Renovation. Painters. Hammering. Very loud."

"At my place, silly," she said.

I spoke slowly, thinking it might help. "Leah, I'm not going to come to your party."

"But it's fate. That's why I ran into you—here."

I could've argued that it wasn't fate but a nail-pulling desire for sexual gratification that brought me here, but silence was the better option.

And I had to hand it to her. She was a persistent bugger. "You *have* to be there. We're going to have pictures, and everyone brings their yearbook."

"Pictures," I echoed, bile flavored with grande mocha rising in my throat.

"What are you doing now? Something in real estate like your father?" she asked.

"I'm a life coach," I said, ignoring the sly reference to my felonious paternity.

"Really?" she said.

"Really," I said, whipping out my card in one smooth move.

"Sheffield? You're married?"

"No, I felt Sheffield had the cachet that I wanted in my profession."

"I can see why. After all, Shields was a little tainted, wasn't it?"

I smiled. "Yeah."

She waited for me to ask what she was up to.

When hell froze over.

"So, are you seeing anyone?" she asked, checking my ringless finger.

"Divorced. Two years ago." I flicked my hair back in what I hoped was a sophisticated gesture. "It was brutal."

"Do I know him?" she asked.

As if I was lying. "Don't think so. He's an investment banker. Travels a lot."

"Of course," she said, still not believing me. "So, you have to come to the party, and we can rake all our exes over the coals."

I took a shot at walking away with some dignity. For once, I was honest. "If you think carefully about it, Leah, you'll realize that we were never the best of friends. Let's just leave it that way, huh?"

"But look at us, two divorced women at a sex shop. Don't you think we can put some stupid high school indiscretions behind us? It's been twenty years, Elle. Can't we all just get along?"

It sounded a lot like something I would tell my clients, but I was smart enough to ignore it. "I don't think so, Leah." I had been the butt of too many jokes to fall for that one again. Leah, and most of her type, were so insecure they needed to chew up every poor innocent who landed in the water. I was poor but no longer innocent, so I quickly changed the subject before she smelled the blood of a fresh kill. "What are you doing these days?"

"I'm a director for our co-op board. On the Upper West Side."

Please note that I'm not one of those social climbers who need to have a view of the park. My tastes are more simple, i.e., a roof. However, I still felt a momentary twinge. Obviously the East Side wasn't good enough for her anymore. "How nice," I muttered, and checked my watch.

She waited expectantly for me to make some other gushing comment, but I was strong and checked my watch again.

"Is it three yet? I've got an appointment I have to make," she said, and I cheered my victory.

"Two minutes of," I said hopefully. "Sorry you have to rush. Maybe we'll do it again sometime."

I was counting my blessings as she turned to leave, but then she swung around, her blond bob flying just so. "Elle, you know something? I have a friend who's a reporter for a newspaper. The *Times*. Why don't we go out together? Maybe she could do a profile on you. Just think." She drew her hand in the air. "Elle Sheffield, self-help guru to the stars."

I wasn't going to fall for the old "Get your names in the *Times*" ploy. The Shields name had been daily news for almost three years.

"Why do you want to do this? It seems incredibly generous and human. Did they fix your heart as well as your nose?"

She gave me a look. A guileless, innocent look. "I was a bitch when I was young, Elle. Let me make it up to you."

She had me trapped. I could feel the jaws of her pity closing around me, squeezing tighter with every flash of her had-to-be-capped uppers. "I don't know," I said, turning my back on the promotional opportunity of a lifetime, simply because it was coming out of the mouth of Leah Webster. But how could you take food stamps from the Enemy and still look yourself in the mirror?

"You have to let me do this," she said, and her eyes held that look that people get—you know the one, where they're walking past the homeless, and it's too late to look away, so they turn all Salvation Army.

"I don't know," I said, my stomach turning tighter.

"Well, there you go. You can't say no."

Yes, I could. "I don't know . . ." I answered, which wasn't exactly no, but given some time, I'd have gotten there on my own. Swear.

She grabbed my arm, her perfectly pink fingernails grasping my yellow cotton in a death grip. I stared into her eyes and saw something I didn't expect to see. *Misery.*

Inconceivable.

For some reason that bit of humanity touched me. Maybe in twenty years she'd mellowed out. And I wasn't in a position to turn down the help. How often did you get a chance to be in the *New York Times*? Good God, I'd be in every Starbucks around the country. It was a heady feeling, because I had always wanted to believe in kismet. This was my chance. My sign. It had to be.

"Let's skip this joint," she said, tugging on my arm. "You can help me flag down a cab."

I glanced over my shoulder, the Garden of Eden no longer so appealing, and felt myself pulled in by the magnetic power of Leah.

"You really think she'd do a profile on my business?" I asked, for the first time seeing a way out of the dark tunnel that was my bank balance.

I must have sounded too needy, because the misery disappeared from her gaze. "I don't know," she said with a shrug. "But I'd shoot myself if we didn't try!"

That evening I was on my way to pick up my mail when Maureen called and wanted me to me climb to the roof. It was a celebration, she told me. Considering there was a flight of stairs to the top, I knew she had to be feeling no pain.

I had a pile of mail in the box, which always makes me feel loved. Most of it looked to be junk or bills, but I took it with me just in case I had something good, like a check from the IRS or Publishers Clearing House, for example. When I pushed open the metal door to the top, I spotted Maureen in the usual corner. She had already started on the bottle; obviously I wasn't a mandatory part of her celebration.

From thirty floors up, New York is a great town; it makes you think you're bigger than life. I had never lived outside a twenty-block perimeter, and there was a curious sense of belonging here. It wasn't the people, but the skyscrapers, so tall and silent. They were family to me, always there when I looked, always nearby.

The management company kept a few plastic chairs up there for the residents. They chained them down about seven years ago when somebody got drunk, threw one over the side, and hit a Mercedes that was parked down below. You think I'm pulling your leg, don't you? Trust me, the dangerous thing about living in the city is that something is always falling. Chairs, rocks, even huge chunks of Washington Heights.

I picked up the plastic wineglass (Maureen is ever practical), poured myself a snootful, and got comfortable in the chair next to her, dropping my mail into a disorderly pile. Publishers Clearing House could wait.

"To L.T.," said Maureen, pinking my glass (which is the plasticized version of *clinking*).

"So my plan was a success?" I asked her, needing to hear the affirmation of my manipulative psychological genius.

Maureen beamed. "It was more than a success. You should have seen her. She hid in her office all day. Took three file boxes off my pile. *Three!* When the two o'clock case meeting started she had me *go in her place*. And L.T., oh, this is the good part. You should have been there. He thinks he's turned her hetero. Tell me why the male ego is always wired to sex?"

"Darwin. Procreationism," I said, starting to crack a smile.

"It doesn't matter. I don't care," she said, and then took a long sip to prove it. "I'm going before the judge next month to argue a motion. I can't believe it. *My very own motion.* You're great, Elle, did you know it? Hey, I know, you should go into the life coach business."

Two wins for the day, first Laci, now Maureen. It had to be a record. "It's nice to be appreciated, Maureen. I'm glad things worked out," I said, trying to keep the envy out of my voice. I was happy for her, but in the face of her very real success, my own maybe-sorta-possibly-if-it-all-works-out success seemed a little far-fetched.

"Why is there no joy? You should share in my joy."

I heaved a sigh, because I knew I was going to have to explain, and I didn't want to explain, but when I start drinking . . . no, I wasn't gonna explain.

But Maureen's a lawyer, and her mind jumps in for the jugular. "Mr. Tierney told me about your rent being late," she said.

41

"I just don't understand it. They should be beating down your door for help. You truly have a gift, Elle. I mean, look at what you did for me. One little e-mail, and kaboom, I've got a motion."

I helped myself to another glass. "You would think that, wouldn't you?" I said, a little more sarcastic than usual. It was the first time I let her hear something like that out loud. I didn't share much with Maureen (other than several hundred bottles of pinot); I'm usually pretty much a closed book when it comes to any problems of my own, but maybe it was the wine talking. Most likely it was my nerves.

"They need you, Elle. The world needs you, it just doesn't know it needs you. Yet." She pointed to a window across the street. "See that girl over there? Look at that face. That's a face that needs a life coach. You should go and talk to her. Put up a flyer in the building or something."

"There're laws," I said. "And the flyer union is really fascist about anybody intruding on their turf. Little Nazis."

"Who cares? There's a goldmine of listless people right under your nose. Look there," she said, counting with her finger. "Two floors down and seven over. See that guy. Yowza. Doesn't he look muddled and directionless?"

I could see the guy. Wearing a white T-shirt, bulging muscles. Watching TV with a beer in his hand. "I think he looks hot."

"Muddled and hot, that's a good combination."

He walked over to his door, and in waltzed Beautiful Girl, who was probably a size two, too. He took her in his arms, and we both sighed.

"He doesn't look directionless," I said. We drank in silence as the happy couple made out on the couch while watching what I thought looked to be *Nip/Tuck*.

"They really should close the blinds," said Maureen when the white T-shirt went flying across the back of the couch.

"Are you kidding? This is probably just their way of getting kinky." My way of getting kinky involved my bunny. My dead bunny. I poured another glass.

"You just need a new angle, Elle. Something to get you noticed."

I sighed. "There is something. I ran into a girl from high school, who has a friend who works for the *Times*. She's trying to talk her into writing a profile on a life coach—namely, me."

"The *Times*? Oh, yeah, I can see why that'd bum you out."

"She was my most hated enemy in high school."

"Treated you bad?"

"She didn't know I existed." *Until my father allegedly bilked her family out of several hundred thousand dollars.*

"Oh, don't you hate that? I was the Fat Girl. So, you were Ghost Girl, huh? And look at us now. I'm still that Fat Girl, but you're not a Ghost Girl anymore, so there must be hope for me, too," she said, and she smoothed her hand over her stomach, the way a pregnant woman would. Only Maureen is not carrying, just large. I suppose extra poundage could be treated like a baby. I know Maureen used her weight as an excuse for a lot of things. *He doesn't like me because I'm fat. I can't get the promotion because I'm fat. I get the rudest clerks because I'm fat.*

All those things happen to me, too, and I'm not fat.

I slapped her on the shoulder because she was turning maudlin, and I was feeling maudlin enough for the both of us. "Of course there's hope for you, Maureen. If you'd just lay off the Yodels, you'd be svelte in no time," I told her.

"Were we talking about me? No. We're talking about you. And your little friend. What's her name?"

"Leah."

"Sounds like a bitch name to me. Leah owes you. Take her up on the favor, work your way to your own life-empowerment empire, and chalk it up to righting the world's injustice system. Works for me."

It sounded so simple when she said it, but I didn't have much to show for all my work so far. "I should, shouldn't I?"

"Of course."

I poured myself another glass. False courage is what Tony always called it. I figured false is better than none. "You're right. It's the chance of a lifetime. All I need to do is visualize myself walking all over her size two body, making my way to the top."

"Size two?"

I nodded.

"Anorexic, salad-eating turdball," Maureen scoffed, but she understood my ethical dilemma. "I suppose you could turn her down, merely as a matter of principle."

"Not a fiscally responsible decision on my part," I said, making a smiley face in the gravel.

"Sorry," she said. "If it wasn't for my medical bills, I could spot you a few months rent. The doctor's got me on some new drugs."

"You've got worries of your own," I said, but I was touched that she even considered it.

I wasn't sure if was Maureen's mood or the wine, but I was starting to feel better. The air was cool and full of spring pollen, but it was a small price to pay for the three months out of the year when things start to bloom inside the city. Sweater weather was just giving way to short sleeves. I love spring. And maybe opportunity was blooming as well.

Maureen picked up my mail and started thumbing through it. "This is the new Bliss catalog? Ah. There's a lot of world problems that can be solved with an hour of Nerve Whacking." Then she held up an envelope. "What's this?"

"You've had too much to drink. It's a letter," I said, and then grabbed it because I don't get handwritten letters, unless they're that faux-script font, designed to fool you into thinking it's a handwritten letter.

"It's from prison," she said, eyeing me with new respect. "A federal institution? That's the big time, Elle. I imagine there's a huge, life-empowerment void in our penal system. You could be just the one to fill it."

I pretended to study the address, not that I needed to. It was nothing that I hadn't received and then promptly spindled and mutilated many times before. "I'm not going to read it," I said, tearing it up into tiny pieces. I noticed Maureen was still watching me suspiciously. "Those cons will write to anybody with an address on the web," I told her.

"Elle, you put your home address on your website? And what are we supposed to do when they fish your dismembered body from the East River? Oh, yeah, this time it's Club Fed, but what's next? Attica? Rikers? Sing Sing?"

Damn. I had to be more careful about lying to Maureen. "I got a P.O. Box now for exactly that reason," I said, and then threw the pieces into the wind, watching them flutter away.

"That's better. I thought you were losing it. You've got to be more careful these days. You never know when a charming sociopath is gonna come knocking at your door."

I gave her a steady look. "I'm careful, Maureen."

"Okay, maybe the crime rate's down, and you don't have as much to worry about. But identity fraud, con games? The white-collar stuff is taking off big-time. Trust me. I know that of which I speak."

"Con men? Swindlers? No man is ever gonna mess with me." I meant it, too. I learned my lesson—the day that Tony Shields, a.k.a. my father, got sentenced to twenty years in the can.

Three

Honesty is the best policy, when there's money in it.

—Mark Twain

The real estate market tanked my sophomore year in high school. We were deep in the era of savings-and-loan bailout and Michael Milken—the junk-bond king, for those of you lucky enough not to remember the movie *Wall Street*. My father was a struggling real estate salesman, and we weren't rolling in the dough, but I didn't give a rat's rear about any of it, because I was trying to survive my days at St. Anthony's Prep by maintaining anonymity. When you're sixteen, you're more concerned with boys, zits, boys, drinking, boys, and MTV. From that little soliloquy, you might think I was quite a little party girl. You'd be wrong. Other girls were out having a good time; I was at home listening to Duran Duran with the door firmly locked (don't ask). It wasn't a great existence, but I was no better or worse off than thousands of teenagers across America, so I didn't complain.

One night, when the Yankees were battling the White Sox, the cops showed up at our apartment and took Tony away, all before the seventh inning. Now, on the surface, this seemed pretty cool, and Dad's mystique grew by leaps in my estimation. All of a sudden, my father had done something illegal. It boggled my sixteen-year-old mind. I imagined he was part of the Gambino crime family or maybe that he'd robbed a liquor store at gunpoint, either of which would make me an instant celebrity at school, and perhaps get me a date with Alan Benefield. If that seems egocentric to you, you're not fully comprehending the nothingness of my days.

Sadly, the truth wasn't anywhere near that exciting. Tony Shields was indicted on forty-seven counts of fraud and grand larceny, most of his victims being the angry parents of my schoolmates. Dear Old Dad was charged with creating fake deeds and reselling condos in Florida that didn't even belong to him. My mother took me shopping to buy a new dress for the trial. It was turquoise with gold braid trim. I detested turquoise, since even before the long hours in the courtroom. When the judge's gavel hammered guilty on the bench, my sentence was decided as well: two years of hell at St. Anthony's, worse than anything I had imagined.

My earlier mousey days would have been a relief; anything was better than the jokes, threats, and graffiti that appeared in permanent marker on my locker. "ROBBER BITCH, DIE" was the most common. I was shunned, both publicly and privately. Invitations to the usual Friday night parties, after-baseball pizza, or even just going to someone's apartment to watch MTV screeched to a halt. There was one girl who stuck by me: Felicity van der Hoffen, from the Netherlands, whose father worked for the UN. His assignment ended my senior year, and I spent that fall semester praying for the 3:15 bells to ring, when I could go home.

I tried to stick it out. My mother sang "Peace Train" to me and plied me with self-help book after self-help book. I ended up with the wisdom of every self-help doctor known to mankind, she ended up prematurely gray.

I graduated six months early, not because of some newly discovered brain cells but strictly for survival. Shortly thereafter, Mom ran off to the Caribbean, and other than my annual "Wish You Were Here" Christmas card, that's pretty much been it.

I had purged most of the memories, but I'd never really outgrown the insecurities, and the past few nights, the temazepam hadn't worked as it should. I'd had a couple of nasty nightmares and woke up with my fist stuffed in my mouth. I wanted to believe my luck was taking a turn for the better. I wanted to believe Leah was actually trying to help, but I knew never to look a gift alligator in its mouth.

But there was something proactive I could do in the interim. I knew the perfect cure for my insomnia, and I shortly thereafter found my way to Babeland in SoHo.

Babeland made the Garden of Eden look like Times Square, mid-'80s. This place was class. Pure class. There were silver balls hanging from the ceiling; what you did with them, I didn't know. The walls were orange, not pink or black or red. All in all, it was like a museum, MoMA, not the Met.

The sun tracked through the windows like prison search-lights, identifying the faces of shoppers with pinpoint accuracy. I stayed in the shadows and gawked. There were more dildos than I'd ever seen in my life (I'd always been faithful to Mr. Bunny), and I was curious about the size of some of them. People actually . . . It truly seemed physically impossible, not that I was one to judge. Still . . .

The salesgirl approached me, a punky-looking redhead in a pair of skintight jeans. I considered making a run for it, but she caught me before I could make my break.

"Do you need some help?" she said casually, as if this was no more than buying fresh semolina at Amy's Breads.

Maybe that was the secret. Maybe I should just imagine I was shopping for bread. "I'm just looking. You don't mind, do you?" I asked.

"Take your time," she said. "I'm Erin. Let me know if you have any questions." And then she was gone, leaving me alone with my imagination.

My eyes found the bunny rack immediately. There he was, the love of my life. My feet moved with a life of their own. For a moment, I could only stare in wonderment. Then I noticed the company he was keeping these days. Next to him was a green space invader, a bear, what I thought was a possum, a fish, and a whale. The whale looked intriguing, large, thick, hungry, but I wasn't tempted.

Erin came over. "The rabbit's the best-seller," she said, with a harmless grin, as if she discussed sexual proclivities for a living. I felt myself blush.

"Yeah," I managed.

"It's mainly for the clitoral stimulation. If you'd like, there are some G-spot products over here." She pointed to a display of toys with prickles, and colors, and balls, oh my. "Have you ever thought about which type of stimulation you prefer?"

"I can't say that I have."

"Some women like the G-spot, and others need clitoral stimulation, and then others like anal stimulation."

I gulped. "Clitoral."

"Excuse me?" she asked.

"I like clitoral stimulation," I said, louder than I intended. Heads turned. I was shamed.

"Then these are the products you should look at," she said, her fingers pointing toward the animal menagerie and a small set of what looked to be bath toys.

I filled my lungs with oxygen and reminded myself that I was an independent, confident, successful forty-two-year-old woman with a satisfying, yet monogamous, sex life. "What's that?" I asked, pointing to the rubber duck.

She flipped a switch on the bottom of the duck, and his bill began to buzz. Quickly I shut him off. "Women like the fact that he can sit by the edge of the tub, and nobody knows." She gave me a secret smile.

"I'd know," I answered, because some secrets needed to remain in the closet.

"Are you looking for something with some power behind it?" she asked, and immediately I was interested. Bunny caught me with an accusing stare, but I turned away. I hadn't committed to anything yet.

"This is the Wahl 7-in-1. It's electric powered, so you'll have to be near an outlet. Some women don't like it, because it packs quite a wallop. Don't be surprised."

My hand reached out to stroke the mighty gray machine. "Seven attachments?" I murmured, my mind already considering the possibilities.

She nodded. "Seven," she answered. "And now if you'll excuse me?" She went off to help a man who was buying a special surprise for his wife, and for some time I considered the Wahl. It seemed heavy-duty, nearly apocalyptical. In the end, I decided I'd have to work up to the Wahl. For now, I would stick with Mr. Bunny.

I sauntered over to one counter and studied the gels. I didn't need gels. Gels involved two sexually adventurous people, and I was only one sexually nonadventurous person. No gels for me.

One of the advantages of Mr. Bunny was that I never lapsed into dangerous daydreaming that involved a significant other, sensually coated in coconut-flavored gel. I didn't have unrealistic yearnings to be in a relationship with Mr. Perfect, be it sexual or otherwise. No, I knew better. I wasn't particularly particular about men anymore, except they couldn't be fat. Or gay. Or under thirty.

My man would have dark hair and melty brown eyes that

fired when he looked at me. He wouldn't say much—I had a talker once, won't make that mistake again—and he would love making love in the dark.

I almost bought the gel, right then and there, not because I was planning on using it but because it was like the size six cocktail dress that hung in the back of my closet. I could put the gel in its little bag, right at the foot of the cocktail dress. Then when I was eighty, I'd clean out my closets and laugh at the madness of my youth. Sadly, I was too old to have dreams, so I packed them carefully away and moved on. I tried not to look directly at anyone else, but my self-control wasn't that strong, and I peeked. There were two senior citizens in the corner, and I swear one of them looked just like my grandmother when she was alive. The same perfectly permed gray hair, the same curious blue eyes, and she was examining some clothing made of leather and chains. It seemed sacrilegious, so I looked away. On the other side, a twenty-something man and woman stood hand-in-hand, looking at the videos. I don't know why I thought that sex shops catered to the single person.

Finally, I gathered my courage. It was time to take the bunny and run. I went to the cash register and cleared my throat. "I'm here for the bunny," I said, before she could pull the thing out.

"I should have guessed," she said, leaving me to wonder why she should have guessed. Did I have "Bunny Lover" written on my face? Or did I look boring and nonadventurous? And why was I embarrassed that I was boring and nonadventurous? Except that I was here, in a sex shop, buying a vibrator. Just the idea gave me tingles. But the good kind.

She pulled one out of the case, and I pretended to study it. For one second.

"I'll take it," I said.

"Blue, pink, green?"

"Pink, please," I said.

"Of course," she said, and once again, I had been relegated to nonsexual deviant.

I handed her my Visa card, and she put the box in my hands. I was already anticipating my quiet time as she ran my card through the machine.

"Miss Sheffield?"

"Yes," I said.

"I'm sorry, but your card's been declined. Maybe you have another one we can use while you straighten out the situation with the bank?"

"Would you take a check?" I said, not willing to part with my purchase.

She shook her head. "I'm sorry. Cash or credit only. You understand," she said, holding out her hand for either fiduciary compensation or the bunny.

It was like a dream as I handed her my purchase. One moment, he was there, alive, in my grasp. It would have been so nice, so pleasant . . . just to forget for seven to ten minutes. It didn't seem like a lot to ask.

"Come back tomorrow," she said. "He'll still be here."

And there he would stay. Locked away in his ivory tower, far,

far away from any parts of me that might really, really need him. I gave him one last glance and took a deep breath.

I wouldn't be back tomorrow. No, I was alone once more.

On Friday, I was scheduled to meet Leah and her *New York Times* Reporter Friend at Arlene's Grocery on the Lower East Side, which is not a grocery store but actually a club. Leah told me that the reporter wanted us to meet her there to do the interview. Why a club? I don't know, but when the possibility of media exposure is involved, I don't quibble.

Tonight I was cautiously optimistic. I'd spent four hours the day before wrangling with a credit counselor at Citibank. Her name was Tashondra, and she was quite personable. After I explained that I was meeting with a reporter from the *New York Times*—yes, *that New York Times*—the next day, she agreed to give me thirty more days and an extra thou on my credit limit. It sounded impressive, even to me.

When I got inside and noticed the amount of skin being shown, I unbuttoned a few buttons on my blouse and tossed back my hair. Once again, the tectonic plates of peer pressure had reduced me to some sort of invertebrate mollusk, fossilized forever, most likely taking a piss.

Leah was dressed to the nines in a micro-miniskirt and much cleavage, and I felt a familiar pang in my stomach. I had opted for a pair of black jeans and a pinstriped blouse. Quickly, I popped a couple of Tums, because I knew that tonight was going to be murder on the old digestive system.

It would be hard to miss Leah, the forty-two-year-old divorcee, who obviously hadn't let go of her more youthful years, dirty dancing with whoever was within striking distance of her pelvis. Was that awful of me, thinking such thoughts about the woman who just might rescue me from financial ruin? Yes, yes, it was, and it felt grand. She stopped dancing long enough to perform the introductions, yelling above the screaming hordes, but I couldn't get the name. I think it was Tracy, and she was there to cover the band since the guy who normally did the music scene was either in Acapulco or out with a head cold. I wasn't sure which.

There was a photographer with her, an older guy who looked as out of place as *moi*. Decked out in khakis and an untucked Hawaiian shirt, he was methodically snapping pictures of the band as they sloshed their pitchers of beer onto the swooning androgynes who were standing below the stage. I stood far from the maddening crowd, because I knew what beer smelled like after several hours of fermenting. Those days were long ago but not forgotten.

Tracy typed some stuff on her BlackBerry, lifting her thumbs from the keys every few songs to direct the photographer.

"I thought she was coming here to see me," I said to Leah, sensing something was askew.

"Did I say that?" she said.

"Yeah, about eight times."

Leah had the grace to look somewhat ashamed—like we all do when caught fibbing.

My little beacon of hope dimmed, and I felt as if once again I'd been played.

"Look, I talked to her about it, but she wasn't sure. But, and this is the important part, she's going to ask you a few questions. Scope things out and see if you're readable. So go out there and impress her. Last thing? Don't mess this up for me, Elle. Tracy Gorman is a very important friend," she said, tapping my chest for emphasis.

"I thought you wanted to make up for old times, Leah."

"I do, but I don't plan on losing all my important friends in the process."

"Thank you for clarifying my place in the food chain," I said, but it was under my breath so she couldn't hear. I needed her, witch that she was.

When the band took a break, Tracy pulled me toward the front bar, where things were forty decibels quieter. I thought it was progress. Leah moved back to the dance floor, proving to all who cared that she wasn't getting older, she was getting better. Whatever.

Tracy took out a tape recorder and clicked the button. "Do you mind? It's easier than taking notes."

I shook my head, pinching myself. I just needed to think of this as the screen test. My big chance. And who knew, it might happen. Miracles are only a matter of rearranging your opportunities. Of course, that had never happened to me, but there was always a first time.

And all because of Leah. It was one of those moments when all reality goes vertical, and suddenly I wondered if my years of assigning blame were real or psychosomatic hallucinations brought on by the need to see evil in others. (My twelfth-grade guidance counselor gave me that one.)

I leaned back against the hard wood of the bar, trying to get more comfortable, which was impossible when packed in between seven twenty-something blondes with the appropriate body types (i.e., ogle-worthy).

No, my self-image was being shoved into the dark shadows of doubt. I dug into my psyche, pushing my root chakra right where it belonged. I would let the rain fall inside my soul. I pictured a sunshiny place, and soon I was wearing confidence like next year's design. Instantly I felt ready for anything, twenty-something blondes (probably fake) be damned.

"What can I tell you?" I asked, taking a cool sip of my beer.

"How'd you start in the life coach business? Is this something you've always wanted to do? I have to be honest, I never heard about this until that feature in *Vanity Fair* a few months back. I would so love to work for *Vanity Fair*. They get such great stories," she said, and I took another sip, studying her for some clues about the best way to impress her.

She didn't look like any reporter I'd ever met, not that I'd met a lot in my lifetime. Short and cute, with a bright, open face and the shoulder-length platinum blonde hair that was so very popular these days. Her tortoiseshell glasses perched halfway down her nose, but the lenses looked fake, so I think she was using them to detract from the California cheerleader look, which probably isn't a good look for a journalist.

I pushed back the hair from my face, not that it did any good, but it made me feel more self-confident, and self-confidence is the first requisite to great undertakings. Samuel Johnson said that right before his second emotional breakdown.

"So how did I start in the life coach biz? Lots of educational training (*six months of correspondence courses*), and then you have this apprentice program (*six weeks of status reports being sent back to the Life Coach Schools of America*). It was very intense," I told her, then took a sip of my beer. "I've known since I was a kid that I was destined to contribute to the lives of others and guide them toward the best they can be."

"Do you ever get nervous about the responsibility? I mean, you don't have a doctorate, do you?"

I laughed nervously. "No, but I've learned a lot about what motivates people over the years, and every human being has it within themselves to find what it is that'll bring them to satisfaction. We're wired that way. We have to chase our dreams." Every cliché seemed to spring forth from my lips, but I couldn't help it. When cornered, others resorted to violence; I used self-help mantras.

"Leah said your father was Tony Shields."

It's always darkest just before it turns pitch black. "You don't mind if we don't talk about Tony, do you? I really wanted to focus on the business."

"But Tony Shields is news. A missing twenty million dollars is news," she said, and I heard echoes of "Kill Shields" ringing in my ears. I pulled at my earring, and that eased the pain. "Elle Sheffield is news, too," I said, trying not to sound snippy but failing. If she had known Tony, she would have known the money was a myth. Criminal mastermind? Not in this lifetime.

Tony and I were never close. He was shy and unassuming, the most unlikely criminal suspect you've ever met. And not a great father figure, either. During the trial, not once did he ask, "Elle, is that a new haircut?" "Elle, are you losing weight?" Not even a simple "How are you holding up?" And trust me, I visited him often enough before he was convicted. The caring father, ha; stuff like that only happens in the movies.

I'd moved on.

Her eyes didn't look happy, but I figured she could tell I wasn't going to budge. "Maybe I'll run the fluff piece on life coaches in the Style section," she said, "but I'm after bigger things."

I gave her a confident smile. "Me, too." She talked about politics (Democrat), she talked about her college (Vassar), and as I watched Leah blithely jumping away on the dance floor, I felt my existence get smaller and smaller.

"Tell me about . . . oh, my God! That's Jake McNichols over there. Did you read his latest book, *When Movie-Star Mothers Go Bad*? It was awesome. The part where you realized what his mother was doing to him, and those other men? I swear, I cried buckets. Buckets. God, I have to talk to him. Maybe he'd let me do an interview. Nobody's gotten him to spill anything yet. You know, in her movies, she looks like such a nice person. Just goes to show that you can't tell about anybody, can you? Listen, it's been really nice talking to you, wish me luck," she said, and then, with a wave of her water (*cheap whore*), she dashed off to chase her dream.

I polished off my beer before switching to Scotch, which was an excellent dream killer.

Why did I even bother? Time after time, things that on the

surface looked real were nothing more than urban myth. Boyfriends? Ha. Don't go there. Successful career? Outsourced to India, replaced by some moron speaking bad English who thought *download* was a scatological term. *Amateur.*

I was ordering another double when a girl was pushed next to me, her mascara blotched in a streak that was very unattractive.

I pulled out a tissue from my purse (another life coach tip: always carry a pack of tissues with you. People cry at the drop of a hat) and handed it to her.

"Here, you've got Great Lash running down to your chin," I told her.

"Why do you fucking care?" she said, rebuffing my tissue.

"Sorry," I said, and went back to nursing my double. Sometimes people are really touchy.

"No, I'm sorry. I shouldn't have been, like, a skank."

"You want to talk about what's bothering you?" I asked, buttoning up my blouse. Cleavage be damned.

She looked at me, from beneath untweezed, scowling brows. "Like what are you, one of those promotional marketing vodka pushers? You just go up and talk to strangers?"

"Forget it," I told her.

"Fuck her," she said, directing a glare to the thousands on the other side of the room. She would be very attractive if it wasn't for that mascara . . .

"Look, at least clean up your face," I told her, sliding right into her problems and leaving mine buried at the bottom of the glass. Tomorrow would come soon enough.

She pushed a mess of black hair out of her eyes and then took the tissues from my hand. "Thanks." Eventually she turned a clean cheek in my direction. "Better?"

"Got it all."

We stood in silence, me moving toward a slow-blind drunk, and her sending death vibes toward a she-devil of unknown species.

"You came out to see the band?" she asked.

I nodded. "They're not bad."

A guy came up next to her, a nice enough kid, with a "Got coke?" T-shirt and torn jeans. "You want a drink?" he asked, giving her a friendly smile.

"Fuck you," she told him.

I gave him a sympathetic smile, figuring I could scam either a new client or a free drink. The way I felt now, both seemed equally important.

He ran away before I managed to snag either.

I ordered another double. When sadness strikes, self-medicate. Next to me, Mascara Girl missed my deep state of depression. "I started out listening to, like, the Strokes and shit like that, but then, it's just so last year. Music is getting so stale."

"Yeah. I remember the days when singers bit off bat heads and pissed on the stage. Those were the days."

"Bat heads? No shit?"

"Ozzy Osbourne," I said.

She eyed me with new respect. "From the TV show? Wow, you *are* old."

"Like Methuselah," I answered.

"I love their stuff. Did you see the new video?"

And yes, now they're naming bands after old, dead Jewish guys. "I must've missed it."

She turned around and leaned against the black polished bar, watching where the band was coming back onto the stand. "Amy's such a whore."

I watched Leah press up against a nineteen-year-old man-boy just barely wearing a pair of baggy jeans. "Definitely."

"He's going to go home with her."

"Probably," I said, as the man-boy started licking Leah's ear.

"I started coming on to him first. I was, like, 'Cool dude,' and he was, like, all 'Yeah,' and I knew we made a connection, and then she skanks up, like I wasn't even there."

"You should pick a new guy," I told her. "Look out there. Who do you want?"

"Like, I just pick anybody?"

"Anybody."

She stuck a finger in her mouth and began to chew on the nail. "He's hot, the one in the Aeropostale shirt."

"Go talk to him."

"No way. He's, like, so beyond me. I'm just, you know, a pimple compared to a god like that."

"You're no pimple," I said, pulling her finger out of her mouth. "Plunge boldly into the thick of life, but without chewing on your nails."

"Do you just make all this shit up?"

I waved off the compliment, because I was used to them. "Nah, some dead guy said it a long time ago."

"A guy. Figures."

"Listen, do this for me," I said, falling into my old routine. It felt good and right. Citibank might not have that much faith in me, but surely I could guide one self-conscious reject to a success. Even a mini-success would be nice. "Close your eyes and think about yourself talking to him. What would you say?"

"I'd ask him if he wanted to hook up."

Jeez, mini-success was going to be harder than I thought. "You're kidding me, right? You just lay yourself out there like a slab of roast beef? Nah. Go over and spill your drink on him."

"That's just, like, evil."

"Trust me, it's been the first step in more marriages than most people realize."

"What if he smacks me or something?"

I stuffed the package of tissues into her hand. "Here, take this, start wiping as soon as you throw it at him. And don't go for the face. Go for the shirt."

"I can't do that."

"What's your name?"

"Joselle."

I sighed. Joselle had more backbone than I suspected. That was okay, I was working my way up to the challenge. "Get a hold of yourself. Start thinking of Joselle the Conqueror. Make him work for you. You're worth ten of him. On a bad day. Think positively. What's he going to say to you after your little 'accident?' "

"He's going to say, 'You fucking bitch. This is my good shirt.' "

"No, Joselle. Focus. Visualize. He's going to gaze into your limpid blue—they are blue, aren't they?—eyes and fall instantly in love."

"I'm not looking for love. I just want to go home with somebody tonight. No commitments. I'm too young."

I heaved a sigh, because everybody is looking for love. Some of us just choose pink, plastic animal figures as the object of our affections. "Let's get back to this guy falling all over himself to get to you. Of course he'd take you home with him. I mean, what guy doesn't want free sex?"

"You think he'll, like, go for me?"

She had the exuberance of youth, and the breasts as well. I sighed. "Like a well-powered bunny."

"I can do it, can't I?" she said, and I could already see the confidence taking hold.

"You can do anything you want," I told her, because after downing three double Scotches, I actually believed she could.

"I'm gonna do it," she said.

" 'Bout time."

She took a shot of my Scotch and promptly gagged. "What is this stuff?"

"You're too young to understand."

As I watched, she went toward Mr. Aeropostale and promptly splashed her beer all over him. It wasn't casually done, either. A moron could have seen right through it, but she started mopping up his chest with her tissue, and, well, one thing led to another, and I chalked up another one in the win column.

"You're pretty good at that," said a voice behind me.

I turned, prepared to be offended, but it was only Tracy's photographer. Jimmy Buffett Fakes Manhattan. "I better be; it's my job. Is that a margarita you're drinking?" I asked, betting he listened to country music, too.

"Tonic water. I never drink while I'm working. You get a lot of bad shots that way."

"And we know the *New York Times* can't handle bad shots."

"I didn't peg you for a snot, although if you're one of Leah's friends, you probably are."

"Sorry. I didn't mean to take it out on the hired help. Elle Sheffield."

"Just call me Harvey."

I clinked his glass. "To bad shots," I said, and then downed my next Scotch.

I was starting to see the world through a Chivas-toned filter, and it looked pretty nice. In fact, Harvey looked pretty nice, too. I gave him a flirty smile. "You in need of a life coach?" I asked.

He snorted. "That crap?"

Obviously a nonbeliever. "You just saw that crap in action. It works."

"Sex without strings. It always works."

I squinted at him, trying to decide if that was a come-on. I didn't think so, possibly because of the "done that" glint in his eyes. "You're mocking me, aren't you?"

He shook his head. "Nah. You're not driving, are you?"

"In New York?" This time I snorted. "Where's your boss?"

"Tracy? She's headed this way. But she's not my boss. I only freelance for her paper."

"So how does Leah know Tracy?"

"Through me," he said, putting down his glass and then taking more pictures of the band.

With my supersensitive perceptive abilities, I sensed he wanted to change the subject. Naturally, I ignored that. "You and Leah?" I asked, trying to get a handle on that picture and failing.

I wanted to like Harvey. I wanted to respect him. He glanced toward the dance floor and winced. Wow. Maybe it had just been a meaningless fling. I could see that.

"Not anymore," he said, his eyes somewhere else.

"You're better off," I told him, and he swung around to look at me, and even through my Scottish haze, I felt the tingle all the way from hips to thighs, right down to the toes.

"The alimony sucks."

"You married her?" I said, not bothering to hide the horror in my voice, all tingles disappearing. This was the one who gave her the money for the perky breasts? In my head, Leah's ex was a stuffy plastic surgeon, preferably thirty years older than she. Yet here was Mr. Florida, only ten years older, but attractive, in a very rough kind of way. And he was Leah's ex . . .

"Past tense," he answered, taking some more shots of the band.

"Tense is right. You look so much more, uh, relaxed, than what I expected from someone she would deign to marry. You know, in our path to getting what we want, we have to find those things that are keeping us from living at our full potential and then jettison them away. It's a freeing experience to get rid of the negativity surrounding—" I started, lapsing into habitual self-help mode.

I stopped when I realized he wasn't listening. Oh, well. My business was doomed anyway. I don't know why I even thought I could ever succeed, when—

"Tracy, are you going to talk to Elle, or do I have to stand here like some *People, Jr.* photog?" It was Mr. Hawaiian Shirt, and he was talking to Tracy.

I gave her my back. "Did Mr. McNichols blow you off?" I murmured. "Pity." I was fed up with narrow-minded snobettes who were only interested in selling more newspapers.

Tracy sighed to Harvey, and I leaned in close to eavesdrop. "I'm not going to do it. I need something with more punch, you know? I'm not sure that a life coach will cut it."

I knew that I was a little snockered, but I still felt the pinch of personal criticism. "I have punch," I whispered, not that anybody could hear me. Or was listening.

"I think she has punch," said Harvey.

"I told you I had punch," I said, just in case she missed it from him.

"She's wasted," said Tracy.

"You should give her a shot. It'd make a good story," said Harvey, and I wasn't sure why he was being so insistent, since he obviously thought my mantras were crap. I mean, he told me so.

Most people don't have the cojones to shut me up, and I admired that about him.

"Why do I listen to you, Harvey?" said Tracy, but I sensed he was wearing her down. In my head, Harvey was gaining more and more points, even if he was Leah's ex.

They continued their discussion, and I tried to listen, but everything was too loud, and the buzzing in my ears was taking over. I saw Leah show up and pat Harvey on the chest. Very interesting. Leah still had the hots for her ex. He looked over in my direction and gave me a smile.

I winked, because somewhere inside me, I still remembered how to flirt with a man.

Unfortunately, the Wicked Witch of the West Side noticed. "You're soused, aren't you, Elle? You always were a lush in high school."

"Better a lush than the human wishbone," I told her.

Harvey moved in between us. Good thing. I could have taken her. Cellulite trumps silicone any time, any place.

Tracy moved into my line of vision. *Damn. Forgot about her.* I smiled innocently. "Nobody wants to give me a break, do they? Oh, it's just fuck Elle, fucking Elle, fucking hell." I started to laugh, but nobody else was, so I shut up fast.

Harvey nudged Tracy, and I knew she was going to cave. I was liking Harvey even more.

I could see the tiny gears turning in her brain. "We'll set up a meeting for Monday. I want to see you sober, in action, and you have to impress me, Elle."

"Of course," I told her, and beamed in Leah's direction.

Her eyes narrowed, and my lightning reflexes took over, where common sense feared to tread. I splashed my drink all over Harvey's shirt.

And that's pretty much where my memory cuts out.

Four

Every great quote about sex was written by a man.

—ELLE SHEFFIELD

I woke up the next morning with a life-altering hangover. I had hazy recollections of Leah's jealous glare, an excess of Scotch (on top of beer—agh!) and Jimmy Buffett, although I was almost positive that Jimmy Buffett had not been the act onstage.

I peered through one eye, ignoring what tasted like year-old Camembert in my mouth. On the other side of my bedroom was a chair. Nothing Chippendale, merely the basic wooden Windsor that my grandmother had left for me when she died. But strangely enough, there was a man in the chair. A shirtless man.

Quickly I patted down my body to see what I was wearing

today. My blue nightshirt and undies. Had I gotten laid last night?

I opened the other eye, just to check and see if perhaps he was a hallucination created from years (it had been almost three) of physical deprivation. He looked real.

Harry.

That's it! It was Harry. No, no. Harry was the Scotch talking.

Harvey.

Oh, my God.

Even the hammer of a killer hangover couldn't diminish the excitement I felt. Real sex—a monumental achievement, even if I couldn't remember it.

But he didn't have the look of a sexually sated man, nor did I have the feel of a sexually sated woman, but there were telltale signs: head dent in pillow next to me, and an organized neatness to the covers, which I knew wasn't me, because I'm a sheet roller, big-time. Maybe I was just too old for one-night stands.

"You alive?" he asked.

"Yeah," I lied.

"No hangover?"

I pasted a perky smile on my face, ignoring the jackhammer that pounded in my head. "None," I said, sitting up straighter. The room began to spin. "That was a mistake."

He nodded, just as a sanctimonious person without a hang-over would do, and headed out of the bedroom. Quickly I searched my emergency nightstand drawer, searching for a mint, or toothpaste, or a box of dynamite to blast the night-afters from my tongue. I found the remains of an Altoid and popped it into my mouth.

It was the most disgusting thing I'd ever tasted, but at least my breath would be minty fresh.

Harvey returned with a glass of tomato juice in his hand. "Drink this."

"This looks like tomato juice. I hate tomato juice. Where'd you get it?" I asked, because I knew tomato juice had never graced this apartment.

"I made a run next door. Trust me."

I considered the wisdom of taking tomato juice from a stranger, but he had that weather-beaten look of a man who knew how to cure hangovers. I usually just took two aspirins and slept it off. I downed the glass in one long gulp, ignoring the heaves in my stomach.

"Perfect. Thank you," I told him.

He put the glass down on my nightstand and crossed his arms over the shirtless chest. I tried not to look but failed. I stared, wading into the luxury of sexual awareness. I was woman, he was man. The covers heated me, and for a hare-brained second, I considered tossing them aside, giving him my most seductive eyelock, and letting nature take its course.

But what if he laughed? Or worse, gaped at my nontucked stomach and unnipped arm flab? Fear is a powerful emotion, responsible for the enduring survival of the human species, and also for pink bunny sales everywhere. It was fear that kept me safely tucked in my blankets.

"You're going to have to do better than that," he said.

"Better than what?" I asked, praying he wasn't speaking of my sexual prowess. I never claimed to be Angelina Jolie, tawdry home wrecker that she is.

"I thought you wanted publicity. The good kind."

Suddenly, I flashed to an image, a headline, my name. In the *New York Times*. A new image replaced it, one of Elle hitting the bottle with a little more muscle than brain. I was screwed, but I thought it was only in the figurative sense. "You took me home?"

"Somebody had to. You started singing 'Margaritaville' and wanted to get up onstage with the band."

The Camembert aftertaste returned with a vengeance. My stomach cramped up, and I knew if there had been any real food in it, I'd be racing for the toilet. Everyone has an Achilles' heel. I'm sure I'm stating the obvious when I say that alcohol was mine.

"I love that song." Not really, but I was at a vulnerable place in my life, and I'd been crushing in a major way and wasn't about to tell him. Being a woman without a vibrator gives you thoughts of weakness.

"So, Harry . . ." I started.

"Harvey," he corrected.

I sighed quietly, because he looked so much like a Harry with a Clint Eastwood squint in his eyes and the pool-hall tilt to his mouth. I thought his mother had screwed up, but I kept my opinions to myself. "Sorry."

"S'all right."

"So . . ." I drummed on the covers of my bed, trying to approach the subject of sex with sophistication and poise.

"No," he stated, very definitively.

"No?" said I, just making sure we were talking apples-to-apples here.

"No."

"Oh," I said, hoping I didn't sound too disappointed. There would've been a great shift in the forces of the universe if I had done Leah's ex. Even for just a few hours. Wrongs would have been righted, sins not quite forgiven, but at least I could triumphantly rub her nose in my sexual conquest. And all without surgically enhanced bazoombas.

But were my questions truly answered? I mean, why was his shirt off? And he had a really nice chest, but it was an older guy chest. A little gray chest hair, muscles that were nice and ropey. *Did I take off his shirt?*

"Where's your shirt?" I asked.

"The remains of the Scotch you'd been drinking were all over it. I put it in the sink."

"Oh. Sorry," I said, and my eyes adjusted to the vision of him in my bedroom. First of all, to understand the harmony of this picture, you must understand that my bedroom consists of a queen-size bed, a chair that is usually covered with yesterday's clothes, and the old nightstand that is usually covered with books I should be reading but never have the time. My single window has a quaint view of the parking garage across the street. It's a rumpled room, and he was a rumpled man.

Currently I had a rumpled life, and if the fortunes were to be believed, I was going to be a rumpled homeless person living in a box down on Tenth Street.

I heaved a sigh, and immediately my stomach cramped up again.

"So, what do you do for the *Times*? Do you cover music?"

"No. Last night I was doing a favor for a friend. I grew up with Tracy's editor. They needed somebody to fill in. Keeps my skills sharp."

"What's the usual work?"

He scratched his chest. I averted my eyes. "I do a lot of still work. Coke cans. Food products. Automobiles."

"You don't look like a car photographer. I pictured you on top of the Andes, or deepest Africa. Something more—gritty."

He seemed exotic and manly, a foreign breed in Manhattan. He seemed like a man who wouldn't let his fears keep him buried under the covers. Actually he looked like a guy who wouldn't hesitate tossing off the blanket and taking what he wanted. I let the covers slip down half an inch, mainly because he inspired me.

His eyes took in the view, lingered, then looked away.

"I used to do gritty, but I'm getting old, and cars pay a lot better. Leah has expensive tastes."

Now, that was a subject I didn't want to touch, so I switched it back to something more palatable: me.

"Did I blow my shot at the profile?" This time, the bad taste in my mouth had nothing to do with alcohol.

He shook his head and put socked feet up on my bed. I

noticed the hole in the left heel. Immediately my heart warmed. "Don't sweat the small stuff. It's no big deal if she decides against it."

"I don't think you understand how important this is to me," I said, wondering if all *New York Times* employees were this arrogant. There was a cookie shop on Fifty-sixth Street that had had a profile done a few years back. They were now franchised in seven states. Good Vibrations was gonna live or die by this profile. "Humor me. Tell me what I need."

He thought for a minute. "You need a good angle."

I suspected that if Dr. Phil ever chose to analyze me, he would say I had a deep-seated fear of success. He would tell me that I used my drinking and various other weaknesses in order to torpedo my chances. I knew my imaginary Dr. Phil was correct. It was easier to blame my failures on Scotch than on me. What if I did get the publicity and nobody came? What if everybody saw right through me?

It was easier to hide under my rumpled covers, alone, and hope the world would ignore me for at least seven years, possibly longer.

However, and you knew there was a however, didn't you? Even stronger than my fear of success was the desire *not* to be laughed at, especially by members of the graduating class of 1985. I shoved my rumpled covers aside (figuratively only). I was gonna get a profile in the *New York Times,* because this time I wasn't seventeen, and I wasn't Elle Shields. I was a Sheffield. It was easy to think these positive thoughts when Harvey was staring at me in such a tasty manner. He was the only trophy in my trophy case, and I wanted to keep him. And since the sex hadn't worked, the profile was the only way I knew how.

"I've got a great story for her. What if I took her on one of my field trips? With my clients."

"Field trips?"

"We go places. I have an organized lesson plan, and in a new environment, my clients seem to process things better. Plus, it builds confidence and promotes a positive outlook on life."

"Where?"

"I'd planned a trip to . . ." I thought to myself, thinking of the relationship books stacked almost neatly against the couch. "The Container Store. One of my clients is trying to get a handle on organizing her things."

"Why?"

"Because clutter can be an annoyance in our lives, and there are four easy steps to cut down on clutter. Question. Location. Organization. Trash. All of your organizational problems can be solved with a quick trip to the Container Store."

He didn't look as if he believed me, but Tracy was the one I had to convince. And I'd yet to meet a woman who didn't get orgasmic in the place.

"Trust me, Tracy will love it."

"When is it?"

"Group meets on Monday. Two o'clock," I said, and realized that none of my clients had "real" problems, the high-profile stuff that would be needed to attract a high-profile readership. My girls had problems that were ordinary, everyday, yawn-inducing problems. I needed to find a disorganized client, something like you'd see on *Oprah*. Tanja had potential, but I needed someone more worthy. Someone like Maureen, who owed me a favor. I smiled; things were looking up.

Harvey checked his watch and then stood. "Ten o'clock. I gotta leave, but I'll have Tracy there on Monday."

He sounded so confident, as if he was used to getting women to do his bidding. Still, he'd taken me home from the club, so I knew there was interest on his side as well. And it's not like he was some hottie kid who wandered the East Village. No, Harvey was all man.

"Thank you for helping me," I told him with a shy smile. "Why did you, by the way?"

"It got me out of taking those damned band pictures."

"Oh. Why did you stay overnight then? Why not leave?" I asked. It took a lot of courage for me to ask that, but I had reason to believe it wasn't to admire my decorating skills.

"You were cute."

"Oh!" He stood there looking at me, and I could feel the tension pulling between us like gravity. "Maybe we could . . ." I shrugged, letting him interpret however he wanted to. I was flexible, it was spring. Who needed a vibrator, anyway?

He shrugged. "I really gotta leave. I've got a daughter to pick up."

"Daughter?" I asked, tasting the soapy cheese taste again. I gotta tell you, it's not pretty.

"Lindsey. She's fourteen."

"With Leah?" I asked, needing clarification to see if the situation was as bad as I thought.

"Leah is the biological mother, yes."

Yes, it was.

"Bound together for life." A kid changes things in a relationship. It chains you to a person. When you get involved with someone who has a kid, suddenly you're all one big happy family. But *involved*? Quickly I stepped back about eighteen mental steps. *Involved* meant pain, rejection, and a cramped-up stomach. Involved? Nah, I wasn't talking involved, I was just thinking of meaningless sex that didn't require AA batteries.

"I'll see you Monday," he said, and I watched him walk out my bedroom door. For a man who I guessed to be in his mid-fifties, he was pretty spiffy. And he wore khakis better than a lot of men. His hair was more gray than brown, and his eyes weren't dark, they were the color of wet cement, but all in all, I approved of the physical package. It was the baggage that came with it that bothered me. He had expensive baggage. Louis Vuitton.

"And Elle?" he said, interrupting me in mid-ogle.

"Yeah?"

"Skip the Scotch this time."

"I'm quitting for good," I said, and crossed my heart. After all, self-discipline was what I did best.

After Harvey left, I spent some time in the lotus position on my living-room rug. It's not something I do often, it's not even something I do well, but it's a lesson I teach, and I think it's important to be able to clear your head. I stared at the eight-by-ten framed picture of me with my parents on the wall. It was taken

Easter Sunday just after I turned fourteen. They're dressed up in suits, and Mother is wearing a purple pillbox hat, and I'm stuffed into a pink ruffled concoction, looking like a marshmallow Peep.

In the picture, if you looked closely at the way Tony was holding his hands, you could clearly see he was grinding away at the skin on his thumb. He'd always been too spineless, never strong enough, like, say, Cliff Huxtable.

I spent my formative years watching *The Cosby Show.* "Escapism" is what the books called my overdone television watching. Yeah, whatever works.

After I had done the lotus position until my thighs ached, I dug through the back of my closet and found my old yearbooks. Why I hadn't burned them, I don't know. Actually, I did. They were my badge of courage for surviving. The proof I needed that I was stronger than Tony Shields.

My junior yearbook wasn't a big book, the whole of St. Anthony's was only 370 students—369 too many, is what I always thought. I traced the St. Anthony's seal on the white leather cover. Embossed, of course.

Inside, pressed between two pristine vellum sheets, was flowing black script. "Relive the Memories." Why would anyone want to relive the Fifth Ring of Hell? I had flipped open the page to Leah Hanover (that was her maiden name) when, speak of the devil, the phone rang.

And yes, it was Leah.

"Elle! You disappeared last night. What'd you do?"

I could hear the vibrato of fear in her voice, which she disguised with a cheerful lilt. "Don't you want to know," I taunted.

"Did things go well with Tracy?" Which was code for "Did you shtup my ex?"

"Fabulous," I answered, and then sighed with heavy satisfaction. "Better than I hoped." Idly I flipped through the pictures, finding Leah on the cheerleading squad, Leah in the Honor Society, Leah on the debate team. I avoided my own picture and slammed the book shut.

"Whew! I was so worried. You were smashed, and I thought, oh, she's gonna screw this one up, too."

"But look how it turned out. I had more fun than I've had in a long time, and she is really nice," I said, my hands caressing the St. Anthony's seal.

"I saw you talking to Harvey by the bar."

"Uh-huh."

"Let's not dance around the truth, shall we? Did you do him or not?"

I could feel her blood pressure rising, threatening to explode. All because of me. I snickered again. Only not inwardly this time. This time I snickered aloud. Softly. Confidently. "Leah, what kind of friend do you think I am? But you are divorced, aren't you?"

"Look, we're all adults here. And there's no reason that we can't handle the situation, whatever vagina Harvey chooses to root around in, but I won't have this affecting my Lindsey," she said, the tension coming through loud and clear.

And now she turned into a supermom, putting her daughter first. Did she remember "my Lindsey" last night when she was pelvic thrusting with Young Mr. Jailbait? I don't think so. Here she was, getting so wound up with jealousy, and I worried that I'd have to call 911 soon. If the traffic was bad, well, who knew what would happen, and then where would Lindsey be? Motherless, that's where she would be. Harvey would be a widower, which sounded so much more appealing than "Leah's ex."

Yes, Leah having a fatal stroke because of her jealousy of me—yes, me—was a nice thought. A coup de grâce after years of painful torment. But I was not a vindictive person, and I still needed her help to get that article, so I gave her an encouraging sigh. "Leah, Leah, Leah. You're making so much out of nothing. Really. Harvey's nice enough and everything, but you know, I'm happy being footloose and fancy-free . . ." I trailed off meaningfully, because I didn't want her to worry. Much.

"I just thought . . ."

"Oh, honey, I know what you thought, but I have no intention of settling down."

"I thought you had been married once," she said, reminding me of my earlier lie.

Quickly I covered. "Settling down *again* . . . Nowadays, with so many divorces, like mine, like yours with Harvey, for instance . . ."

Reminding her of her failure in marriage seemed to provide less of a sting than me sniffing near her territory—correction: past territory. I could tell because I couldn't hear her breathing anymore, so probably the chances of her having a heart attack and keeling over dead were greatly reduced.

Easy come, easy go.

"So when you gonna see Tracy again? You *are* gonna see Tracy again, aren't you? The way you were acting last night—"

"Monday. She and Harvey are going on a field trip with my group."

"A group?" For the first time, I heard the slightest trace of awe in her voice. "You have a group?"

"Yeah, it's my most popular program."

"Is this in a classroom setting?"

"Oh, no. That's too formal. When you get too many people together, the quality of sharing is diminished. Everybody starts to clam up. I keep it small; there's about seven that usually show up. The financial rewards are more limited that way, but I don't think we should put a price tag on personal success."

"Tracy would like that, I bet. A real slice-of-life moment. Although it'd be nice if your group were a little bigger, you know? You need to show her that you're not some boffo with an online degree."

"I don't know, I really like to keep the group small."

"Well, it's your article. I'm just telling you what I know about Tracy. She writes success stories. But if you're not interested . . ."

"I'll make sure they all show up," I said, doing addition in my head and realizing that Barbara plus Joan plus Tanja equals three. Although, there was Maureen. If I had her play up the limp, it would lend a certain "triumph over physical challenges" aura to the whole thing. That could work. If only I could drum up some more live bodies . . .

Frank! He would do it. After all, his days were pretty empty.

"Oh, listen, I have to run. I just wanted to call and see how it went with Tracy."

I bet you did. "Leah, I know we weren't the best of friends at school, but I want to thank you for doing this for me. Introducing me to Tracy—and Harvey." I feigned an emotional sniff. "It's just the nicest thing anyone has ever done for me."

Too late. She had already hung up.

On Sunday morning, Mr. Tierney, who manages several apartments in my building, rang my bell. I peered through the peephole, hoping it was Harvey, but instead it was my landlord expecting his rent.

I quieted my breathing so he wouldn't hear me and waited until he went away. The experience weighed heavy on my conscience, because in the past, my honesty separated me from Tony Shields. I could remember listening to the phone ring in our apartment, waiting for my father to pick up. But he never did. It was Mom who always answered the phone, telling the callers that Tony was out, even while he sat in his La-Z-Boy, reading the *Times,* pretending he couldn't hear the whole conversation.

I never picked up, because I had moral principles, and I refused to lie, but then, one day, the unthinkable happened. I forged a note to my teacher, saying that I had been sick the previous day. It was so easy. I justified my white lies, because nobody got hurt. Lately I worried about the slippery slope I was skating on. But I shrugged it off as a matter of survival. Queens was calling my name, or, even worse, Wilmington, Delaware, home of myriad credit card support opportunities and also a cost of living forty percent lower than Manhattan (I told you the credit card counselor was helpful). But I could do this. I just had to visualize the lesson of a lifetime.

Then the bell rang again, and my stomach cramped up like bad sushi. I was living on the edge, and I wasn't a live-on-the-edge sort of person. It's easy to take risks when you're twenty and living in a studio on the Lower East Side. Even when you're thirty, you know you still have time. But starting over when forty is gunning for you like a cabbie on Park? That's not so easy, my friend. Chances are not infinite; someday they start running out.

The ringing stopped, and I rubbed my arms, feeling the chill of age in the air. I told myself to get a life, which is exactly what I was trying to do. I called Maureen, and we argued about whether she should play (a) pitiful disorganized girl, (b) poor disabled girl who wanted to lose fifty pounds, or (c) poor disabled girl who wanted the partner spot at the firm. Eventually she convinced me that no one would believe she *was* a pitiful disorganized girl; however, I had the last word when I told her the last thing she wanted was to have her ambitions splashed across the *Times* where anybody could read it. If they happened across the weight-loss goal, then they'd probably believe it, and as a bonus, if she got fired, it made great fodder for a discrimination lawsuit. Please note that she did negotiate me down to a thirty-pound goal instead of fifty. I let her win that one.

So now my group was up to a big four, which wasn't quite

where I wanted to be. A life coach needed the patina of success coloring her world. With only four marginally disenfranchised women, I really didn't have the cultural rainbow that I felt the *Times* would require.

But a gay man . . .

Now, there was a subject to give my rainbow a little purple. I called Frank, but alas, he told me he had a date the next day. A coffee pas de deux that he was very excited about. I gushed something appropriate and hung up, scratching purple off my rainbow. The tart. I was stuck with my four, but we were strong, and we were invincible. Actually, I supposed it was better for business if they were vincible.

On Monday, I slept in, using the few extra zzz's to keep my stomach in line. I dressed, took my early afternoon coffee, and gathered my materials. It was now or never.

The Container Store, which is to some people (myself included) Utopia, looms high in every woman's dreams and was just the rejuvenating silver bullet I needed. I don't understand this need to compartmentalize and organize our lives, because we're so piss-poor at it. Perhaps that unfulfilled longing is why the Container Store ranks only behind my vibrator as the thing I would want most on a desert island.

When I made it to the bright-blue-awning-shaded building, Barbara and Joan were waiting outside the front doors. Joan was blowing her Virginia Slims in the face of every annoyed pedestrian who walked by her. According to Joan, the air belongs to the polluters. Words to drive your Hummer to. I admired her convictions.

"Good afternoon, ladies. We'll be having a guest in the session today," I said, deciding to tackle the tough parts right up front. It had been a strategic decision on my part to defer this news until this moment. I knew my group; they wouldn't have showed.

Barbara, no surprise there, went instantly on alert. "I can't speak in front of a stranger," she said, looking nervously at the jostling crowds around us.

"This stranger is a reporter. For the *New York Times*. She's very nice. Come on, Barbara. Be a sport."

Her lips set in a tight line. A storm was brewing. "I'm not a sport. My personal life is not meant to be bandied about on the subway."

"They never use real names in these pieces. No one will ever know it's you."

She gave a little shake of her head. "I still can't talk in front of a stranger."

"A stranger is only a stranger until they're your friend," I told her.

She looked at her watch. "We start the session in ten minutes. She'll still be a stranger."

Why now? Why couldn't she be a bit more flexible? "Look at Joan, she has no problems."

"I know. That's why she doesn't care if the *New York Times* sits in on our session."

"Barbara, Barbara, Barbara. I need you to do me this favor. Think of it as a commercial. For Good Vibrations. Think of your part in this as an actor."

"I don't have to talk about my real goals?"

I shook my head. "Nobody has to know."

"All right. I'll do it. But call me Babette, instead of Barbara."

I gave her a confident smile. "Whatever you want."

After that, I pulled the ladies inside, where we waited by the return desk. All around, hundreds of women were hypnotized by the promise of housekeeping perfection contained in this one store. Aisles and aisles of boxes and bags, splashes of color, accessorized with sharp chrome and white. I sucked in a breath, nearly succumbing to the siren's song of a flawless life.

I was shaking it off next to a row of steamer trunks, when Maureen made her entrance, dragging a limp leg behind her. I gave her a pointed "Don't overdo it" glance, but she just waved and started rubbing her calf. (Little-known fact: Maureen played Maria in Skyline High School's version of *The Sound of Music*. The lure of the stage has never left.)

There was still no sign of Tracy, but I wouldn't let the fear rule me.

Surrounded by the ladies in the group, people who all occupied a place of well-adjustedness that I liked to believe was several levels below my own, my confidence began to grow.

Of course, Tanja was late. But poor girl, that's why she needed me.

"Have you been waiting a long time? You all look sorta wilted. You were outside, weren't you? What kind of idiots wait outside in the heat? Sorry, shut my mouth for me, will you? They shut down the C line for repairs. No flyers, no notices, just kaput."

I put my steadying hands on her shoulders. "Tanja, you're going to be fine. We haven't been here long. Swear."

"You're sweating like a dog."

I took out a tissue and blotted my forehead, telling myself I wasn't going to get nervous. I was a master of organizational time management, and I would use the remaining moments to do a little prep.

"Okay, everyone. At each session we define our goals, and the goal for today is to make me look good, make me look effective, and make life coaching look like the hottest thing since Earth and Wind discovered Fire. This is really important to me."

Joan pulled out another cigarette, preparing to light it. "We'll be on our best behavior, Elle. You can count on us," she said, as I politely took it and put it back into her solid gold ciggy case.

"Thank you, Joan. Coming from you, well, that touches my heart. Now, speaking of behavior, here're the rules. One, there will be no whining," I said, pointedly looking at Tanja. "We will all be positive, self-assured, and well on our way to achieving weight loss, job satisfaction, and more free time than we ever dreamed possible. Got it?" Heads nodded, and I was feeling pleased. "Any questions?"

"Do we have to do this?" asked Barbara, starting panic butterflies in my gut. Still, if there was anybody in the world I depended on, it was my group.

"Anybody who wants to can walk away now. I know you all come for the motivation, but I wouldn't have asked the favor if I didn't consider each and every one of you my friends."

It shocked me to hear those words come out of my mouth, but they were true, and dammit, they were motivational, too. Even I felt inspired.

I waited, my heart beating like a drum, to see if anyone would walk.

Nobody did.

"Any more questions?" I asked.

Barbara raised her hand. I lowered it. "Remember, we need to stay casual, Barbara."

"Babette," she corrected.

"Babette. What's your question?"

"Larry wanted me to get a new lint brush while I was here. Will I have time after, or do you think I should do it now? It's the little round one, with refillable sheets. He likes to use it for his suits."

"I know just what you're talking about," said Maureen. "Do they sell those here? I have three wool suits, and the dust lint is murder."

"That's what a lady in his office said."

"You two can look together afterward," I said, wanting to nip the personal conversation in the bud. "Maureen, you're walking around so well."

She paraded in front of me. "New drugs. They're amazing."

Joan looked intrigued. "Really? What kind?"

I coughed and diverted the conversation. "Today we're all business. Remember, what is our goal?"

"To make our esteemed royal highness look good," said Maureen in her best dronelike voice.

"So how is L.T. today?" I asked, with a superior brow quirk to remind her that she owed me. She had the grace to look ashamed, just as Tracy showed.

I locked my shaking hands behind me. "Oh, you're here. Glad you made it."

She looked great, dressed in a flowery sundress and flats, both of which made my yellow silk blouse wilt. She'd changed her glasses from tortoiseshell to a summery pink plastic look. Very chi-chi.

"Where's Harvey?" I asked her, looking past her down the closet organization aisle.

"Why would Harvey be here?" she asked.

"I assumed that the reporter and the photographer would hang together." She was looking at me, completely clueless, and my hands started shaking even more. "You know. Big *NYT* reporter, hot on the story." I stammered. *Elle, pull it together.*

Her eyes clued in, and I heaved a sigh. Last thing I needed to do was to appear ignorant.

"We usually work separately," she said. "He's off shooting a dinner plate at the studio."

Well, hot tamales. I guess I knew where I fell in his priorities. Somewhere below Fiestaware. I swept my disappointment aside; I'd save it for later when I had a nice bottle of pinot (or Scotch) well in hand.

I clapped my hands, shaking off the negativity. After all, my ladies were here, and we were a darn good team. "Today we're talking about paperwork." I rounded up my charges and led them back, *back,* back to the far end of store, where a stylish wooden selection of office accessories awaited. Tiny drawers, shelves, and letter holders. The women (Tracy included) were entranced.

"How many of you are drowning in paperwork?"

Everyone but Barbara raised a hand. I looked at her. "You don't have this problem?"

"La-Larry doesn't like for me to look at the bills."

Maureen shook her head. "I wish I had a man who didn't want me to look at my bills. Don't you feel nervous, though? Not knowing anything about your situation. What if he died? Who would take care of you?"

Barbara's eyes bugged out. "I couldn't survive."

Maureen, feminist that she was, stood ready to argue. It was just too much to ask her to leave the lawyer at home. I cleared my throat, and she got the hint.

Tracy didn't seem impressed, so I rushed on. "Okay, that's a nice bonding moment, I'm glad to see we're making some progress, but let's talk junk mail. Americans dispose of four million tons of junk mail each year. That's a lot of credit card applications. But there's a way out. It's my patented one-touch system. The goal here is to touch paper only once."

I pulled a bill from my bag. "See, I go to my mailbox, pick up the letter, and if you're like most people, the letter gets put in a pile or buried under another pile or, worse, shoved in a drawer where it's never heard from again."

I kept going, demonstrating the Elle Sheffield sort-slot-fix-and-trash technique. Tanja volunteered to play helpless head of household confronted with too much paper, and she did a fine job, squinching her forehead as she opened bill after bill. By the end of the exercise, Tanja wasn't so confused, and I suspected that even Tracy benefited. I rubbed my hands together, feeling pleased.

"That's our lesson part of today's session. Now I'll talk to Tracy for a few minutes, and why don't each of you find something that will improve your life?" I shooed them away, the knot in my stomach unraveling. I had done it.

We had gone through the lesson without a hitch.

"Elle, wait a minute."

Strike that. I could sense the hitch approaching. "Sure thing," I told Tracy. "Ladies, hold up. I don't think we're done."

Tracy pulled out her tape recorder. "That was too canned. Bor-ing. We need to use some more personal stories. Maybe a success or two? Anybody?"

The word *success* was met with a broad silence. "What do you mean?" I asked, even though I knew exactly what she meant. I just had to stall for time, to think, to plan.

"Well," she said, and then pointed to Maureen. "What are you here for?"

Maureen coughed. "I'm here for my . . ." she looked over at me, pleading.

I pleaded right back.

"My weight," she said. "I'm trying to lose fifty pounds," she said. What a pal. I grinned.

"How much have you lost?" asked Tracy.

"Three," said Maureen. "But I'm brand-new to the group. With Elle's guidance, I can see my way to a more svelte me."

Okay, so I wasn't Weight Watchers, but still . . .

Tracy jotted down some notes and turned to Tanja. "What about you?"

"I'm trying to meet men."

"How?"

"I ride the subway a lot. Scan the Missed Connections notices and see if anyone noticed me."

"Any hits yet?"

Tanja scratched her head. "Not yet; men don't like me."

"How has Elle helped you?"

"I've thought about putting in an ad of my own. And there's this cute guy on the F train that I'm working up the courage to meet."

Tracy glanced over at me, and I smiled weakly. These weren't the success stories that the *Times* needed, and I knew it. They wanted job promotions, pay raises, weight loss in triple digits.

She looked at Joan. "What's your story?"

Joan coughed. "I have lung cancer, and I'm dying. This group is my support. They're my friends."

I shot Joan a big thumbs-up behind Tracy's back. Death was always a big seller. It was just the touch of violin schmaltz that I needed. Joan winked.

Tracy looked skeptical. "I'm sorry. That's very touching. If it's true."

"Oh, come on, who lies about something like that?" I said, shaming her with my look.

It worked. "Sorry, we have to really double- and triple-check our facts now. The world we live in." She turned to Barbara, but her voice was gentle this time. "And you?"

"My name is Babette. And I'm working on developing my own home design show."

I flinched. *Uh-oh.*

"Have I seen any of your work?" Tracy asked. "Babette? That's a very unusual name."

Barbara began to stammer. "I like c-c-color, and big patches of light."

Tracy's voice sharpened. "Where did you go to school?"

Barbara's lip was vibrating faster than my heart.

I stepped in to avert disaster. "She has some training in France. Many years ago. It's been a lifelong dream of hers to create objects of beauty for other people's enjoyment."

"Is this true?" asked Tracy.

I willed Barbara to do something. Nod. Speak. Bark. But Barbara stared blindly into the light of the oncoming train.

"Come on, we don't have all day. Is it true or not?" Tracy snapped.

If it was anyone but Barbara. Heck, even Tanja had fangs.

I could see my future sinking lower and lower, right there in Barbara's terrified eyes, because for once, somebody was getting hurt because of me. I had called myself a friend, but was I really? Or had I turned into a vindictive opportunist, just like the rest of the St. Anthony's graduating class of 1985?

My hands stopped shaking, my stomach relaxed, and I caught Tracy's attention, something I had failed to do before.

"I think you should leave her alone," I said. "She's had a hard life and doesn't respond well to authority."

"She's going to have a tough time in design," said Tracy.

At that, one lone tear hit Barbara's eye.

There are times when you're faced with tough choices. Two divergent paths, one of which is usually marked DETOUR. I wanted to keep my mouth shut, but I couldn't. I really wanted the profile, but at what price?

"That's enough," I said. "She's not a designer, she's an ordinary housewife, and she doesn't want a reality TV show. Barbara, uh, Babette would hate being on TV."

Barbara looked at me, gratitude in her eyes. I waved it off.

"I fired my maid," she said.

I shot her a disbelieving look. "You fired Imelda?"

She nodded. Only once, but there was a steely glint in her eye that was new. "Congratulations," I told her, and then turned to Tracy. "Her maid was stealing from her. This is our first breakthrough." I gave Barbara a hug. "It's gonna be okay," I whispered in her ear.

And it was going to be okay. A calm peace came over me, chakras past and present floating to their rightful places. These women needed me right now, and I wouldn't desert them. I couldn't because they were all I had.

"We're not a lot of flash in this group," I said to Tracy. "We're mainly just four average women trying to keep our heads above water. I don't know if you still want to do the profile or not, but I'm not going to lie to you, or have my ladies lie to you, either. We're who we are, and if that's not newsworthy, that's fine, but it's groupworthy, and that's what counts."

Tracy clicked her pen and tucked her notebook in her purse. "That's touching, but not what our readers expect. I'm sorry, Elle."

She turned and started walking toward the door. That was it. My last chance at making it in New York.

"Here's your Visa bill, Elle," said Tanja, handing me the fat envelope. "You really should see a credit counselor."

I could hear the voice of Tashondra telling me that I'd do really well on the phones at Citibank, I could hear Leah snickering just over my shoulder, but even that wasn't enough to make me go after Tracy. There wasn't anything I could do.

We all looked at each other, and it was Barbara's disappointed face that finally did me in.

"I screwed it up, didn't I?" she said.

Her words were the same words I used on myself over and over again. I gave her a big thumbs-up. "We're not dead yet, Barbara."

I ran after Tracy.

There was only one way out.

Five

Honesty is the virtue of pretty much nobody.

—ELLE SHEFFIELD

You want the interview with Tony Shields?" I asked, arms akimbo, bravado completely feigned.

Her eyes sharpened behind the perky pink lenses. This was a woman with ambition. I recognized the species.

She nodded, and I held up my negotiating finger. "Do the profile. My terms. No lies. And I'll get you an exclusive. The truth about the missing money. But you have to run the profile first. That's my condition. When that runs, then I'll let you talk to my dad."

"I can't guarantee that," she said, never blinking once.

"Can you guarantee some of it? For instances, take the 'lies' part. You can lie on my father's story all you want; in fact, I think your readers would find it far more interesting."

"You don't think the money exists, do you?" she said, wearing her hard-hitting reporter face.

I started to laugh. If she knew how very unrich we were when I was growing up, she wouldn't even be asking the question. Oh, we didn't starve, and I was at prep school, but all the great clothes, European vacations, culinary extravaganzas? Not in our household. "Maybe I'm wrong," I said, mainly to keep her interested.

Her little white teeth chewed rabbit-style on her lip.

"Do your best," I told her, while I still had her on the hook.

"You'll set up the interview for next week?"

"I'll do it as soon as I get home," I promised. It was a phone call I wasn't looking forward to, but if Barbara could fire her maid, how hard would it be for me to call my father?

That's a rhetorical question; I'd rather cut off a finger than see Tony again. Mainly because I considered him a loser and didn't want to grow up to be just like him. He was a convicted criminal; I could live with that. But if we had lived Gotti-style with a big town house and the coolest clothes and the priciest friends, I would have been happier. I would have felt as if something worthwhile had come from his indiscretions. But he did the crime, and I ended up doing the time, right along with him. There's something wrong with that picture.

And the worst sin of all was that *he never even cared*.

I shook off my doldrums, because the past was the past, and the future was looking brighter than ever. Maybe something good could finally come from my father's screwups.

"He has to cooperate fully," she said, but I could see the excitement in her eyes. She wanted the interview bad.

Strike one up for Elle.

"He will," I said, picturing a franchise in my future. Actually, a few decent months' worth of income would tide me over nicely. I followed her out into the sunlight, my steps perkier than before. I pulled out my sunglasses, because I was stepping out from the shadows of the Shields legacy.

It was about time.

I got a new client that afternoon, Stephanie Burns, a serious overspender who needed help getting her finances under control. I spent two hours going over line item by line item, showing her how much that daily café mocha was hitting her bottom line. Finally I gave her the pièce de résistance, upping the deductibles on her renter's insurance, an automatic extra fifty buckaroos in her pocket each and every month. Yes, that's me, problem solver extraordinaire.

Leah called me later in the day and wanted to get together for drinks. I suspected she wanted to interrogate me more about Harvey, but I told her that I was meeting a "male friend" at the Blue Fin that night for drinks. Okay, it was just Frank, but if I had thought that was any of her business (or that I could get some mileage from it), I would have told her. Frank felt bad that he'd had to turn me down and was buying alcohol to make up. I like the way he thinks.

The Blue Fin was a glass-lined aquarium in Times Square, only instead of fish, it housed men and women in search of a hookup. We squeezed past three model types (*hate* them) and a dynamic duo in suits.

Right off the bat, Frank ordered two tequila shots and I knew I was in trouble. I looked at him carefully, so caught up in my own euphoria that I had missed the squinchy lines around his forehead earlier. Trouble. I knew the look. I'd seen it in my mirror often enough.

"What's wrong with you?"

"He shot me down," Frank answered, downing the drink with one jerk of the hand.

"Did he tell you why? Hips too wide? Extra lines around the eyes? You're not funny enough?"

He shot me a huffy look, but I knew what I was doing. Anger was always preferable to wallowing in your depression. "I'm too old is what he said. He's looking for someone younger. Do you think I'm too old?"

"Can you explain why men do this to . . . other men? Doesn't it seem unfair to you? Men are jerks; that's all it is—present company excluded, of course."

Quickly I downed the shot and felt the worm blaze a path of fire down my throat, metaphorically speaking, of course. He held up a finger to the waitress, signaling another round.

Promptly I popped some Pepto-Bismol, 'cause I could see where we were headed. I had promised Harvey that I wouldn't drink anymore. However, Harvey hadn't called to check and see how abstinence was working for me, and Frank was a friend in need of sympathy drinking.

"Would it make you feel better if I told you that I had a man at my apartment on Saturday, and I don't think he touched me? Except the part where he cleaned me up after I poured a drink on his shirt."

"That's an attractive come-on. I haven't tried it before," he said, trying to be caustic and uncaring, but I saw through the charade, and my gut twisted for him. It could have been the tequila, but I didn't think so.

I looked him square in the eyes, because he needed the hard, honest truth. "Frank, you need new blood. You've got to go out and meet new men. This guy's a jerk; he'll only break your heart. When's the last time you went out for drinks?"

"You mean besides now?"

"Yes, besides now."

"Saturday," he said, as the waitress came by, glasses clinking on the table, and Frank downed his quickly.

"Oh. Well, maybe you just need to be more aggressive. A little more eye contact, some touching. Touching is always good."

His shoulders schlubbed even lower. "I'm old, Elle. Men don't want old men."

"They don't want old women, either, but do you see that stopping me?" I said, downing my next shot, partially for effect, partially for courage.

He gave me one of those X-ray vision looks. "Are you looking for honesty here or zealous denial?"

I saw his point. "Denial works for me."

"Thought so."

We clicked the magically refilled shot glasses together, and Frank smiled. "L'chaim."

"Screw life. Let's toast to love."

"I'd be happy with a torrid affair," he said, his eyes watching the bartender appreciatively. "Preferably with Brad Pitt."

"Me, too," I said, and downed the shot, nearly choking on the fire.

"Just have a quiet evening alone with Mr. Bunny."

I nearly choked again, but not from the fire. "How did you know?"

"I found him buried under the couch cushions one day," he said, completely blasé, as if he'd discovered a week-old bagel instead of my most private possession.

"Why were you pawing through my couch?" I asked.

Frank, who obviously handled his alcohol better than *moi*, looked offended. "I wasn't pawing. I sat on him."

"Oh."

I should have been appalled, or at the very least embarrassed, but the alcoholic haze made me feel warm, fuzzy, and safe. Tracy of the *Times* was going to run the profile, my business was going to struggle no more. I was now officially a winner in life. I figured I could tell the truth.

"You're too late," I told him. "The rabbit died."

"Sorry."

"Yeah, I need a new one," I said, tracing circles on the tiny table with my glass. Just as soon as I was back on my feet financially, I was gonna go back to Babeland, because my trophy case of sexual conquests was empty, and I was feeling the emptiness, and I mean that in the most literal sense.

"Why don't you try a live version instead?"

I looked around at the press of flesh in the room. Some were older, but most were younger than me, with firmer flesh, with better hair, with better clothes . . . you can see why me and my bunny were close.

"I considered that," I told him, as I watched one young, virile stud flirt his heart out with a young, nubile nymphette.

"But?" said Frank, obviously not seeing the writing on the bathroom wall, which surprised me, since he was just complaining about said writing not two seconds ago.

"What if I'm too old?" I said, as the nymphette tossed back her hair and laughed. I turned away, because green eyes aren't good for the soul. "I'm going to replace my pink pearl Casanova. I've been shopping. Haven't found the right one yet," I told him, putting a positive spin on the truth.

"Looking for Mr. Goodbunny," he said, cracking himself up.

"Not funny, Frank. Just think, it could be you," I snapped, because it's not funny when it's your absentee sex life under discussion. He saw my point, stopped laughing, and ordered another shot.

Once again, the glasses were magically refilled. And no matter what you've heard about the things that happen in Times Square, it's always magical but never cheap.

"I'm glad you're buying tonight," I told him.

"I know. I've seen your bills."

"I've been meaning to talk to you about that. You're putting them in the wrong piles. You had my Visa bill in my junk mail pile."

He tried to look innocent, but that's a stretch for Frank. "I thought you might actually look at it that way."

This time it was my shoulders that sank. "What do you think I should do?"

He raised a brow. "You're asking me for advice?"

"Hypothetically, yes."

"First we have to scarf enough to cover the loan payment and the rent. I can cover the loan payment for you."

I was deeply moved by this gesture of unselfish kindness, even if I suspected it might be his tequila talking. Frank gets more dramatic as he drinks, not that I'm one to throw stones.

"I won't take your money. Besides, you're working for free anyway. Do you ever feel like there's a little raincloud following you around?"

"They have a word for that."

"Cursed?"

"Paranoid. Your problems aren't any worse than anyone else's, Elle. Get out there and meet some potential clients."

I remembered Leah inviting me to her party and immediately felt a hot knife stab in my gut. "Maybe I should put up some flyers?" I said, because even cold calls were preferable to revisiting old acquaintances.

"That only works if you're a band."

"Why are you not helping? You're supposed to be helping."

"I'm not the life coach," he reminded me.

I knew he was kidding, but the best laughs are the honest ones.

We sat in our own comfortable silence, watching the inner workings of a Monday night happy hour. Over in the corner, a secretarial type was making eyes at a broker type, who was making eyes at a model type, who was pretending to ignore them all.

Frank tapped my arm. "There's a guy checking you out."

I didn't believe him for a sec. "You're just trying to make me feel better, but it's working."

"No, really, turn around."

I started to move, and he grabbed my hand. "Casually. Don't want to make it obvious."

Slowly I turned, inch by inch . . . whoa, tequila moment. I found myself staring into the sexiest brown eyes this side of a beagle puppy.

"Elle?"

The sexy brown eyes knew me? "Yeah," I answered, trying to focus on the live male in front of me.

"Elle Shields? Oh, God. It's been what? Twenty years?"

"Do I know you?" I asked, because even though I was pretty sure, I wasn't completely sure that the tequila hadn't transformed some dweeby insurance salesman into a ringer for a high school crush.

"Alan, Alan Benefield."

"Alan Benefield," I repeated, testing it, tasting it, *loving it.* Did I remember Alan? Yeah, baby, he was right up there with Shaun Cassidy and Mick Jagger (the early years). Alan had been gorgeous, built, and popular. In short, he had absolutely nothing to do with me.

If I had run into Alan two days ago, I probably would have turned and run. But today, flush from Tracy's to-be-done article,

Stephanie's financial overhaul, and also three shots of tequila, I looked my school years in the face and said, "Bring it on, baby."

"Alan . . ." I trailed off, snapping my fingers.

If he asked, I could have told him that he used to live on Sixty-seventh Street right near Lex and had a springer spaniel that he walked around seven at night. Not that I noticed or anything.

"From St. Anthony's," he said, looking slightly peeved that his name hadn't been rolling off the tip of my tongue. Then he looked at Frank. It was one of the testosterone rock-paper-scissors moments, but Frank was low in the testosterone zone, and Alan knew. How do people know? Frank was classy, well dressed, but not in a pink sort of way. I don't know, but Alan knew.

"This is Frank," I responded. "He works for me."

At that, Frank kicked me under the table. I deserved it and reveled in the pain. I reveled in the respect in Alan's sexy brown eyes as well. Alan looked at Frank and grunted.

Frank stood up. "I think I'll earn my keep and get another round. Alan?"

Alan nodded. "Beer. Something light. Took off forty pounds with the South Beach Diet. What do you think?" He patted his gut.

The said gut was clothed in some really nice fabric, a dark blue suit, possibly tailored. He had the brown hair to match the eyes, although he was doing the Trump comb-over thing, probably to cover the telltale signs of a receding hairline. I liked that little bit of vanity, that need to preserve his youth.

I wondered if women found him too old. Probably not. I

balanced my chin on my palm and gave him a goofy smile. "You know, Ralph Marston once said, your goals, minus your doubts, equal your reality. Just goes to show that drive is a very powerful force within the human psyche."

"Who's Ralph Marston?"

"I don't know, but I think he was a very smart man."

Alan nodded. "What are you doing these days?"

"I'm a life coach," I told him with my modest "Don't go on about it" smile.

"Listen, maybe we could have dinner tonight. I'd love to catch up on old times. Just the other day I ran into Leah Hanover . . ."

At that moment, Frank walked up and handed me a glass. "Elle, a martini. And for Mr. Goodbunny, a light beer."

I gave him my evil eyes, but he just smiled. I knew he was hurting, I knew I was about to desert him in his time of need, but there are times for loyalty and times for shallowness. Usually after three drinks, I'm as shallow as they come.

The waitress walked up and placed the check in front of Frank. "Here you go, sir."

Frank looked at the check, then looked at Alan. "So what do you do, Alan?"

"I'm a hedge fund analyst."

Frank looked impressed. "I've read about those in *Forbes*, but didn't know they actually existed outside their confined captivity on Wall Street."

"It's not something you dream about when you're a kid. I wanted to be a baseball player."

"Baseball players make a lot of money," said Frank, his hands inching toward the check. "I was just talking to Elle about how we're at the point in our lives when people either make it or break it. Know what I mean? It seems like when you hit middle age, you better have made your mark, or else you're nobody."

"I do all right," said Alan, pulling the check away before Frank could take it. We all watched as Alan slid his American Express card inside the leather check case.

It was Centurion black. I may not know the hottest fashion designers, but I *do* know the latest trends in credit cards.

I did a little happy dance in my head. Oh, God, there was hope for finding a man who was (a) attractive, (b) single, (c) successful, (d) not a dweeb. Frank saw the joy in my eyes and winked.

The waitress, spotting the card, immediately swept it up with a fawning nod of the head. *Go ahead and kiss his ring, why don't you?*

"I'm packing it in for the night. Getting too old for this," said Frank, rising slowly, rubbing his back. It really was too bad he was gay. He and Maureen would make a perfect match.

"Take the day off tomorrow," I told him. "With pay."

He blew me a kiss. "You're a sweetheart," he said, and with one last longing look at the bartender, he left.

"We're on for dinner?" asked Alan.

"Of course," I said, grabbing my bag in one smooth motion. "Where to?"

"Wherever you like," he said with a smile.

I closed my eyes, feeling as though I were staring into the

sun. The possibilities blurred in front of me, like little spots of color. When I opened them again, I was drunk. Not on tequila. No, tonight I was drunk on dreams.

We ended up at Per Se. How he got us in, I don't know. However, it was a Monday, so maybe it was just a slow night rather than superhuman powers of persuasion and/or cash.

Per Se was a sleek, contemporary restaurant in the Time Warner Center that smelled of money and air freshener. That's what happened to this city once they banned smoking. The ticklicious smell of pure money began to float to the top of the ozone. When you went to restaurants, you came out with clothes smelling of money. When you went to the bars and paid eighteen buckeroonies for a top-shelf martini, you'd develop a stale, Chase Manhattan bank-vault scent.

Currently Alan smelled of money as well, but I suspected that was his own aroma, rather than the spray-on version of Extra Loaded. I sniffed appreciatively, feeling a special extra zing between the thighs. I'd been without my vibrator for nearly two weeks now, but this wasn't only about relieving some stress. This was about playing in the big leagues. I shot him a slow, satisfied smile.

"Tell me what a life coach does," he said, while I feasted on flounder seeped in the most perfect Gouda sauce. It wasn't heavy or florid, like a lot of cheese sauces. Instead, it was light and tingled on your tongue.

I suppressed my moan of delight and swallowed. "I help people achieve their goals."

He twirled his wine just like they did in the movies. I myself had switched to water (sparkling). This was one night I didn't want to end up puking on his undefiled white shirt.

"Do you focus on one sector?" he asked.

"Beg pardon?" I said, wiping away the bit of sauce that was stuck on the corner of my mouth.

"Specialize. You know, weight loss, career counseling, etc." I was touched that he understood the biz so well. Not only handsome and rich but perceptive as well.

"No. I do it all."

"You look like you love what you do."

"I'm happy," I said, which before today would have been a lie, but I was starting to be hopeful about my life. Opportunities were plopping themselves in my lap, which was something new for me. Even better, I had offered Tony Shields up as a media sacrifice. Life was good.

"How about you? Do you like your job?"

"Oh, yeah. I've been really lucky."

"Isn't that nice," I murmured, because I wasn't surprised that Lady Luck favored people like Alan. "So, besides your job, what have you done with yourself in twenty years?" I asked, fishing to see if he was married, and I figured he knew I was fishing, but that was okay, because I wanted him to realize I had some standards.

"I got married right out of college, but we divorced eight years ago. She didn't like how the job kept coming first."

"You're just driven," I said, defending his shallow need for material goods and success.

"You're just being nice."

"I know," I said, happily devouring the last of my flounder.

"What happened to you after school? Did you go to college?" he asked, as the waiter whisked his plate away.

I could have told Alan I got a degree in MIS from CUNY, but I wasn't about to explain the whole layoff thing; that chapter was closed. Instead, I got creative. "I backpacked through Europe. I felt like I needed to find myself. I went all over the place. Italy. France."

"Did you see Sacre Coeur?"

"Nah. I skipped the touristy spots. I wanted to meet real people, in little towns, get to know different cultures." I spread my hands in front of me. "I needed to open my mind."

"I can understand. After what happened at your father's trial—"

"You'll understand if I'd rather change the subject," I said, not wanting to taint the delicious aromas in the air with the stench from the past.

"Tell me more about your business. It sounds like you're doing really well."

"I get by," I said modestly.

"Lots of clients?"

"Oh, yeah. I squeeze in some individualized, high-intensity sessions between my regular schedule. I call it Pilates for the soul."

"Catchy."

Modestly I looked down at the table, then peeked up from under my lashes. "In fact, I was just speaking with a reporter from the *Times* today."

He looked just as impressed as he was supposed to be. Oh,

God, I'd made an impression, and I hadn't even been drinking. "I think it's great that you're going after your dreams. I thought my life was shot to hell after I killed my pitching arm."

"How did you end up on Wall Street?"

"Family dynasty," he said with a disarming smile. "But I know what I've done; let's talk about you."

"Sure. What do you want to know?"

"Did you ever get married?"

And that was another topic I wanted to avoid. My love life, or lack thereof. I shook my head sadly. "There was one. I thought he was pretty special, but he died recently," I answered, my voice tinged with sadness. My bunny was very special, and I could see that replacing him was going to be a real bitch.

Alan's deep brown eyes filled with sadness. "I'm sorry. Was it an accident?" he said, which touched me, because it meant he thought I was capable of attracting a man whose life expectancy had yet to be reached.

However, I felt I should be honest. "Old age, mostly."

His hand reached across the white tablecloth and covered my own. "You need somebody younger. Full of life."

"That's what my friends have been telling me." I shot him a meaningful glance. "I think it's time I listened."

"Be careful out there; there're a lot of wolves in the woods. When you're vulnerable, like you are now . . ." He trailed off, pulling his hand away with a sigh. What a charmer.

"The wolves don't scare me. It's all the Prince Charmings."

"Why?"

"When you run with the wolves, you know exactly what

you're getting. With a prince, it's anybody's guess. Sometimes you get the happily ever after, but sometimes it's *Romeo and Juliet* without the Romeo."

"You're very cynical, Elle. I don't remember that about you."

"I'm surprised you remember me at all," I said, finally daring to bring it up. I was riding so high tonight that I could take most anything.

"Oh, I remember you. And that blue sweater you used to wear," he said.

My pulse shot to the moon. "That old thing?" I laughed, wondering if I still had it.

"All the guys knew who you were. There's a party coming up with some people from St. Anthony's. A few of us still get together. You should come. Leah told me she invited you."

Two invites to the same party in one week. A new world record. I shrugged, because I still had an exposed nerve, but . . .

Notice the *but,* which translates to "The jury's still out on that one."

The waiter came and whisked the plates away, dusting away the crumbs. I was left staring at a pristine white tablecloth, nothing to indicate untidiness at all. It was all about the image. When I was younger, I let everyone see the real me, crumbs and all. Over time I'd learned that everybody had a white tablecloth of their own. As soon as the crumbs appeared, you immediately dusted them away. It'd be nice if other people could overlook the crumbs. Yeah, if wishes were taxis, we'd all ride in the rain.

We ordered dessert and coffee, and while we were waiting, I

found his eyes on me, more often than not. "You're staring," I told him.

"You've grown up so nicely," he said.

"You're a liar, but I love you for it."

"I'm intrigued by your business. If I were a client, what advice would you give me?"

"What do you want?" I asked him.

"You."

I swallowed, my fork tapping nervously against the white tablecloth. I laid one hand over the other, so he wouldn't notice.

He covered my hand.

"Oh," I said, because he had floored me.

"So?" he asked, giving me the bedroom eyes. Every woman can recognize the bedroom eyes, but the trick is to ascertain the motivation for said eyes. *Is it because he's wasted?* No, because he'd only had one glass of wine. *Is it because he wants something other than sex?* I ran through my list of things that I could give (other than things that involved sexual favors) and suspected the answer was no.

That left one thing: Alan was proposing a torrid affair.

How deliciously slutty.

I'd never been a slutty individual; before tonight I couldn't slut my way out of a paper bag. See, unless you have zero self-respect, and I do mean *none,* you have to be fairly sexy to be slutty. *Sexy* was not an adjective used to describe me. Loyal. Yes. Cheerful. Yes. Cute. Yes. Sexy. No.

Yet the words of Ralph Marston echoed in my head: "Your goals, minus your doubts, equal your reality."

My goal for tonight was simple. I wanted to get laid. I wanted to have sex with a man, not a machine. A great-looking guy who carried a black AmEx card and liked to listen to me talk about my dreams.

If we were lucky, he'd have gel, preferably in a tropical coconut scent.

Until two days ago, I wouldn't have dared talk about my dreams; that was what my clients did. *My* dreams were stored away in a box, one of those fancy keepsake things that hold champagne corks, ticket stubs, and love notes that were never sent. Tonight I was going to open my box (both figuratively and literally), and I wanted to touch my dreams. I wanted to let my mind free to imagine. Free to imagine without the fear of getting hurt.

Which is not to say that I didn't have doubts. Was I too fat? What the hell did he see in me? What if he'd lied about his divorce and was just looking for a fling?

I glanced at his ring finger, and there was nothing there, not even a tan line.

A fling.

So what the heck was wrong with a fling?

Nothing at all.

If I may share a personal bit of wisdom here, when you're forty-two, you look life square in the eye and realize that the odds are slim you're going to find an ideal mate with minimal hangups and/or physical defects. It's another chapter I've closed. But I'm not dead yet, and I still had needs.

Your standards shift downward, right along with your boobs.

Of course, I would have to get naked and expose those boobs. And my tummy bulge, which had nothing to do with childbirth and everything to do with the freshly baked bread from Mr. Lombardi's on Eighty-first Street. And the back of my thighs, although if I positioned myself just right, I could avoid that unsightly embarrassment.

It was enough to send me right back into the arms of my vibrator.

"You're being very quiet," Alan said, which startled me, because I had millions of conversations honking in my head, and I think my heart had suddenly developed arrhythmia. I stared into those bedroom eyes that would soon see me in all my flaccid, untoned glory.

"Do you mind if I order a drink?"

Because men never say no when their date wants to get drunk, he immediately summoned the waitress. "Whatever the lady wants," he said, with a smile that said he knew exactly what I wanted.

"Chivas," I told her, not looking Alan in the eye.

"You really like to mix your drinks," he said, which I construed to mean that I was an alcoholic, not that there's anything wrong with that.

I downed the drink quickly, staying silent until I felt the soothing warmth of narcosis dull my worries.

"Better?" he asked.

I gave him a smile that said, "Don't worry, you'll still get yours," and rubbed my thumb sensuously against his palm. "I'm very bad," I told him, which was about as close to foreplay as I got.

He laughed, and he picked up my hand, inserting his thumb between my two fingers. Then he began to rub.

We were having finger sex.

Oh, God.

I needed my anxieties to just calm down. Tonight I was Cinderella. All right, a slightly tipsy, slutty version of Cinderella, but I believed in the alternative version of the story, where our princess-to-be drank Scotch out of the slipper instead of trying it on, mainly because her arches had fallen—among other things.

I considered downing one last drink, but my not-quite-firm stomach was already feeling the effects, and I really wanted this one night.

To have sex.

There was no reason for panic. We were going to have sex.

Batteries not included.

Six

Turn out the lights, the party's over.

—VARIOUS SOURCES,
ALL WOMEN OVER THE AGE OF 35

We stood in front of the Time Warner Center, arguing about where to go, his place or mine. Cars whizzed by, but I would have none of it. He was voting for my place, and I was stubbornly insisting on his. Finally I won the argument with the "I'll never believe you don't have a wife and kids unless we go to your place" piece of logic. Also, my place was a wreck, but I didn't tell him that.

"What if you have a husband tucked away?" he asked, as he single-handedly wrestled a cab to the curb. My hero.

"Would I be having tequila shots with a gay man on a Monday night if I were married?" I said, as I plopped into the seat.

"You got a point," he said, and gave the cabbie an address down in the West Village.

His place was an old converted warehouse, with no traces of the warehouse left, except for the outside. We passed through the doorway, protected only by a single gold key. At the back of the tiny room, there was a gray elevator and one unmarked button. As I entered the anonymous space, I knew how Alice felt at the Rabbit Hole. We took the elevator to the fourth floor, and suddenly we were there—a very airy, minimalist sort of loft, with very little furniture. Other than the bed.

"So," I said, eyeing the bed with trepidation.

"So," he said, taking off his coat and loosening his tie. "Want a drink?" he said, and it was a testament to my gurgly stomach that I refused.

"I'll pass," I told him, casually kicking off my shoes but hiding them under the retro-looking sofa. Next to the sofa was a Lucite table, no drawer, and a funky-looking blue glass lamp, completely impractical and very pristine. On the east wall, there was a huge print, the old diner picture with the counter worker, the dame, and the world-weary man. Opposite that was the view, a full-size window looking out over the Hudson. I curled up on the retro sofa, tucking my feet underneath me.

He strolled over to the bar, where he plucked two ice cubes from an ice bucket (how come the rich have permanently unmelted ice?) and poured two fingers of Scotch on top.

"Nice place," I said, trying to fill the dangerously meaningful silence.

"It's okay. When I was married, we had a place in Westchester, but I lost it in the settlement."

"Still," I said, looking around, "this is not bad. City lights, city action."

He sat down next to me (not too close), and I noticed he had ditched his shoes as well. I also noticed that his socks didn't have holes in them. "I miss the quiet."

"I've never lived outside the city; never wanted to," I said firmly. It wasn't just the tequila talking, it was Elle. I had struggled my entire life to make it in this city, my own Holy Grail. There are other people, less stubborn and probably a little bit smarter, who might have packed their bags, but not me.

Not yet.

Alan smiled his nice, successful smile. "With your business it makes sense to keep it local."

"Yeah," I said, watching as he drank the Scotch.

"Why haven't I heard more about you?" he asked.

I thought about telling him the truth, that I'd done nothing talk-worthy, but tonight the universe had shifted. This was the life I should've had. "I've been keeping on the down low, you know?" I murmured.

"This is the part where I kiss you," he said, and I closed my eyes to wait.

It was a nice kiss, very comfortable, like a down comforter on a cold winter's night. He pulled me closer, and I felt my stomach lurch. It was part nerves, part Chivas, part coffee, and part chocolate soufflé.

I pulled back.

"Problem?" he asked. "We don't have to do anything you don't want to."

"The mind is willing, but the body is weak," I told him.

"It's been a long time for me, too," he said.

"I don't believe that."

"Seriously," he said, and his arms tightened around me. "Relax, Elle. It's been over twenty years in the making."

"Build up the tension, why don't ya?" I said, struggling to recapture the romantic magic, while my less-than-firm parts jiggled in fear. "You wouldn't mind if we turned out the lights, would you?" I managed to ask.

He touched a finger to my cheek. "You're having some issues with this, aren't you? If you'd like, we can just wait. I'll call you, take you out to dinner, maybe dancing or something."

Now everyone who's heard the phrase "I'll call you," raise your hand. Thought so. I reached behind me and popped off the funky-looking lamp. The lights were dimmed, but not enough.

His hands moved to my blouse, and I knew I was at the point of no return. I didn't want to be a coward. I didn't want to have a monogamous relationship with a little orgasmic doodad. I wanted to be a part of a brave new world that actually had sex with men.

I could do this.

Oh, God, his hands were at my bra.

Just one click, and—

—my breasts swung free.

Sneakily he distracted me from my unadulterated exposure by kissing my neck and whispering in my ear.

"I love the feel of you," he said, his hands touching me, and I swear, it was like we were making out in the back of the gym. "You're so soft."

Slowly I began to relax, to enjoy the feel of his hands on me. He didn't use the used-car-salesman approach like other men who slept with women over the age of thirty-five. His technique was—quite nice.

Feeling a bit daring, I unbuttoned his shirt and discovered something marvelous: the extra roll of flesh at his waist. It was neither big nor unsightly, instead it warmed me all over. My Mr. Right Now had a minor case of love handles.

He pressed me back into the cushions, his lips still working over my neck. "I hope you don't mind making out on the couch, Elle," he said. "You were a high school fantasy for me."

And in every high school fantasy, a boy must try for third base. His hands went to the buttons on my pants, only to discover that I had no buttons, only an elastic waistband. I tensed up for a moment, because the lights were still brighter than what I wanted, but he shushed me with his mouth, and I kissed him back.

I could get used to this kissing stuff. My last carnal visitor (the talker) wasn't much of a kisser, always lapping me up like a dog's bowl of water, but Alan had finesse. His fingers crept lower, and my hips were moving on autopilot. They knew the drill, but the weight on top of me, two hundred pounds of man, well, that was new.

I felt his finger touch me, gently, and I nearly shot through the roof. His skin felt hot and alive, and I swear I could feel the blood pumping through him. It was so unusual, this joining of woman to man. He slid my pants down over my hips (no small task, that), and I didn't even object. The lights weren't as dark as I would've liked, but I was even willing to overlook that. I was caught in the throes of actual lust. A moan escaped my lips, as his hands crept beneath my practical cotton Jockeys.

I felt the start of my orgasm begin to take over (when you're used to the rabbit, speed is not a problem), and I let myself fall. It was a gentle one, no fist pounding or screaming involved. But it was nice, comforting. There's something about the humanity of sex when two people are conjoined.

We moved on to bigger and better things, and I do mean bigger and better. He doffed his pants, and there I was, flesh to flesh with Alan Benefield, who was a certified card-carrying member of St. Anthony's Preparatory Jock Elite.

He moaned aloud, and I cried at the sheer beauty of that sound. I had Alan Benefield on his knees, in the metaphorical sense only, although the night was young. Tonight was more than just a sexual encounter for me. This was a redo, a chance to whisk away all the crumbs from high school and start over.

Guilt crept over me, because I suspected I was more turned on by the idea of Alan Benefield than by Alan Benefield himself, but I was turned on by something that was taller than seven inches, and happiness was bursting forth from places it usually didn't burst forth from. In short, now wasn't the time.

I felt his body jerk, and he collapsed on top of me, and for a few minutes we just lay there on his retro sofa, in his West Village loft, and I knew how Cinderella felt, just before midnight when all the guards were looking for the prince, and he was out in back of the castle, getting a little somethin' somethin'.

"Thank you," I whispered to him.

He rose up, looked me in the eyes. "For what? I got the better end of this deal."

I smiled, as if he was right. But actually, fifteen minutes of sex had just done more for me than fifteen years of therapy ever could.

Tonight I was healed.

I awoke the next morning to the smell of freshly brewed coffee. Instantly, I knew I was not at home, because I didn't own a coffee maker (my kitchen was truly killer small). I stretched, my muscles protesting with the movement.

I could hear the television in the kitchen, and I gathered up my clothes and ran to the bathroom to get dressed, just in case Alan decided he wanted to see me nude in the cold light of morning, without the judgment-impairing influence of alcohol. I locked the door. It seemed best.

Quickly I threw on the pantsuit, brushed my teeth, and then stared critically at my wrinkled and shameless outfit in the mirror. Silk is not conducive to being thrown over a chair all night, and it looked like either (a) I'd spent the night out, or (b) I had been dressed by Don King. I shrugged because I had no choice, and to be honest, it'd be kinda nice for the world to know that I got laid last evening.

In the West Village.

In a loft.

Ha. Take that, Ms. Leah Weber.

I scoured through his bathroom drawers, looking for something to help erase the lines around my eyes. There are women who carry every cosmetic known to Cher in their handbag. I'm not one of them. Eventually I found some suntan lotion with aloe, which was better than showing up looking like a hag.

I needed to stake out the situation before I decided on the best approach, so I crept down the hallway and peered into the kitchen. Alan was sipping a cup of coffee, reading the *Wall Street Journal,* and watching CNBC on the mini-television perched just over the island. Note that his kitchen was *not* killer small. Unfortunately, he was dressed in a suit, already wearing his shoes.

Okay, I could connect the dots: breakfast was gonna be short.

He saw me, shot a perfunctory smile in my direction. A smile that had as much heat as Antarctica in summer. I wiggled my fingers in a flirtatious wave. Alan looked startled and buried himself back in the *Journal.* I cleared my throat. His head stayed buried. I considered trying something else, but I'd played this part so many times I knew the role by heart. Something died then, the neurotic Cinderella fantasies that one night of sex had metastasized into something dangerous.

I took a deep breath, mentally preparing my lines, and then scurried in. I kissed the air in his general direction, a nice touch of carelessness and sophistication.

"Did you look at the time? I can't believe I slept so late. You should've gotten me up earlier. I have an appointment in an hour!"

Alan clicked off the television and sighed. "All right. But I insist on taking you home," he said, his eyes never leaving the paper.

You remember how I told you about last night being better than ten years of therapy? Well, I'm taking all that crap back. This whole ping-pong thing is why I spent so many months celibate yet satisfied.

Still, I wished he didn't look so good. He smelled like after-shave and soap, and his hair was still damp from the shower. At least he was still wearing the comb-over. If it was tousled and rumpled, I think I would have beggared my pride.

After all, he had a loft.

I forced a smile. "Crosstown and uptown? During the morning rush?" I said, because I wanted to give him one last chance to act as if I was something more than Vagina-on-a-Stick. Maybe he wouldn't cave so easily this time. Maybe I was reading the signals all wrong.

"I have a meeting on Eighty-second Street at eleven o'clock. It's not out of my way at all," he said, flipping the page to yesterday's market wrap-up.

I smiled tightly. "How convenient. Why don't we get going, then? No telling what's up with the subway today."

"Subway?" He looked at me in horror. "We'll call the service."

"Yeah, that's what I meant," I said, still trying for poised and sophisticated.

He speed-dialed the service, and I clicked back on the TV, pretending to be fascinated by the morning market predictions.

The trip home was completely uneventful, so I won't bore you with the details. To be frank, I don't know why I tried. It was possibly because of Frank that I had tried (and that little part of me that didn't want to be a loser in love), but trying is for those people with a modest chance of success. Namely, actresses and supermodels.

I tried to make small talk, honestly, I did, but it kept falling flat, and I was all small-talked out. With each passing mile, I knew I wouldn't be back to the loft in the West Village. I popped my last PB chewables to calm down the nervy stomach, because if not, I'd be puking my guts out all over Alan's clean white shirt.

Alan wasn't Harvey. He'd care, and not in a good way.

His cell rang, and I pretended not to listen.

"The presentation is all ready."

"Yeah, I'm on my way now."

He shot me a polite smile.

"Not long. Traffic's easy . . ."

And so is Elle.

"Not a problem. Talk to you soon."

He snapped the phone shut. "The office."

"Do you spend a lot of time on the phone?"

"Not really," he answered, and then stared out the window. I got the hint.

When we got to my building, I was surprised that Alan got out. I wasn't expecting that. I was expecting a casual wave and a meaningless "Call me."

Instead, he was opening my door. Artie, the doorman, didn't blink an eye at my appearance. I tried to look as if I did this all the time, but Artie knew better. Alan didn't.

"You don't have to walk me in," I told him. I didn't bother putting the extra little coyness in my voice this time. Seemed like a waste.

"I have to take you upstairs, Elle," he said. He walked back to the driver, said something, and the driver drove off.

I was puzzled, confused, slightly hungry, and really wanted a shower. Unfortunately, I had no idea why Alan had just sent off his driver. I mean, the guy had a business meeting in—I checked my watch—an hour.

An hour?

So what was I? His mid-morning coffee break?

I gave him a nervous smile, because maybe I'd been too hasty earlier. Maybe he was just as bad at the whole man-woman thing as I was. Not likely, but I considered it, all the same.

Do you see what I'm doing here? Whipping myself into a frenzy over possibilities that every women in her right mind would dismiss. It's the wrong mind that gets us into trouble every time.

Why do we do this to ourselves? Why do women get in such a frenzy over the mating *dance* and men get in such a frenzy over the mating *act*? We shouldn't have to. This is why God invented the pink pearl bunny.

After today, I was hanging up my vagina and heading for Babeland.

Of course, that was assuming that Alan didn't have carnal intentions when we got upstairs.

Oh, God, I'm such a wuss.

We got into the elevator, an awkward moment for both of

us. I stared at the numbers over the door. When we got to my floor, my keys were ready, and I let us into the relative safety of my apartment.

Immediately I was hit with the stack of self-help books leaning against the couch. I had forgotten about that part, in my worries about having a man notice the effects of gravity on my flesh.

"Nice place," he said.

"You're too kind," I told him, laying my jacket on top of them. "I've been going through my wardrobe and deciding what to donate to the shelter. I do it every spring. Clutter. It's the devil's handiwork."

He sat down on the couch and gave me a friendly look. I wasn't feeling friendly, so I took my usual brown chair.

"So who's your appointment with this morning?" I asked, crossing my legs oh so casually. Keeping them tightly closed.

"It's a friend of a friend. I'm trying to get him to change brokers."

"Ah, a little sales call, huh? I figured you'd just sit behind a desk all day and punch numbers."

"Nah, I hit the pavement just like every other joe," he said.

"These are hard times for us all, aren't they?" I said, even though I lived in a postwar one-bedroom that was just this close to being "too far uptown," and he lived in the West Village. In a loft.

"Why don't you change your mind about Leah's party?" he said, and his smile turned nice. "Please."

The whole thing was right out of *The Twilight Zone*. Last

night had been like a dream. This morning, not so much. And he was *still* pushing the party? What did I look like, a masochist? "Oh, I don't know," I answered. "This is my busy season at work."

"The spring?"

"It's the perfect union of tax day and bathing suit season. Gives everybody the woolies."

He quit trying after that, and I wondered if he remembered what I looked like in the nude. Judging from the tension in his face, I thought so.

After another twenty minutes of strained conversation, I couldn't take it anymore. "Listen, I don't mean to kick you out, but I've got a client to see," I said.

Thank God he took the hint, which made me wonder why he had come up here in the first place. I wasn't sure what he wanted, except that I knew with soul-stirring clarity that it wasn't me. "Sure. Let me call my service," he said, and pulled out his cell phone.

I could have told him that Artie would get him a cab, but he was already on the phone.

"Another ten minutes," he said, after he hung up.

Another ten minutes of hell? I was considering walking out of my own apartment, when the buzzer rang.

There was a good possibility it was Mr. Tierney. However, I heaved a sigh of relief and pressed the button.

"Visitor, Miss Sheffield."

"Send them up," I said, not even bothering to ask who it was. It could have been Hannibal Lecter, and I still would've showed him up. Murder by cannibalism was preferable to this awkward silence with a man who was suffering from the post-traumatic stress of seeing my naked body.

When the doorbell rang, I ran and flung it open. Literally. No exaggeration here.

Unfortunately, it wasn't Hannibal Lecter. No, it was Harvey.

Seven

There are no good girls gone wrong, only bad girls found out.

—MAE WEST

N ow, isn't this a nice surprise," I said, wishing that I had taken the two seconds necessary to change from my "spent the night out" clothes.

He looked from Alan to me, back to Alan, and then finally at my calla lilies print on the wall. "I shouldn't have come by. Leah insisted. I tried to call."

Note the "Leah insisted" part. Not "I wanted to see you," not "I was worried." No, nothing like that.

I glanced over at the answering machine blinking like a fire engine. The red indicator said I had twelve new messages. Twelve? What if they were all creditors? Or Mr. Tierney? Of course, maybe those calls were from Harvey. Maybe he was just trying to save face in front of Alan.

Harvey saw the glance. "I called a couple of times, but most of those are from her. You can check."

Okay, not trying to save face at all. No, the other face around here needing saving was mine. I looked at Harvey, doing my best slutty tramp imitation (not hard in my currently wrinkled dress). "God in heaven, what happened? She won the lottery and decided to tell *me*, who we all know is her best friend," I said, very proud of myself for the snippiness in my voice. The little girl was growing up. And growing claws.

Harvey shifted on his feet. "She knew you saw Tracy yesterday and tried to call last night. Then she called me, and I told her I hadn't heard from you, so she waited another two hours and then called me again. And after I worked really *hard* to convince her that I hadn't heard from you"—he shot a meaningful glance in Alan's direction—"I told her I'd check in the morning." He shot me a faux smile, and trust me when I say that Harvey doesn't do faux well. "So here I am. And I see you're okay, so I'll just be going," he said, backing into the hallway.

Alan stood up. "I'm sorry. This is really awkward. Alan Benefield."

"Harvey Weber. Pleased to meet you."

"Weber? You're Leah's husband?"

"Ex," said Harvey painfully.

Alan winced. "Yeah, I've got alimonies of my own to worry about. Child support?"

"One daughter."

Alan pounded him on the shoulder. "Sorry about that. None here. The ex said it'd ruin her shape. At the time, I thought she was being selfish and egotistical. Now I see she was saving me about fifty grand a year. I don't remember Leah saying where you worked."

Harvey shoved his hands into his jeans pockets. He wasn't the social chatterbox that Alan was, and I could see his face closing off. "Photographer."

"Harvey works for the *Times*," I said, butting in. I didn't want Harvey to sell himself short. In a bit of late-night insomnia, I had Googled some of his older work. He was very good.

"Need a financial advisor?" asked Alan.

"I thought you were a hedge fund analyst," I said.

Alan smiled. "I had hoped you were listening. I do both for the firm."

"Good to know," said Harvey.

Alan pulled out a card, shook hands with Harvey, and palmed him the card, all in one smooth move. I could learn from this technique. "I better go." He held his pinkie and thumb to his face and made the international sign for phone. "I'll call you," he said to me, and then walked out my door.

Normally I would have written Alan off just for saying it. But he did walk me back to my apartment. He did sit on my couch. All in all, Alan was a big jigsaw puzzle piece. With a très cool loft.

I turned my attention back to Harvey, who looked awkward and uncertain, which seemed to be a new look for Harvey. "It went well yesterday. The group meeting with Tracy. She agreed to do the piece," I said. I didn't mention that I had to bribe her with an exclusive on my father. Yeah, Harvey would find out about that soon enough, but I preferred to keep my pride intact. At least the illusion of it.

"Tracy called and told me," he said.

"Oh," I answered.

"I should go," he said.

"Wait," I said. "Look, I'm sorry. It's been a bad morning."

"I should go," he said—again.

"Can we talk?" I asked, and the instant the words were out of my mouth, I knew it was a mistake.

"Sure," he said, panic flashing in his eyes.

"Water?" I asked, but he shook his head.

I made a long production out of getting my own glass of water while I figured out what exactly I wanted to say. Two men had just been in my apartment, both of whom were not in my league. On the one hand, there was Alan. Rich, handsome, blast from my past, but doesn't-do-mornings-well Alan. And then there was Harvey. Bohemian, rugged, formerly married to Leah, only-came-by-because-my-ex-wife-sent-me Harvey.

Lastly, there was me. I, who had never dallied in sexual juggling games before in my life. Might I give you a bit of advice? Forty-two is not the time to start.

Yet Harvey captured my rather prurient imagination, and I suspected he knew.

I suspected, from the way he sometimes wouldn't meet my eyes, that he had dabbled in some prurience as well. Harvey struck me as a man on a first-name basis with prurience. I suspected he liked his women fast and loose, although how the heck he ended up with a stick-in-the-mud like Leah was beyond me.

But Harvey looked about as happy to be in my apartment as Alan had been.

So why were they there?

I sighed, my stomach heaved, and I really missed my bunny. "I'm sorry Leah sent you all this way for nothing," I said, coming around the corner and settling in my favorite chair.

Then I cocked my head to the side, mainly to hide the slight dongle beneath my chin, awaiting his response. Harvey's not a fast talker, so I waited a bit.

Finally, he deigned to speak. "This isn't easy for me, but you should know something. I like my life the way it is. I've got freedom to stay up as late as I want. Nobody there to nag me about the dishes piling up in the sink. I see my daughter when I want." He stopped and rubbed a finger over a piece of thread on my couch. "I'm not looking for anything now, and you have vulnerable eyes."

I widened my vulnerable eyes, trying to erase all hints of vulnerability. I wasn't vulnerable. Not anymore. I had been vulnerable. But now I was hard, strong, able to withstand whatever crap life chose to throw my way. "Don't you worry about me; I'm as tough as nails."

For a second, he looked me in my eyes, but I guess the strength was too much for him, because he looked away. "Alan seems like a good guy. You should go for it."

It wasn't the most romantic thing he could have thrown out there. In fact, I knew, with a crystallizing moment of clarity, that Harvey would never be a part of my life, and it hurt. I liked the way he always seemed at ease with who he was. Maybe if I stayed around him, some of the easiness would wear off on me, too. Unfortunately, unless I kidnapped him and chained him to my bed, I suspected it was not to be. Alan's morning-after behavior had given me pangs, but nothing like this. I hate pain, I don't like talking about pain, I don't even like thinking about pain, but this time I'd slipped up. Not again. No, right now I needed to be alone, preferably behind a locked door where none of the world could intrude.

With a regretful sigh, I stood, the universal sign for "Why don't you leave now?"

"It was really nice of you to be so concerned," I said, and I was very proud because there was no sarcasm in my voice.

He ducked my glance away. "It was Leah."

My eyes narrowed. "Nice of her, then." Okay, there was sarcasm that time, and I'm sure he heard it.

"I'll go."

I didn't argue, just smiled politely. I had learned early on that a smile could hide a heckuva lot.

He jammed his hands into his pockets, his shoulders slumping as if he were carrying a big weight. Welcome to my world, bud.

Harvey gave me a last look. "I'm sorry," he said, summing up all his shortcomings in two words.

"Build a bridge," I answered, because I was tired, I hurt, and I wanted someone else to hurt, too.

• • •

As much as I detest pain, it truly is a wonderful motivator. I spent thirty minutes with my head buried in my pillow, refusing to cry. Instead, I lay there, my mind pushing out the dark thought and concentrating on the good. There was good. The profile was good. My love life sucked, but I was okay with that. Soon I could go bunny shopping, and balance would be restored.

I popped some Pepto and called Mr. Tierney to explain my current situation. I told him I was good for the rent, business was starting to pick up, and the *New York Times* was running a profile on Good Vibrations sometime within the next two weeks. He thanked me for my honesty, told me that I had another two weeks but not a moment longer. I told him very clearly and politely that two weeks would be more than enough.

And it would be. I knew the power of positive thinking, and right now, I was the most positive thinker on the planet. This time, I wasn't going to wimp out. I was going to ride the wave of success for all it was worth.

Next up, dear old Tony.

Going to visit my father in prison wasn't the highlight of my life, but I'd been in lower spots. And all I needed to do was get the green light for an interview with Tracy, and that should be a piece of cake. Didn't everyone want to be in the *New York Times*? I knew I did. It only seemed logical that Tony would want his brush with fame as well. Of course, he'd already had one, and that got him twenty years in minimum security, so he might not have been as enthused.

I popped four Peptos, and although they settled my gut, they didn't help my unsettled heart.

The prison guard frisked me with his metal detector, which would have been fun if he hadn't been twenty and blushing the entire time. I gave him a maternal smile and restrained myself from patting him on the head.

"I'm here to see Tony Shields."

"Sign here. No sharp objects, no weapons, and no sexual contact."

"He's my father."

The guard shrugged. "You never can tell. Dames really go for the prisoners. I don't judge."

"Let's just get on with this," I told him, as I pulled open a cut in my heart that hadn't been touched in a long, long time. My mind and my heart worked in perfect tandem. Any problem that was too hard to face got ignored.

Money. Men. My father.

You would think my earlier experiences would have made this one a walk in the park. However, my feet didn't want to move.

"Coming, miss?" the guard asked.

I concentrated. Once, twice, and soon my feet were cooperating.

I was led into a large visiting area lined with tables. There weren't the glass dividers you see on TV, which disappointed me. I sat in the black plastic chair and tried to get comfortable.

Tony came in through the back doorway, and I got my first sight of my father in working-class blues. I'd expected zebra stripes or prison orange, but no, he was dressed in jeans and a work shirt with a name tag over his chest pocket.

It was easier to focus on the clothes than the face. His hair had turned steely gray, but he was still the same skinny man I remembered. He smiled when he saw me, his eyes holding none of the prison shadows I had hoped to see. "Pookie Girl!"

"I'm not seven anymore, Daddy," I said, sounding exactly as if I was eight.

He reached out to touch me, and I scooted back. "Pookie Girl" had cut through one wall of defenses, and we were only thirty seconds into the reunion. Quickly I recovered. "We're here to talk. Got any prison-type diseases since you've been in here?"

His eyes shut off, and this time I saw the shadows. "Sorry," I said, not sorry at all. He hadn't cared about my pain, so why should I care about his?

"I got in over my head," he said, *still* making excuses.

"Fifty thousand dollars is over your head. Twenty million is stupidity. Congratulations, Tony. I never knew you were that much of an idiot."

"Is this why you came? To lay into me?"

"No," I said quietly, because after forty-two years, I finally needed something from him.

"Then why?"

I met his eyes evenly, no vulnerability there. "I need your help."

"Sure, whatever I can do," he said, still choosing to lie to me. "Did you get my letter? Almost time for the parole hearing.

You'll be there, won't you? Say something good about your old man?"

His smile ate into me like acid. I wanted to tell him to go to hell. One letter in twenty years, and then only because he wanted me to do something for him.

However, here I was, visiting for the first time in twenty years, only because I wanted him to do something for me. The apple doesn't fall far from the tree.

I took a deep breath, inhaling federal prison air, visualizing a sweet, green meadow, one I could run into and never see Tony Shields again.

Nine months of online life coach training came to the rescue, and I gazed at my father as if he were a means to an end and nothing more.

"I'm trying to get my own business off the ground," I told him, neglecting to mention that I'd been working on this single task for the last four years. "A reporter from the *New York Times* wants to do a feature on me, but she needs to talk to you, too." Then I smiled sweetly, just so he could remember that I was his only Pookie Girl.

"No."

I laid my hands out flat on the table, my skin turning pale from the pressure. "What do you mean, no? This is the *Times,* Tony. You could be famous."

"I don't want any fame, Elle. I've paid my debt to society. I'm up for parole next year, and the good warden willing, I'll be out. I don't want anyone digging up the past. It's over."

I blinked, not believing that after all the hard work I'd done to get to this point, he was just going to say no. Why did I think I could count on my father? *Stupid, stupid, stupid.* "I thought you would be willing to help."

"Find somebody else," he said, his eyes avoiding my own.

"I don't know any other felons who were responsible for having bilked most of the parents of the senior graduating class at St. Anthony's Prep out of twenty million dollars," I answered.

"I thought you believed in me. You, of all people, knew we were never rich."

"If I believed in you, don't you think I'd have visited in, say, the last two decades? No, I never thought you were innocent. Just incompetent."

"I'm glad to know you thought so highly of me."

"Can the violins. They clash with the ambience." I knew this would be a mistake, but still, you'd think for once he could have delivered on something. I stood to go.

"Don't leave, Elle. Don't you have time to stay and chat?"

I wanted to scream then, but we weren't a family of screamers. The Shields family never yelled or screamed, cried only rarely with fat, silent tears muffled by a pillow and a firmly locked door.

"You really expect me to just sit down and discuss sports?" I said loudly, as close to screaming as I got.

"The Yankees have done good this year."

He was trying to wear me down. Talking baseball touched a soft spot. "They do good every year, Daddy. Things change in twenty years."

"Haven't you ever wondered how I was?"

I gave him a hard look. "No."

He rubbed his chest. It was a new move for my father. I wasn't the only one who had hardened up over time. Three years ago they had a special on Court TV that I discovered while channel surfing. A mug shot of Tony had flashed across the screen, timid and vulnerable.

I don't understand why so many people believed that this ninety-pound weakling could steal a cool twenty mil. This wasn't George Clooney or James Bond.

This was a man who couldn't work the microwave.

Not that it mattered; they didn't have microwaves in prison.

He looked at me with my own blue eyes. "Why does it have to be the press?"

"You owe me," I said. "Do it for your darling daughter."

He shook his head. There were many times I had hated my father: the night of Tiffany Morgan's party, two weeks before graduation when my ten announcements came back marked "Return to Sender," and the day I stood at LaGuardia, waiting for Mom's plane to return from the Caribbean. But those were a pale shadow of the black rage that shot through me now. If I had had a shank in my hand, I swear I could've killed him.

I was tired of being vulnerable.

I was tired of being a victim. I was taking charge, being aggressive, chasing my dream. Twenty years too late, but what the hey?

No, I was going to be tough, steely. I would do whatever it took. "Want me to speak on your behalf? That's the price, Dad. Talk to the reporter, or I swear I'll have every one of the parents of the St. Anthony's graduating class of 1985 at your parole hearing, and I'm sure they won't be kind."

He raised his voice, not screaming, though. "You really hate me, don't you?"

"Yes," I said, and didn't even hesitate.

"All right, I'll do it."

"That won't make me not hate you," I told him, just so he knew that would never change.

He nodded. "I know."

It took me about two seconds once I reached the sparkling fresh Connecticut air to dial Tracy on my cell. My fingers were shaking, partially because the conversation with my father had lasted about ten minutes too long, partially because I could see the wealth of ten thousand Life Coach University graduates just within my motivational fingertips, and partially because the keypad was itty-bitty. She answered on the second ring.

"Tracy. I did it. You're cleared. Visiting hours are Tuesday through Sunday, from ten to four, and you'll have to clear it in advance. He's ready."

"He'll talk about the money, right?"

"Sure," I said, as if we were rolling in it. "Do you have all the material you need to run the profile?"

"I think so. I submitted the article to my editor yesterday. He said they'd run it a week from Saturday."

Saturday? "I don't mean to be telling you how to perform your journalistic operations, but don't you think Sunday would be better?"

"Elle, I know this means a lot to you, but I'm just a little fish in a big saltwater aquarium, and we're lucky to get Saturday. Okay?"

I swallowed my objections and muttered something agreeable. She was doing the profile. I was golden. Okay, it would run on Saturday. Big whoop.

I flagged down a cab to get me back to the train station, leaving the rigid confines of the federal institution far behind me. I didn't plan on coming back.

That piece of my life was over.

Hallelujah.

$\mathscr{E}ight$

I believe that the Good Lord gave us a finite number of heartbeats and I'm damned if I'm going to use up mine running up and down a street.

—NEIL ARMSTRONG

The rest of the week passed quietly, and if you read that to mean that neither Alan nor Harvey called, you'd be batting a thousand. I looked back over my actions, but barring an extreme makeover, Elle edition, I couldn't see how I might have prevented any of it. And to be fair, why should I be second-guessing my actions? It wasn't me who turned into a Frigidaire appliance. It wasn't me who "liked my life the way it was." No, I was the one with the "vulnerable eyes," which pissed me off to no end. In fact, I got myself so pissed off I nearly broke down and returned to Babeland to buy a toy, but I shamed myself into staying away. Mainly because my credit was still in the toilet, but also because I was going to be strong. However, I did go through half a bottle of Chivas, two packages of Pepto-Bismol, and two temazepam in my quest for strength.

And ignoring the negatives (many), there were the positives (one). Namely, my business. On Sunday, I bought the *New York Times* and skimmed the sections. Just in case the profile on Good Vibrations broke early and I needed to be prepared for the torrent of calls that were going to overwhelm my modest infrastructure.

At mid-morning, I got a call. An emergency appointment with Laci "My Boyfriend's Married, Why Won't He Get a Divorce?" Anderson. A NYC fireman had asked her out, and she wanted to go, but she worried that David might think she was being unfaithful. I kid you not.

"Laci," I told her, "what if the fireman is your fate? Your one true love."

She looked at me through the clueless eyes of someone who has a fantabulous life but doesn't know it. "You think? I mean, he's hot, and built, and I like the way he eats me up with his eyes . . ."

Aghh! At that moment, I wanted to hit her. I'd never hit anyone in my life, but I had to clench my pen till blisters formed. Not two weeks ago, Harvey had looked at me like that, and in that one, short, marvelous moment, I had been wanted and desired.

"Has your fireman been married? Have any kids? Does he enjoy his freedom?"

She pushed back a few strands of hair from her eyes. "No, he told me something popped inside him the first time he saw me."

My hand jerked against the coffee cup, spilling mocha on my mercifully mocha-colored pants. However, the coffee was hot, and it burned like hell. I sat frozen until the pain passed and then gave Laci a tight smile.

"When something pops in a man, and it's not his penis, you run, don't walk, to see what's what. Where do you want to be twenty years from now, Laci? When you hit forty?"

She stared at her hands, the long pink, pearlescent nails, and then she nodded. "I want to be successful, confident, and happy. Like you. Maybe."

I blinked. Twice. "That's a really . . . perceptive thing to say," I answered, with a completely straight face. "What if your fireman—what's his name?"

"Tom."

"What if Tom is your future? You could be successful, confident, and happy, and have someone to share all that happiness with, too."

"What if David's my future?"

I sighed. "How old is David's wife?"

"Forty-two."

Of course. "When you hit forty-two, don't you think he's going to start looking again?"

Her smile turned goofy. "He says I'm the only one for him."

"You mean besides his wife?"

Tiny, elegant tears welled up in her eyes, and I swear I felt like I kicked a puppy. However, in my own defense, Laci needed a good kick in the size two buttocks. They don't call it tough love for nothing.

"You hate me," she said. "You think I'm stupid."

I gave her a tired smile. "You're not stupid, Laci, but you've got one great guy, who hears 'pop' when you walk into the room, and then you've got a loser guy who's making you sit on the bench during the prime years of your life."

Comprehension dawned in her eyes. "I should call Tom."

I nodded. "You should call Tom."

Even as I was speaking, she was starting to dial on her cell. I walked away with a smile on my face. God, I love my job.

Monday's appointment with my group was at the reservoir in Central Park. A time-out for exercise, in order to revitalize our minds and our souls. JFK once said that the lack of exercise in America was a menace to society. 'Course, he said that in 1960, when the Cuban Missile Crisis was just a twinkle in Castro's eyes.

But today wasn't about Castro, or missiles, or dead presidents. No, it was about the joys of nature. The park in April was gorgeous, sporting every color in the rainbow: greens, yellows, pinks, oranges, and purples. There were daffodils everywhere and the scent of the magnolia trees heavy in the air.

However, I wasn't here to sightsee. Today was all about feeling the burn.

In the spring, the sleeves came off, midriffs were bared, and sweaters were no longer required. Barbara and Tanja both needed firming up, and I figured the exercise would do Joan good, too.

I had changed into my best gray sweats and was doing my warm-ups up when Tanja jogged up, wearing the glow of success. I immediately knew something was akilter.

"Guess what I did today," she said, not expecting an answer. Of course, I spit out the most preposterous thing I could think of.

"You put an ad in Missed Connections," I said, a gentle reminder that in order to achieve our dreams, we actually do have to lift a finger, and not that finger, neither.

Her mouth dropped open. "How did you know?"

"*Oh. My. Gawd.* You really did it?" Immediately we were jumping up and down like a couple of little girls. A man gave us a leer, so I stopped. As soon as the perv was gone, I gave her another hug. "Tanja, I'm so proud! Tell me everything."

She started to talk, but I felt we should wait and share the success with the others, possibly inspiring them to try something radical on their own.

Five minutes later, when I was dying to hear all the details, Joan and Barbara finally made it. Joan looked fab in a white running suit, with a subtle yet sparkling line of silver running down the seams. I felt shamed until I glanced over at Barbara, who looked frumpy, like me, but in a more comfortable, stylish way.

I gave her a smile. "Tanja has some news. Tanja, share," I ordered, deciding to start the session off on an uplifting note.

"Now it's my turn?" She clasped her head in her hands. "I saw this man on the F train this morning. He was, like, looking at me, you know? And he had the good smile, his teeth were a little crooked, maybe some coffee stains, and then he had this curly dark hair, and skinny. But not in a druggy way, I can't stand that. When he looked at me, at first I looked away, but then it was, like, you know, magnets. I had to look at him. He caught me looking, and so I looked away, but then I looked back, and he was looking again. So I pretended to read my newspaper, but when I got to the Saks ad—God, can you believe their prices on shoes?—I looked up again, and guess what?"

"He was looking at you," we all said together.

Tanja hit me on the arm. "God, it's like you were there!"

"Did you talk to him?" I asked.

She blushed pink. It was the first time I realized that Tanja was a very attractive young lady if she'd just do something a little more with herself. Maybe I should schedule a session at Sephora.

Her hand fanned her face, more spastic than graceful, but this was Tanja, after all. "I couldn't talk to him. I was going to, I even rode two extra stops, just to work up my courage, but then it was, like, totally late, and I knew I'd get fired if I came in late again. My boss already hates me, he's a total loser. And so when he got out at Twenty-eighth Street, I hopped off, too."

"It sounds incredibly romantic," said Barbara. "You were so brave."

Joan clicked her tongue, lighting up her cigarette at the same time. "But you still didn't talk to him, did you?"

Tanja looked shocked. "Of course not, he would've run."

"Just tell us about the ad, would you?" I reminded her before the entire afternoon was shot.

Tanja nodded. "I did it."

I gave her a high five and considered making a small celebratory speech, but this was Tanja's moment, not mine. And speaking of moments . . .

Barbara had fired her maid, Tanja had made steps toward meeting a guy, and Joan . . .

I turned to Joan. "It's your turn."

She took a drag on her cigarette and then started to cough, a clever way of avoiding an answer. I crossed my arms over my chest and waited until her spell was over.

"For what?" she asked, trying to be Miss Innocent Ignorant. Joan was neither innocent nor ignorant.

"You have to get control of your goals," I told her. "We've all had our successes. It's your turn. What do you want, Joan?" I asked. Since she had started with the group three months ago, she'd never once told me how she needed help. I took her money politely and didn't ask. But throwing good money after bad only works when you're running for congress, and I was turning over a new leaf. "So what do you want?"

Joan just shot me a bland look, resplendent in her designer sunglasses, spiffy sweats, and Marlboros. "I have everything I want."

I grinned at her because I figured she wasn't ready. Nobody has everything they want. "You're always good for a few laughs, Joan, baby, but don't think I'm gonna let that diversionary tactic get us away from the subject at hand, which is you."

Joan smiled from behind Hollywood dark lenses. "I wasn't joking. What're your goals and successes?"

"To make a success of my business. To help others realize their dreams. To make a difference."

"But what about you?"

"My business is my life," I answered, then shifted on my heels, pretending to stretch.

Tanja, sensing the momentary weakness, joined in the feeding frenzy. "But you always tell us we have to balance our personal selves with our professional selves—how if you're not personally successful, you can't be professionally successful."

I backed up until a tree cut into my back, and the pain helped me to recover my normal poise. I had taught these ladies everything they knew. They wanted to spout useless homilies? Ha! I was the queen of useless homilies.

I power-walked over to the track, a woman with a goal. A successful goal. "The first step to personal achievement is to give the body the time and respect it deserves. The muscles in the limbs are tied directly to the muscles in the mind. We're only going to do a mile today. A brisk walk. Feel the sun on your face." I began walking confidently down the path, cocking my head until I heard the sounds of power-walking feet behind me. And yes, glory be, my girls were following. Then I looked back for real, checking out their progress.

"Tanja, keep your arms moving. It increases your speed."

Tanja obeyed.

"Joan, put the cigarette down. You'll be winded before you go half a block."

Joan shot me the finger. I waved back. "Keep the rhythm."

I was back in charge, the fearless leader, guiding the blind through the dark pathways of self-doubt, and nobody would ever question my abilities again. Power flowed in my veins, warm and luxurious.

As we walked, joggers ran past us, cyclists biked past us, and at one point, a roller-skater landed Tanja flat on her ass. She regaled him with a colorful litany worthy of a Red Sox fan.

"That's it! We're doing great now," I shouted encouragingly, trying not to limp because my new walking shoes were killing my feet. Note to self: always break in the shoes first. Of course, that would involve exercise.

When we reached the half-mile mark, Tanja stopped and struggled to breathe. "Everybody, take five," I said, and handed her the water bottle. "Drink. You need to hydrate the muscles. And it's great for your skin as well."

"You don't need good skin if you're dead," she managed between heaves.

Barbara was barely winded. "Elle's right. Even at your age, you need to protect your skin. Cancer." She clasped a hand to her face. "Oh, remind me. I need to pick up the suntan lotion for Memorial Day weekend. We're going upstate. Larry would never forgive me if I forgot. He's so sensitive."

I pointed a finger at my girls. "You all think you can talk me out of our exercise. Oh, no, my friends, this is the new and improved version of Elle. Stronger. Harder. Faster. And it can be you, too. I'm gonna tell you a little story. About a president. Not too long before he was elected—the second time around—he said that defeat doesn't finish a man—quitting does. Those are words to live by, Tanja. You, me, everybody here. We can't be defeated. We can't quit. You just have to keep going. One foot in front of the other."

"As if I'll ever be president of the United States," muttered Tanja.

I gave her a big-sister smile and slapped her on the back. "One foot in front of the other," I told her.

She didn't look happy, but she set off with a bounce in her step and with more energy than before. I trotted in behind her.

"Pick up the pace, Joan, you're slowing us down."

Joan kicked it up a notch, possibly two, and I struggled to keep up. "Who was the president?" she asked.

I glanced behind me, making sure that Tanja was out of hearing range. "LBJ."

"I thought it was Nixon," she said.

"Nah. He got credit, but LBJ said it first."

"You sure?" she asked.

I nodded. "Come on, we've got to set an example," I told her.

"I think it was Nixon. LBJ didn't say jazz like that."

"Can you just leave it alone?"

"Yeah, yeah, whatever," she said. "I'll race you to the Tavern on the Green. Loser buys martinis."

"Alcohol's bad for the skin," I reminded her, leaving her in the dust. After all, there were free drinks at stake.

We sat at a white wrought-iron table outside, toasting our excursion with martinis and dark chocolate cake. Tavern on the Green was old-school New York, the grande dame, still resplendent, albeit with an excess of powder and blush. On a late Monday afternoon, the empty tables merely looked lonely, a fabled institution showing its age. Some of my favorite times were spent here when I was a kid. My grandmother (also of excessive powder and blush and Chanel No. 5) used to take me here once a year in the spring. We threw on our best dresses, and once I even wore a hat. It was a mistake I haven't repeated, but I look back on the memories with a smile.

Today was about making new memories, and I looked over my ladies. Tanja had taken her first step toward actually developing a social life. It wasn't world peace, but small successes build to great ones. And Tanja wasn't the only one. I had taken some steps as well. Doing the article with Tracy and having real sex with a real man—once.

"So what lessons learned can we take away from our experience today?" I said, raising my glass and tasting the sharp bite of the vodka.

"Exercising is much easier than I thought it'd be," said Joan, spooning a bite of strawberry parfait into her mouth.

"All it takes is a little self-discipline. And you follow it up with a lucrative reward system," I answered. "Barbara, how's life at home without the maid?"

I watched her fiddle nervously with her neckline before she began to speak. "Larry hasn't figured it out yet, but he did ask if Imelda was still doing the mirrors and glassware. He thought there were streaks."

"What'd you tell him?" I asked, gently yet firmly moving her hand back onto the table where it belonged.

"I told him her mother had passed away," she answered.

"Not bad, Barbara. We'll turn you into a pathological liar yet," said Joan.

Barbara took a sip of her martini, pretending she wasn't pleased. I knew better.

"Did you go shopping? Buy something fabulous just for yourself?" asked Joan.

Barbara pulled out a strand of pearls from underneath her sweatshirt. "Look at this. They're matched, and they go perfectly with the black suit I have for Larry's company do's." Quickly she tucked them back beneath the fleece.

"You should wear them out," I told her. "They go nicely."

She shot me a look. "You never wear pearls at lunchtime. It's tacky."

"I love pearls," said Joan. "I think you should wear them out."

"We'll vote," I said. "Democracy rules. All who think that Barbara should wear them out, take a drink."

Tanja lifted her glass. "You're a total pansy, Barb. For once in your life, be bold," said she who had never been bold in her life.

Barbara touched the little gems and smiled. "You really think I should?"

Joan took a drink and immediately broke out into a fit of coughing.

"We're gonna have to call 911, aren't we?" I said, thinking that maybe we'd tackle Joan's smoking next.

She took a gulp of water until the wheezing stopped. "If the paramedics are good-looking, I can fake a heart attack." Then she flashed a very knowing smile. "I have before."

"Ladies, we need to stick to our schedule." I pointed to my watch. "Disorganization is the sign of an unfocused mind."

Tanja pulled the olive off the pick and popped it into her mouth. I pretended not to notice. "Can't you quit for one second?" she said. "Let us have some fun?"

I pulled the pick from her twirling fingers, mainly because now I *was* irritated. "I am here to help you, motivate you, and push you toward the previously unobtainable. Not to have fun."

She glared from under short, stubby lashes. "I was just suggesting . . ." She caught my deflecting glare.

There was a long, uncomfortable silence, and I felt some guilt. However, I kept the walls up for a reason. A life coach needed to remain detached, uninvolved, in control. This was the reason life coaching was my perfect vocation. Detachment was my middle name. Tony Shields had taught me that painful lesson, and I had learned it well.

There was much clinking of glasses, but finally Barbara spoke up. "So, T, are you gonna talk to Mr. Curly Head tomorrow?" she asked, completely ignoring my speech on our purpose.

Tanja's mouth dropped a good inch. "Are you, like, for real? Of course not!"

I threw up my hands. They were hopeless, but secretly I was pleased. Hopeless meant the group would be together for the long haul. I made a vow to myself to loosen up, at least a little.

"Tanja, you gotta talk to the guy. Flirt with him a little, at least. Drop your bag on his feet or something."

With the way her brows locked together, you'd think I had suggested she flash him. "Look," she snapped, "you can't force me to do something I don't want to do."

"But I thought you wanted to," I explained patiently.

"I just wanted to place the ad. And I did. Subject closed. Thank you very much."

Joan patted her stylish coiffeur. "It must be true love. She's very touchy about him, isn't she?"

"New do, Joan?" I asked. "It looks nice." It was no lie; her hair was shorter, and there were highlights there. It made her look younger, happier, or maybe that was just Joan.

"It's Felix," she answered, and then lowered her sunglasses. "I think I'm in love."

Barbara was instantly intrigued. "So do we get to meet him? Have we read about him in the papers?"

"He's just a lowly hairstylist," she answered, sunglasses back in place.

"A stylist? You're dating your stylist?" I asked.

"Dating your stylist? That's very practical," said Tanja. "But he's not gay? All stylists are gay."

Joan raised her glass. "Not all of them," she said, in a tone that indicated she had firsthand knowledge.

Still, I worried. Joan was loaded and lonely. We knew it, the world knew it, and that included her hairstylist. "We'll have to meet him," I told her, but right now, I wanted to head home and take a nap. All that exercise had really gotten to me.

161

"When're we gonna be in the paper?" asked Tanja. "It's been forever."

"It's only been a week. Tracy said it would run on Saturday."

Even Barbara looked excited. "This Saturday? Do you think we'll be famous? Maybe they could do a movie? I think Cameron Diaz should play me."

We spent the next twenty minutes happily casting ourselves in a movie and drinking an extra round since Joan had so graciously picked up the tab.

After the waitress cleared the table and the sun was starting to go down, I stood, albeit slightly unsteadily. "We're doing a special session. Friday night. Club Night, ladies. Dress appropriately."

"I gotta ask Larry; I'm not sure if he'll let me out."

"Tell him you're meeting your lover. That'll give the old man a good scare," said Tanja, ever ready with the useless advice. I gave her a smile because she reminded me of me at that age.

"Larry's not old," stated Barbara firmly.

"Age is totally a state of mind," said Tanja.

We all glared at her, because when it came right down to it, our age wasn't a state of mind; it was a state of denying gravity.

That night Alan called. I nearly fell off the couch when I recognized the voice, but I was a cool customer. He wanted to go out on Friday, and I explained about Club Night. I waited for him to suggest another night, but he missed the telepathic waves I was sending over the phone line. I suppose I could have asked him to come with the group, but I was afraid that with a man around, I'd regress from strong, fearless leader to sappy, submissive female, and I couldn't bear for my ladies to see me in my weakened state. I had to stay strong. I was their role model. Sorta.

We talked a little about the rest of the group from St. Anthony's, not that I cared, but I listened politely, and Alan had a way of telling stories that made me almost care. I couldn't figure out why he called in the first place, although I suspected he was as fascinated by the idea of me as I was by the idea of him. He considered me a driven, ambitious entrepreneur, a woman who took life by the dingleberries and squeezed. That was Elle Sheffield, but Elle Shields was never buried too far below, and I think he knew that.

And don't get me wrong, I salivated over the idea of having a date/affair/relationship/whatever with Alan Benefield, hottie from my past, but the reality wasn't nearly as appealing as the fantasy.

After he hung up, with a fine amount of regret and longing in his voice, I stayed up late, watching *Letterman,* and boxing up my relationship books for Frank, who was due to come in the next day.

When he showed up, he looked tired, and though he was usually a very sharp dresser, today his jeans were wrinkled, and his shirt was definitely last year's style. But he still had enough zest to give me a saucy wink and cut right to the chase. "How was last week?"

"Let's leave certain things private, shall we?" I answered, with a smug grin that said I had been pounded six ways to Sunday.

"So good you can't talk about it, huh?" he asked, jealous sparks in his eye.

I savored the moment of being an objet d'envy, and then remembered my less selfish tendencies. "How're you doing? Did you meet somebody?"

He shook his head. "I told you. I can't win when it comes to men."

I knew just what he was going through, because it was Alan who called, but it was Harvey I wanted. "You got to believe, Frank." I pounded the box with my hand. "And for reading pleasure, a whole shelfful of instruction manuals. I figure it can't hurt."

"Thanks, Elle. You give me hope."

I chucked him on the shoulder. "Hey, Frank, hit the books, huh? What do you think, I'm running a charity here?" I said. "And speaking of charity cases . . ." I began to hum "We're in the Money."

"Something happen?"

"The article is running on Saturday."

"You think this'll work?" he said.

"Of course it will. It's the *New York* Freaking *Times*. If I get a profile in the *New York Times,* and the people don't come flocking to my door, then I should just quit now, because that means I'm a failure. But you know what, Frank? I'm not a failure," I said. "And neither are you. We're gonna get through this together. Right?"

He studied me for a minute, looked at his computer screen, and then looked back at me. "Right."

I was working on some e-mail consultations when the phone rang. I wasn't even afraid to answer, which tells you much about my optimistic state of mind. It was Maureen, who sounded pan- icked. I considered opening a bottle, but I was trying to cut down, and with my impending financial crisis coming to its conclusion and two men—well, at least one—calling me regu- larly (sometimes), it seemed like a good time to try.

Maureen came running through the door a few minutes later, shaking her head, her hair flying every which way.

"It's a nightmare. A disaster. The end of the world as I know it," she said, and I knew it was pretty much the end of her world because she was pacing with no noticeable limp or dis- comfort.

Frank looked at me. "Last time I checked, the world was doing okay. A few nukes, global warming, mass genocide, but other than that . . ."

Maureen glared at him and then collapsed in my chair, but I liked that Frank was making jokes. Nothing like someone else's misery to cheer you right up.

"I think they're having an affair," she said, all in one long breath.

"L.T. and Dykezilla?" I asked, and then winced in Frank's general direction. "Sorry."

"It's all right. Make fun of my sexual persuasion, and I'll tell her about . . ." He trailed off but made Little Bunny Foo-foo signs.

"Do and die," I told him, and turned back to Maureen. "I don't believe it. He's not her type."

"Not her type? Puh-lease. A cow would be her type if it would further her career. There's no ladder too high for her to climb, no body too warm for her to step over."

"You think she'd really sell out in order to move up?"

Maureen squinted up her eyes. "Let me think . . . ding, ding, uh, yes!"

I took a spot on the couch and steepled my hands together in my counselor look. "But why is this a disaster? I thought you wanted her out of your hair. She's out of your hair."

"You don't get it. It's worse. They're always taking these long lunches, and do you know who gets to take care of all the crap while they're out? *Moi!* That's who!" As she was talking, her hands got more and more animated. More so than usual.

"Maureen, calm down. Relax. With your blood pressure, we could be in serious trouble." Handling people in distress was a new one for me. My clients didn't have distress, because they usually didn't do enough to cause distress. I liked it that way; it kept my life simple. "And think of this. It's a great way for you to take the Mancusi case. I think everything has fallen right into your hands. You're just being pessimistic."

"There're only twenty-four hours in a day, Elle. I can't do all the discovery, and the depositions, and take care of all the motions, too."

"Maureen, you're selling yourself short. Johnnie Cochran has the same twenty-four hours that you do."

"He's dead."

"Well, before he died, he had the same twenty-four hours."

"And he had a whole team of legal assistants to help. It's just me," she said, pounding her chest for emphasis (like I couldn't sense her panic).

"So what do you want me to do?"

"Can you kill her for me?"

I stared. She sulked.

"I thought not," she said, "but I needed to ask." She turned to Frank. "Would you?"

"How much will you pay me?" he answered. I glared. "I could be a hit man. Did you see *Collateral*? He had a killer wardrobe. I could do that, and I bet the pay would be better than what I make here."

"You two, be quiet. We're not getting anywhere. Maureen, can't you just live with the situation? I have some great tips to ease tension, and I'll loan you my squeeze ball."

"I can't live with the situation. If the stress doesn't kill me, the putrid nature of their relationship will."

"Then be proactive. Change jobs," I said, because the situation seemed obvious to me.

She crossed one leg over the other and began kneading her calf. "It's my medical problems. Nobody wants to hire a fat woman with a preexisting medical condition."

"Okay, so if we can't kill Dora, then what can we do?" I asked, trying to guide Maureen into establishing her own solution. It's very important to let the client take charge of her life, especially when you have no great ideas of your own.

"Her death would be so much easier to handle. She's always cooing and telling him how great he looks, and ewww . . ." She trailed off with a shudder.

"So, if the affair—excuse me, the alleged affair—ended, wouldn't that solve your problems?" I said, because Maureen refused to be sidetracked from the kill-her-boss mantra, which, although I sympathized, was considered illegal in the great state of New York. She was a lawyer, she should know.

"I suppose so, but a crowbar couldn't pry those two apart. How am I supposed to end it?"

I pondered some more and realized I was going to have to find a solution for her. *Again.* "What about significant others? Is either one of them involved in a relationship?"

"L.T.'s married. There isn't anyone, animal, mineral, or even vegetable, that would take on Dora in a monogamous relationship."

That was promising. "Okay, so what if L.T. thought that his wife was onto him?"

Maureen made a face. "You actually want me to tell her? She's probably nice, although I'm thinking she's a little slow. I mean, married to him? Gotta be. I couldn't tell her. Hell, I'm responsible for throwing those two crazy kids together in the first place."

I sighed. "You don't have to tell her. Just make him think his wife is *about* to learn the truth. It'll scare him straight."

Frank lifted his head from the computer. "Being scared straight won't work."

"Thank you, Dear Abby."

"I'm just trying to help," he answered.

"Fix my books, will ya?"

"God, you're so demanding."

It was true, so I turned my attention back to Maureen.

"You know, L.T. is just enough of a spineless wonder for that to work," she said, her eyes in some far-off place. "But I've got to be very careful." She stood and started pacing.

"How's your leg doing?" I asked. "You're walking a lot better."

"The new drugs are great. It doesn't bother me at all," she said. She stopped her rounds and flashed a smile. "Gotta go," she said, running out the door before I could stop her. Not that I was going to, you understand. Self-reliance is one of the best lessons that a life coach can give. Feed a man, and he comes back hungry. Teach a man to fish, and he'll open up a sushi place in Tribeca, make boatloads of cash, and never go hungry again.

On Friday, the group was meeting at Xanadu. It was a new place downtown, small and not as jumping as, say, Arlene's Grocery, but since Tanja was the only one under the age of thirty, I thought small and quiet(er) was the way to go.

I sat at a table by the front and waited for the others, pretending that it didn't bother me that I was sitting alone in a club. I even kept my foot from doing that "I'd like to dance" bobbing that you see on the feet of lonely women everywhere. Pathetic.

It would have been easier if I'd been nursing a Scotch, but I stuck to tonic water. I figure, if it's good enough for Harvey, it's good enough for me. (That, and I remembered what happened the last time I ended up drunk in a club. Far be it for me not to learn from my own lessons.)

Tanja and Barbara came in together, a couple of birds flying solo. Tanja had dressed for the occasion; her T-shirt had little baubles on it that spelled: BITCH. Barbara had worn a white silk suit that looked great coming in but was going to be murder to clean after the first drunk got too close. However, I did notice she was wearing her pearls.

Pleasantries were exchanged, and while Tanja spent her time scoping out the place, Barbara told me the latest on Larry.

"I've been a little worried, Elle. He's been great recently. He brings me flowers, and he even brought me a bottle of my favorite wine."

"Barbara, you're making lemons out of your lemonade."

"You don't understand. What if there's somebody else? He came home late the other night, said he was working late, and then he picked at his risotto. He loves risotto, Elle, the way I make it with spinach and a little extra parmesan. Something's wrong."

Poor Barbara. There are just certain people who aren't happy unless they have something to worry about. "Were there any perfume smells?"

"No."

"Any calls that he doesn't want you to hear?"

"He's always been that way. Takes his calls in the study. Says it's very important."

"Oh, but he's only worked late that one time, right?"

"Larry is as regular as a clock," she said, and I could see some of the tension leaving her face. "I'm being silly, aren't I?" she said.

"Yes, you are," I told her, pleased that she was starting to figure things out by herself. And it only took about half a century. The night out on her own would do her good, establish her independent spirit.

We were discussing the niceties of a clean house (right) when Joan arrived, Felix on her arm.

I tried to keep my jaw from dropping, but it was difficult. See, when she mentioned Felix, I thought fortyish, nice dresser, and fawning. Instead, Felix was younger than Tanja, and did I mention that Felix was a stud?

Seriously. Long, blond, underwear-model hair. His shirt was open to his navel, exposing a well-pec'd chest, and he wore these tight, tight black pants. Not leather, thank God, or else I would have had a heart attack. As it was, I was getting a little faint.

"Joan, glad you could make it," I purred, rising to kiss her on the cheek. I held out a hand to Felix. "And you must be Felix."

He didn't bother with the hand, he kissed me on both cheeks. Very continental. "You are Elle?" He shot Joan a fond look. "She has told me much about you."

The accent was definitely eastern European. Fresh-off-the-boat, looking-for-a-green-card eastern European. I flashed him a polite smile. "She told us just as much about you," I said.

"I think she left out his age," commented Tanja. We were all thinking the same thing but politely ignored her.

"So you do hair?" asked Barbara, always gracious and ready with the chitchat. "Joan's hair always looks so nice."

Felix lifted a proprietary hand to Joan's layers. "Yes. It is fabulous, is it not?"

"Fabulous," said Barbara, nodding politely.

Joan patted his hand. "Felix, honey, go get us some drinks, would you? Martini, with a twist. Ladies?"

We gave him our orders, and she waited until he was out of earshot. "Isn't he divine?"

I cleared my throat, because I felt that I, as the leader, should say something insightful, yet rational as well. "Joan, I have concerns," I started out.

Tanja leaned in. "He's got to be after your money."

Joan gave us a long-suffering expression. "I expected congratulations, not lectures. You all are my friends. Act like it."

And that was that, she shut us all up with three sentences, but I knew there would be major behind-the-scenes discussion when she was out of earshot.

When Felix got back, I lifted my glass of tonic water. "To new beginnings."

"To happy endings," added Joan. We clinked glasses, and everyone pretended to be thrilled. There were some awkward silences, although Felix knew how to keep everyone entertained. Tanja was making furtive eye contact with a student type across the room, so I nudged her. "Go talk to him. You're the only one here young enough to dance."

Felix took Tanja by the hand. "Come. We will fix it for you," he said, being so nice that it cemented the fortune-hunter image even further in my brain. Nice men were a myth.

Soon Tanja was dancing with Mr. NYU, and Felix was dancing cheek-to-cheek with Joan. The floor was relatively small, tables scattered around, and most of what they were playing was multigenerational jazz.

I watched them dance and shook my head. "It's trouble."

Barbara bit her lip. "I know. Still, he seems very nice."

"Too nice," I said.

"I don't think she's gonna listen to us," she said, watching the two with a dreamy smile on her face.

"No, we'll just have to wait to make our move," I said quietly. Already my mind was spinning. I never suspected Joan for the gullible type. Out of all of us, she was the one most likely to take care of herself. What would a young, studly immigrant want from an older, although nicely well-preserved wealthy lady?

Tanja came back and sat down, having chased off her would-be suitor by critiquing his career choices. So there we were, sitting like bumps, when I noticed a presentable man in a business jacket making eye contact with someone at our table. At first I thought it was Tanja, but then I realized that I was the target of his approach.

I smiled politely but not encouragingly. I don't like bar games, they make my stomach gurgly.

Just as I was figuring I had run him off, he came over and introduced himself. "Would you like to dance?" he asked.

At this point, I gave him a critical once-over. He didn't dress as nicely as Alan, he didn't have that animal magnetism of

Harvey, he wore glasses, which turned me off, but I thought I was being shallow, so I told him yes. We went out to the floor, and he didn't try to touch me, for which I was grateful. Actually, he was an okay dancer, much better than me, which is another reason I had never been fond of the whole club scene.

"What's your name?" I asked.

"Mark," he said. "Mark Brooks."

"It's nice to meet you, Mark. I'm Elle. Elle Sheffield. What do you do?" I asked, working carefully to avoid touching anyone around us.

"I'm a jeweler."

"Very impressive," I said, nodding my head. It was amazing; here was another nice man as well. Suddenly they were falling from trees. I'd heard that urban myth that said when you don't want men, they come after you like flies, but I'd never believed it. Until now. Of course, poor Mark didn't do anything for me, but he didn't repel me, either. Maybe dating was easier than I imagined.

"What about yourself?" he asked.

"I'm a life coach," I answered, studying him objectively. He had nice eyes behind the glasses. Very kind. Probably went to church. Probably Protestant.

"I should have guessed. You have that self-assured confidence. I bet you're very good."

I graced him with a regal smile because I knew I was good. It was the reason I got up in the morning. "Thank you."

The song ended, and I decided that I had faked a rhythmic

talent for long enough. "Do you mind if we sit this one out?" I asked. I fanned my face. "It's very hot."

"Do you mind if I sit at your table?"

"Not at all," I said magnanimously, hoping that he wasn't one of those hard-to-get-rid-of types.

Which of course he was. He sat at our table for two hours, discussing diamonds with Joan. I nursed my tonic water, wishing desperately for a drink, but the last thing I wanted was to end up wasted and waking up next to Mark, so I stuck to my water and made forty trips to the ladies' room.

It was in between two of these breaks that I felt a hand on my foot. Mark gave me a shy smile and put my foot in his lap. I wasn't sure exactly what he expected me to do, but I knew darn well that if he expected me to start playing footsies with his privates, I was kicking him off the table, polite or not. But instead he started stroking my ankle. Very weird.

"You have very pretty feet," he whispered. "It was the first thing I noticed about you."

I faked a coughing attack, telling myself that unless I wanted to end up a little old lady with a box of Mr. Bunnys, then it was time for me to loosen up. And it wasn't as if it was *that* strange. Foot massages could be very cute and relaxing.

Mark started to unbuckle the straps from my sandal, which transformed cute and relaxing into creepy and homicidal. I put my foot firmly back on the floor.

He shot me a "How dare you" look, and that was it. Group or no group, I was about to make a scene.

I stood up and pointed in the direction of the door. Mark ignored me, although Tanja gave me a weird look. "You can leave," I told him, poking a swordlike finger between his shoulder blades, and *still* he pretended nothing was going on.

Asshole.

I hooked a finger in his collar and poured Joan's cosmopolitan right down his shirt. This time Mark didn't ignore me anymore.

"You bitch! Why didn't you just ask me to leave?" Then he stormed off, *finally* taking the hint.

I sat down at the table and gave my group a confident, successful smile.

Felix looked at me quizzically. "Have you always had these anger issues with men?"

I looked at Joan's empty glass. "Felix, honey, I think Joan needs a drink."

We didn't discuss the subject anymore.

The next morning was Saturday. Saturday. *The* Saturday. I got up at five A.M., and jogged down to Starbucks, just waiting for someone to recognize me. There were no takers, but it was early. I sprang for a grande-sized latté, knowing it would earn Frank's wrath, but hey, the calls were going to start flooding in. I just knew it.

I paid the barista, settled myself in a chair, and began to look for the newstype that was gonna change my life. Page by page, line by line I went. Past the article on the new submodern conservationalism esoteric architecture movement. Past the latest food review by the esteemed Miss Hesser, past the crossword, past the Cartier ads, and eventually past the last page.

Not to be deterred, I went section by section, page by page, line by line, until I had read the entire *New York Times,* ads included.

Nothing.

I sighed. Well, it was no wonder no one had recognized me. *Tomorrow. And the Sunday edition would be even better.*

When I got home, I crawled back under the covers and took a short three-hour nap. I figured I could call Tracy later to see what was what.

A ringing disturbed me, and I picked up the phone, murmuring a sleepy hello into the receiver.

"This is Good Vibrations?" said the voice.

"Yeah. This is Elle Sheffield. How might I help you?"

"This is Sandy from Office King. I saw the article in the paper, and I thought I'd call and see if you needed any office supplies for your home-based business? We're running a special on toner this week, and for companies in the area—"

I shot out of bed. *Oh, God. This was it.*

"You're kidding! You saw the article? What section was it in?" I raced for my copy of the paper. I must've missed it.

"The Weekend Shore section," she said.

I glanced down at the paper in my hand. "The Weekend Shore section? Is this something regional for the Hamptons?"

"Jersey. The New Jersey Shore."

Okay, I was totally confused. "Is that a local edition?" I asked.

"They only print one," she said, starting to get a little huffy.

That's okay, I was starting to get a little huffy, too. "Excuse me. Exactly which paper did you see this article in?"

"Community Living: The Jersey Shore Way."

Nine

Most writers regard truth as their most valuable possession, and therefore are most economical in its use.

—MARK TWAIN

Who was the writer?" I asked, still thinking the whole thing was just a misunderstanding, or maybe a practical joke.

"Tracy Gorman. You talked to her, right? She's knows all about you."

"Yeah, I know Tracy. We go way back," I said. Maybe not far enough. "I don't suppose this was a syndicated reprint?" I asked quietly.

"I don't know, but about that toner."

I'd had enough of Sandy and her toner. I'd had enough of thinking that the blue skies were coming. I'd had enough of pretty much everything.

"Sandy, you should think better of yourself than cold-calling people from a Jersey weekly," I said, sounding really cold, and really mean, and really tired.

"I know. I really suck at this. It's just that I'm trying to work things out with my parents, and it was the only job I could get while I watch my little girl," she explained, making me feel like a total heel.

I sighed. "Sandy, go home. Your mother and father love you," I told her, because I figured they might. That was the way it was supposed to work, even though sometimes it didn't.

"I know, but they don't understand me."

She had parents who loved her. Parents who lived in a normal house, in a normal town, somewhere in Normal, USA, *and they didn't understand her.* Well, fuck that. I wish those were my problems.

"Do me this favor. When you hang up, I want you to call them and just ask if you can come home. Promise?"

"But then I have to—"

It was so easy to rearrange her life, to wave my magic advice wand, and *whoosh,* her problems would all disappear.

"Nuh-uh-uh-uh. No buts. Unconditional love. It's a two-way street. Promise me."

"I promise."

"Good. Now, do you have the number for the paper? I need to have a little talk with the reporter." I had solved Sandy's problems and was now prepared to take care of my own. Unfortunately, I wasn't sure that I could. I damned sure knew that nobody else was gonna do it.

When I dialed the paper, I got through to Tracy's voice mail. She was the features editor at the paper, wasn't that nice? I was the features patsy.

"Tracy, this is Elle Sheffield. I tried to call you at the *Times,* but they said you didn't work there anymore and gave me this number. I have big news to tell you. I found the missing twenty million. Give me a call, and I'll give you a scoop."

She called back twenty minutes later.

"You found out," she said, not even trying to deny her culpability. Smart girl.

"News flash. Yes. What were you thinking, or did Leah think this up all on her own?" I asked. It was a rhetorical question. I knew.

"I really thought I could make it work, Elle. I give you my word. I pitched the article about your father to a friend of mine at the *Times*. He said no. I thought I could negotiate a deal for the profile. I didn't set out to screw you. I thought it would all work out." She even sounded sincere.

"Well, it didn't," I answered flatly.

"You're mad."

"No, Tracy. I've learned that anger is a useless emotion and stems from frustration in trying to charter a course through the troubled water of our everyday life. *Of course I'm mad.* I needed this profile, Tracy. I counted on this profile. I have rent due this month, and last month, too, and I assumed I would get the publicity I needed to get me over the rough spots."

"Sorry," she said quietly. "I really tried."

"Sorry? Do you want to see if my landlord will accept an apology in lieu of a check? What did the *Times* say?"

There was a long sigh. "They said Tony Shields was ancient history. And then I pitched your whole life coach business, turning the world around one head case at a time, but they said you needed a hook. Maybe if you were a nude dancer, or your father was a terrorist, or something sexy like that."

"Leah put you up to this, didn't she? Come on, tell me. I can handle it. She wanted to mess with my mind, didn't she? Set me up for the big fall."

"You're not giving her the credit she deserves. It *was* her idea, but she was just trying to help you. She said that I could get the article, and then they'd do the profile, and you'd never have to know."

It almost sounded nice, and if I didn't know Leah as well as I did, I might have believed she was actually thinking of me. "I'll just have to call Leah and thank her for her thoughtfulness," I said. I knew I wasn't going to talk to Leah. I'd never lost gracefully, mainly because it ate me up on the inside when I did. Of course, I never won gracefully, either. Mainly because I just never won.

The anger pretty much died then, and I was left with cold resignation and major stomach upset. If I were younger, more energetic, a little prettier, I might have kept trying, but I was back firmly in reality.

Tracy was younger, more energetic, and prettier. She still had it in her. "I'll make it up to you. I swear," she said, still trying.

Oh, yeah. Once again, mainstream media is out of touch. No point in delaying the inevitable anymore.

"Sorry. Gotta go. Gotta new place to find. A new move to arrange. Busy, busy, busy, busy. See you around, Tracy. Don't call me. I won't call you."

I spent two hours staring at my bottle of Scotch, thinking that one bottle just wasn't enough. I wanted a drink so bad I could taste it, but something held me back. Probably the same thing that had held me back my entire life. I had tried this time, too. Really tried. For once, I had poured my heart and soul into something. For once, I thought I was on the right track. But something happened. Just as it always did, and the train never left the station.

Was I doing something wrong, or was I born under the wrong star? A person doomed never to succeed at anything? Was this some sort of cosmic justice for Tony's crime? The cosmos wasn't supposed to work that way.

I didn't know the answers to anything. Hell, the one thing I knew was that I needed a drink.

Instead of Scotch, I downed four tablets of Pepto. It didn't help.

Eventually, when I realized that the Pepto wasn't going to fix my problems either, I picked up the phone, called Mr. Tierney, and gave him my official notice. He was very nice and polite about the whole thing, much nicer than I would have been, but I suppose that's why he was gainfully employed and moderately successful at what he did.

My next call was to Tashondra at Citibank. I had a feeling me and Tashondra were gonna be good friends. She talked me through the jobs section on their website and promised that she'd put in a good word to her supervisor for me.

There's a time in your life when you set out with goals and big plans for the future. Forty-two years of age is not that time. When you're forty-two, big plans and passion will only screw you.

I called an apartment service in Wilmington. I didn't have much in the way of a deposit, but thank God I didn't have any pets.

Then I went to my room, locked the door, buried my head in the pillow, and this time I screamed.

I spent the afternoon organizing my closets, sorting them into three piles. Trash, charity, and pack. I didn't have that much stuff, but you'd be surprised what you can stuff into a one-bedroom when you're my age. A lot of clothes you can't wear anymore. Camisole tops that looked too young. Miniskirts that wouldn't go over the hips. And then there was the one pair of stilettos that nearly broke my ankle. I put them all in the charity pile. Someone else could have them now.

My next step was to call a couple of my old acquaintances from the database company. We had a nice chat, caught up on what was going on in our lives (I lied), and then I tactfully inquired if they knew anyone looking for a top-shelf tech support rep (the answer was no). Next, I asked if they knew anyone who needed a life coach (again, no). I didn't keep many friends for this very reason. Most were well adjusted and married, and I ended up feeling depressed after being around them. I went back to my packing, and then Maureen came down just as the sun started to set.

I opened my door, and she barged in after me. "Come on in," I said when she plopped down in my chair.

"You can't leave."

"Bad news travels fast."

"No, you don't understand. You can't leave. I need your help."

"What's wrong now, Maureen?" I asked.

"L.T. is pressuring Dora to move into a love nest down by the office. Can you believe it? I'm going to hurl. I'm done for. Kaput. My workload has increased threefold, I'm not sleeping well, and my doctor is very worried."

I ignored the medical problems and went right to the meat of the matter. "L.T. told you his plans?"

"Oh, God, no. She told me that. In her office. Over bagels and coffee."

I pushed aside the bags of clothes and made room for myself on the couch. This was gonna take a while. "You're speaking to Doris? She's confiding her most private business with you? First you set her up for career annihilation, and now you're bonding over breakfast?" It was all fascinating. Much more fascinating than an unemployed middle-aged woman.

Maureen wiggled her hands. "Oh, you know. I felt guilty, and I wanted to know what was going on, so I took her to lunch. God, the woman can talk. Chat, chat, chat, chat, chat. Anyway, she was talking about how she loved her house in Sleepy Hollow, and now he wants her to move into the city so they'll be closer. And she was going on and on about how she thinks Larry's a creep. He's always telling her what shoes to wear, how to write her briefs, the way she needs to handle the Mancusi case. I can't help it. I feel sorry for her."

I nodded in a thoughtful manner. This I could handle. "What are you going to do? You created this problem, you wanted to have more exposure at the firm. It seems to me that you got exactly what you wanted." It was a little harsher than usual, but I'd had a bad day, and I figured I was allowed.

"A problem we created," she said, and I chose not to argue with her reasoning. "What are we going to do now?"

"Take two temazepam and call me in the morning, will ya?"

"I need your help."

"No."

She pushed the hair back from her face, and there was real worry there. "L.T. thinks his wife won't notice that he's suddenly working twenty-four/seven at the office. It's like watching a drunk on the subway. You know he's going to fall, but you can't look away."

"It's his problem, not yours. You might have lit the match, but he's the one sniffing the gasoline," I joked, because she was still making too much of nothing. So she was going to have to work a little harder. It certainly wouldn't kill her. And she had a job.

"What if Dora sues him?"

"Did she say she was going to sue him?"

"We're lawyers. It's what we do."

At that point, I considered asking her to leave. I considered turning my back on our friendship and abandoning her in her time of need. But I knew I couldn't.

That sounds so noble, doesn't it? So courageous and brave. Me, in my time of anguish and need, setting out to help my fellow (wo)man.

Yeah, you saw through that pile of crap, too, didn't you? The truth was—and I fully admitted it—I had to fix just one more problem. Just one little high to lessen my own pain. Alcohol didn't work; food had never done it for me. No, I had to have people need me, and when I sat there, flapping my jaws, telling them "Do this, do that," well, for that moment in time, I was important. Other people have fear of spiders; myself, I'm afraid of not making a difference. There are worse things, I suppose.

I settled in, feeling my own pain start to numb.

"You're creating more problems than you need," I told her. "Here's what gonna happen. He's gonna ask Doris to make the move. She's gonna tell him no and never speak to him again."

"They work together," said Maureen, not seeing the big picture.

"So one of them will quit. Ipso facto, no affair at work. Ipso facto, Maureen gets her normal, pedestrian job back the way it was, she'll take over the Mancusi case, and everybody will cheer her and probably give her a fat raise. You have nothing to worry about. People in affairs gone wrong will run. It's statistically proven." I dusted my hands. "Problem solved."

"And what about the wife?"

"Leave it alone, Maureen. Just like Doris said: Larry's a creep," I said. "She's better off without him, and she'll probably never know. What was he thinking, having an affair at the office . . ." The words died in my mouth. Actually it felt as if roadkill died in my mouth.

Normally, it wasn't a possibility I would even consider. But the day that I'd had? The life I'd had? I figured paranoia wasn't a bad thing.

"Maureen, what's L.T.'s last name?" I asked, putting a smile on my face, because it was crazy. No way. How many Lawyer Larrys were there in Manhattan? There had to be a gazillion.

"McKee, Lawrence Taylor McKee."

My stomach began to cramp badly, but I was still smiling. "Do you know his wife's name?"

"I don't remember. He never invited me to any of their parties, but Dora says she's short, blond, an older woman, kinda mousy. Started with a *B,* I think. Bonnie, Belinda—"

"Barbara?"

She snapped her fingers. "That's it." Then she looked at me. "How did you know?"

I made a run for it. "If you'll excuse me, I think I'm gonna be sick."

Ten

Great achievements are made from great failures. Unfortunately, great achievements are a statistical anomaly, usually involving someone else.

—ELLE SHEFFIELD

After Maureen left and I had cleaned up the mess I made in the bathroom, I sat down amidst the bags and boxes and took a hard look at the mess I'd made in Barbara's life.

The one thing that I knew, that I depended on, was my ability to help others. Maybe I'd never cure cancer or discover a new alternative energy source, but I knew in my heart that I did good and that I had made a difference. Not a huge difference—sometimes it was so small that you wouldn't even notice unless you were looking.

I was always looking.

Other people would've laughed at my success stories—God knows it wasn't going to get me on *Oprah*—but at night, when I was alone, I could look back on my day and know that my mark on the world existed.

That's all I wanted. It was enough to make me happy.

But Barbara? She was my first client, the one who first suggested I have group sessions, the one who always made me feel that I improved her life, at least for that one short hour. Never any questioning my methods or whining about getting her money's worth. Barbara accepted me just as I was. Unconditionally.

She was my friend.

I knew I wasn't gonna leave, not until I cleaned up that mess as well. In my gut, I knew I was a coward, but even cowards had lines they wouldn't cross and rules they wouldn't break. For me, I would never run out on a friend.

I needed clients, and I needed them fast, preferably well-heeled, deep-pocketed ones in desperate need of achieving their dreams. I knew just the person who would deliver.

Leah.

And this time it was personal.

I told her she was buying me dinner at Balthazar, and she didn't even blink. I figured it might be the last decent meal I was gonna get for some time, and it seemed right that she should pay . . . a lot.

The Paris-style brasserie was packed, with mountains of people jockeying for position at the front. I had only been there once before (Restaurant Week '98), and it looked just as crowded then. The room was loud, everybody yelling and only the hostess looking calm (probably good drugs). I saw Leah yoo-hooing me from across the room, and I breezed past the kerfuffle.

I sat down and got right to the point. "You set me up," I said, keeping my voice firm and steady.

She blew an air kiss across the table. "I was only trying to help you, Ellie. It was obvious you're not good at blowing your own horn."

"Did you ever consider telling me the truth? Just telling me that Tracy worked for some two-bit newspaper instead of the *New York Times*?"

She shook her perfect blond bob. "Nope. Not for one little moment. It doesn't matter if you get a profile in New Jersey or New York." She tapped her head. "It's all up here, Elle. You have to think better of yourself."

"My self-image is fine, thank you very much."

"Not from where I'm sitting."

"Can we not talk about my self-image?"

"Fine," she said, and held up the menu. "What should we order? I think I'm going to splurge and have dessert, too. Have you tried their escargot? Escargot is the only reason God made snails. It's divine, but all that butter? But still, an extra thirty minutes at the gym, and the wages of snails will be worth it. What about you?"

"I'm still angry," I told her, my voice not quite as firm and steady.

The menu lowered. "Don't be such a stick in the mud, Ellie. You got some free publicity; I bet the phones are going to be ringing off the hook any moment now. Ring, ring, ring." The menu rose. "Or the bar steak. I get it just for the *pommes frites*. Whoops. There goes another thirty minutes on the treadmill. Bad, Leah, bad, bad, bad."

"Can't you just say you're sorry?"

The menu lowered. "Can't you grow up? I tried to do something nice for you, and it didn't work out like I wanted. End of story." The menu rose.

I wasn't sure if she was mentally unable to comprehend the rankness of her actions, or if she was a malicious backstabber who had plotted revenge for the last twenty years. I doubted she had even spared me a thought in the last twenty minutes, much less the last twenty years, and her moral compass had always been wonky. In the long run, it didn't matter; all I needed was to get her to my way of thinking.

"Maybe the short ribs," she murmured.

My way of thinking was going to take longer than I thought. I cleared my throat.

"I think the steak. Definitely, the steak."

"Leah."

The menu lowered. "Yes?"

"I'm going to give you a chance to make it up to me. I'm looking for clients. You've got connections. Maybe you have a women's club I could speak at. I have some great motivational talks I wrote."

"Nope."

"Book clubs?"

She wrinkled her nose. "Hate to read. No time."

"People in your building? You're on the board," I told her, because I wasn't going to let her wiggle out of this spot.

She clicked her tongue. "Ellie, Ellie, Ellie. You're going about this all wrong."

"Now you're trying to tell me how to run my business?"

"Well, it's not like you're doing a good job of it. Somebody's gotta help."

I took a deep breath. "You want to help?"

"You need someone to help you with promotion."

"And that's you?" I asked. "The *New York Times,* whoops, it's only *Community Living.*"

"Don't be snippy. First we have to work on your networking skills." She lowered her voice. "They suck."

"And yours are good?"

She waved at a couple across the room. "Daphne! Tommy! Call me!" Then she turned to me. "The best."

I was tempted to walk out on her, but sadly, she was my last, best hope. Ideally, I could fix Barbara's marriage before things got worse or my landlord kicked me out, whichever came first. And *then* I could walk out on Leah.

But for now . . .

"So what am I doing wrong?" I asked in a low voice, one hand shielding my eyes.

"You mean, besides everything?" she said in not-so-low voice.

"Yes."

"First of all, you have to start with your friends. If anyone is going to give you money for advice, it's people you know."

I lowered my hand and glared. "My friends either can't afford me or they're already clients," I snapped.

"Not all of them," she answered, raising her water glass and giving me a look.

Oh, I could see where this was headed. We were back at the Fifth Ring of Hell. "I'm not going to the party," I said, and then repeated myself just in case she thought she could wangle me there, on display like a circus monkey. There was one of two plans running around in Leah's brain. Either she wanted me for some elaborate Pygmalion scheme to relieve her own boredom, or else—the more likely scenario—she had never forgiven me because after Tony's deals, her father could only afford a Town Car instead of a Ferrari. Boo-hoo.

"If you don't go, then you don't want those clients as much as you say you do. Seems a shame when you have a golden opportunity put right in front of you," she said, tapping a crimson fingernail on my bread plate.

"No."

"Well, okay," she said, taking my plate and stacking it on hers. A waiter came forward. "Would you like some *pain*, Mrs. Weber?"

"Certainly, François," she said, and he placed a crusty roll on her plate.

The man nodded in my direction. "And you, madame?"

Leah put a hand over my space. "Ellie's not having anything tonight. She's going to sit all alone, nursing her grudge like a toddler with his binkey, wasting away until she's just a tiny, tiny skeleton. But it won't matter, because she's got principles, and that makes her happier than the rest of us."

You'd think François would be accustomed to crazy people in this city, but he scurried away like a cockroach at dawn. I sighed. "I can't do it. I won't subject myself to the misery of a group of people who made my high school experience into a B-list horror movie."

She waved a hand. "Honey, that was twenty years ago. I'm lucky to remember where I left my cell phone." She patted her bag. "There it is. I tried to help you, Ellie. They will, too. Mimi Hall is a top fund-raiser for the Democratic Party, and her husband is a huge golfer, and Paul Obermann does something with money. Banking, stocks, insurance, it's all the same to me. It's not like the Kennedys or anything, but there's gold in them there hills, if you get my meaning, and I think you do. Why do you think I keep up with everyone? It's certainly not for the sparkling companionship. You have to be practical. If you want to survive, you have to play the game."

"I won't."

"Put the past behind you, put it all the way in Hawaii, lounging out on some deserted beach, if you have to. Anything. You're going to be stuck in mediocrity if you don't get out there and try."

"I can't."

She shook a finger at me. "Of course you can. You're Elle Sheffield, world-famous life coach."

I laughed. "You really believe that?"

"It doesn't matter one itty bit what I believe. What matters is what you believe. After that, you just sucker everybody into thinking it's true."

It all sounded simple coming from her mouth. I could almost believe it. Who was I kidding? I wanted to believe it. I wanted to take in her words with a long breath and never exhale.

Here I was sitting across from a woman I didn't respect, sometimes hated, but she was saying the right things. A Scottish politician once said, "I would rather be an opportunist and float, than go to the bottom with my principles around my neck." I wasn't Scottish, but in my past my blood had been heavily influenced by the Scotch, namely Chivas. It all sounded very rational—to Don Quixote, maybe.

However, I wasn't going to jump on her little bandwagon without insurance. "If this is another prank, Leah, I swear, I will call Harvey and have my wicked way with him until he passes out from an OD of sexual pleasure so extreme that they will write manuals and memoirs and make a movie about the whole thing. You get my meaning?"

She laughed. "You're just teasing me, aren't you?"

I stayed silent and tough.

"Aren't you?"

Not a word.

She rolled her eyes. "Such a cynical mind you have, Ellie sweetie. I really try to do the right thing. Sometimes it ends up a little wrong, but my heart's in the right place. Please. I'm giving you a great opportunity. This one is all yours to screw up." Then she smiled as if she thought I would.

I only hoped she was wrong.

* * *

I had a purpose, I had a goal, I had hope. In spite of all of Leah's flaws, and there were many, she had gotten one thing right. I needed to take advantage of my old friends, using *friends* in the loosest definition possible. I could do that.

So I spent the next week rehearsing a sales pitch and trying to starve myself to fit into my size six cocktail dress. A fasting diet was not difficult since my checking account was currently sitting at $163.47. Trying to exist in New York on $163.47 was like smiting a nine-headed Hydra with a new manicure. Every time you lop off one bill, there's another waiting to kill you or muss your polish, whichever comes first. However, after canceling my cell service, turning off cable, and meeting with clients at Schurz Park instead of Starbucks, existing was attainable, assuming you didn't include rent.

On Wednesday, Maureen showed up, not even calling first.

"Your problems are not solved, but they're not any worse," she said in her opening statement.

"What do you mean?"

"Dora finally grew a spine and told L.T. she wouldn't move to the apartment. She told him that theirs was a physical connection only." At this, Maureen made theatrical gagging gestures.

"But is she gonna stop seeing him?" I asked, thinking, Would it kill anybody if just *one* of my problems was solved?

Maureen shook her head. "Nope. She's holding out for a fat settlement. Apparently there's an oceanfront place in Cape Cod she's got her eye on, and she thinks she can get him to deal before the summer season is over."

"She tells you everything now, huh?" I said, noticing that Maureen was making friends left and right. She was a good networker; I never knew that before. And it looked as if she was losing weight.

"Pretty much. Apparently I'm the calm eye in the middle of the whirling dervish that is our daily office environment," she said, sitting down in a chair, my favorite one, of course.

"Does that mean she's doing more work?" I asked, because Maureen didn't seem calm. And I swear the flawless complexion had a pimple.

"When she has a masochistically ambitious fat cripple with a myriad of health problems that she can order to do it for her? What sort of card-carrying slave driver would she be then? Would I be here? Would my blood pressure be 140? Would I be getting by on less than three hours of sleep and a strong dose of Adderall? No, ladies and gentleman of the jury, I would not."

"You're taking Adderall?" I asked, and suddenly it was all starting to make sense.

She jumped up from the chair and started pacing. "Can't you tell?"

Sure enough, she was all but dancing. "I didn't think it worked for pain."

"The OxyContin is for pain. Adderall is for energy," she said, shooting the hair out of her eyes with a practiced flick.

I thought about my words very carefully. It was true, she was doing great, but drugs? "Maureen, as much as I think this medically manufactured personality is a vast improvement, I feel like it's my duty as a responsible human being, who happens to care about you, to say this is a very dangerous line you're walking."

She made some sort of Janet Jackson dance move, which I took to mean she was just saying no to me.

I kept my tone light and supportive, but it wasn't easy. "I can't let you do this to yourself. You're going to either have a heart attack before you hit thirty-five, or else you're going to Hollywood yourself into a size two body, and then I'd have to put the serious hurt on you myself. Either way, it's not good."

She collapsed into the chair. "I know. But it's tempting. Aren't you tempted? I've lost twenty pounds, and even Artie is looking at me with man eyes. I'm no longer just the fat girl in 12B. You don't have my weight issues, but haven't you ever wanted an endless supply of energy?"

I knew what she was looking for: an answer to all her problems—instantly. We wanted to solve them all in thirty minutes or less. Some people looked in the pharmaceutical section, some in the liquor store, and some of us looked to the winsome eyes of a pink pearl bunny.

"Be careful," I told her.

"How's the money holding out?" she asked, electing to change the subject from parental-style lectures. I didn't blame her.

"It's not," I said, rubbing a hand over my eyes.

"Just think, all those preppy friends of yours from school. Mark my words, Elle, they owe you. Just guilt them into helping you. Give 'em the big puppy-dog eyes and remind them of all their past wrongdoings. It'll work."

"I wish it was that easy."

"All you need is to believe," she said, echoing Leah's words. I would have been more moved if she was the same old, frumpy Maureen. The new dynamo wore me out.

"You're the one with the energy. Help me get Larry back with his wife."

"He won't go back, Elle. According to Dora, Barbara is a sexual scud."

The bastard. "That's just what he tells her to keep her doing the nasty. That's what all the married men do."

"And when was your last affair with a married man?"

"I read. I know the lines."

"You're such a babe in the woods, Elle. You need to pick up some life experience," she said, really starting to piss me off.

However, pissed off or not, I knew I could count on Maureen. "Life experiences, my butt. I just need to get Barbara back with Larry."

Maureen, the eternal pessimist, shook her head. "Not gonna happen. As long as Dora's waxing his wick, he's happier than a hot dog in a bun. I'm sorry, because Barbara seemed to be a nice lady."

I bit back a particularly vicious curse. It just wasn't fair. Everybody out there was getting laid, Alan hadn't called me back, Harvey, well, Harvey had never called, and I couldn't afford my favorite bunny. The entire world revolved around sex . . .

Suddenly, it hit me.

"What if she developed a sexually transmitted disease? What if, for instance, she made an appointment at a clinic, and then, let's say, hypothetically, she sent an e-mail to a friend, confessing said illness?"

"You're kidding, right?"

"No," I answered, a little defensively. "I think the idea can be finessed."

"This is the real world, Elle. You can't just go out there and claim that someone has genital herpes. And what's Dora gonna do? She's gonna flip and deny the whole thing—"

I steepled my fingers. "But of course."

"But L.T. won't believe her," she finished, awe in her voice, finally seeing the beauty of my plan. Now who had the life experience?

"You'll send the e-mail?" she said, ducking responsibility to the bitter end.

"She's your boss," I stated flatly.

"Okay, but we have to use your computer."

"I cut off my broadband connection," I said, not mentioning that I'd switched to the cheaper dial-up, although the connection speed really did suck.

"You Luddite, you. What am I going to do? No, I know what I can do. I'll use my own computer. They can't track it to me, right?"

"Brilliant idea, Maureen, you're completely safe. Now, if you'll excuse me, I have crunches to do. I have to lose seven pounds by Saturday night."

She bounced up from the chair. "You want some of my Adderall? It's better than exercise. Who knew?"

I politely declined, and after she left, I staggered to the floor and assumed the position, shamed into doing things the old-fashioned way.

One, two, three . . .

Only seven thousand more to go.

By Saturday I was down three pounds and could wear the dress, although it still looked too tight. I figured another five hundred crunches, and I'd be there. Yeah.

Then, about ten A.M., the phone rang.

Leah.

"You're gonna have to put on your big-girl panties and host the party tonight. I came home from the liquor store, which I was doing all for you, honey, which I think proves my heart is in the right place, and I stepped into my little hallway with the most beautiful parquet floors, teak, which are now ruined, and if you knew how long it took me to pick out those floors, you would know how stricken I am."

I made a face into the phone. "Just because you got a little scratch—"

"A little scratch? They're not scratched, they're under water, and I ruined a pair of Italian leather sandals as well. They were my favorite magenta ones, and do you know how hard it is to find a decent magenta sandal with a sensible heel?"

I sat down because it seemed wise. "Why is your floor under water?"

"My upstairs neighbor, careless hussy, passed out in her tub, it overflowed, and now there's water everywhere. The insurance inspectors are coming out today to take pictures."

"Did she drown?"

"No, damn her. Suicide attempt is what her neighbor said. Good thing she's not here, or I'd finish it myself. They shipped her off to some private hospital in Maine. Maine! That's like wandering in the wilderness. Good riddance. I swear, that's it. You don't mess with the board in this building. A complete flake. Suicide. I knew she was trouble. I told them to turn her down, you know, I can spot the bad seeds—"

I glanced around my apartment. I might be an optimist, but I wasn't completely divorced from reality. "Leah, I can't have the party at my house."

"We don't have a choice. If you saw my foyer, you'd see the truth instantly. It just makes me want to cry. The pain."

"Can't we rent someplace, or can't one of the other people do it?"

"Ellie, Ellie, Ellie. We have to control the environment. We have to create a showcase for you. A little silver here. Cut flowers. Crystal. Maybe chrome, instead. Crystal is so old-fashioned, and you don't have an old-fashioned bone in your body. Wait till my decorators get done with it, they can do truly wondrous things. You won't recognize your own nest of domesticity." She sounded serious.

"My apartment is the size of a closet. It won't work."

"Think and become, Elle. Just be there and be fabulous. Gotta go. Ding, ding. Inspector's here. See you tonight. Kiss kiss."

She hung up on me, leaving me nine hours to make over my apartment. I looked around, knew I needed help, mainly to pre-clean before the decorators arrived.

I called Maureen but got her answering machine instead of the live version.

I was gonna have to handle it all on my own.

I hate that.

Less than twenty minutes later, the invasion started. First up was a confused but appreciative Asian kid in a Red Sox cap, struggling to hold four huge boxes.

He bowed a couple of times, and I nodded. "I bring your food," he said, letting the bags slip to the floor.

I looked at my couch with Frank's books, the dining table coated with the pages of the *Wilmington News Journal,* and shook my head, seeing futility wherever I looked.

No, I was gonna stay positive.

"Give me just a minute," I said, and threw the newspaper into the trash. "There. Just put it here."

"Needs refrigeration. Mr. Washington be here at three o'clock to start work."

"Sounds great," I said, still faking positive for all I was worth.

He smiled and put down the packages. "Thank you, I leave," he said, not moving anywhere toward the door. I dug through my purse, pulled out a five, and handed it to him.

"Thank you for your help," I said, hoping he realized I was giving him most of my life savings.

"Thank you, missy. Have a nice day."

"Right back at ya, bub."

After he left, I took the boxes and unpacked them. Everything looked great. Little hot dogs, some sort of puff thing, chunky sauces, and mini-quiches. It was cocktail heaven. I sampled a mini-quiche, remembered the four hundred crunches I still had left to do, and reluctantly put the foil back in place.

The containers were huge, and not designed for my itty-bitty apartment-sized fridge. No matter how I pushed and shoved, there was no way all of them were going to fit.

Well, that was a fine shift in the refrigerator space-time continuum. However, when life hands you lemons that are too big for your refrigerator, you make lemonade, usually in your upstairs neighbor's kitchen. I called Maureen to see if she was home yet, but I got her machine.

I heaved a sigh and hung up. I guess Dora had her punching the clock on Saturday. However, lemonade was still in my sweaty grasp. I had a spare key.

I loaded up the boxes and the key, elevatored up two floors to Maureen's place, and unlocked the door.

And was immediately sprayed with a lethal can of Lysol.

"Elle!"

"Maureen." I choked through the Fresh Breeze fumes. "You're not supposed to be home." I put the bags on the floor, hoping that Lysol wasn't toxic to hors d'oeuvres. Not that my guests were my friends or that I truly cared.

She lowered the can and looked about as guilty as a lawyer can manage to look. "You can't just break into people's apartments."

I held up the key. "If you had answered the phone, this wouldn't have happened."

"Why're you here, Elle? You're not supposed to be here. I'm

swamped," she said, wrapping her arms around her waist. It was then, after the Lysol fog had cleared, that I realized Maureen looked like hell. So I told her so. It was the drugs. I knew it.

"I've got all this work to do this weekend. What are those?" she asked, pointing to the bags, and this time she didn't answer her own question.

"Party emergency. There was a flood at Leah's. Probably God, but I try not to judge. It's now at my place. In less than seven hours. You have to help me."

"I can't, Elle," she said, having the grace to look somewhat shamed, although her eyes were all bugged out.

"You can't?" I said, trying to guilt her into cooperation.

"I can't."

"You really can't?" I asked, my voice increasing in volume, in direct proportion to my pulse. "No, Maureen. This is partially your fault."

"Are you out of your mind? You must be out of your mind. I've got to go through all these discovery documents," she said, pointing to the file boxes that lined the floor, right next to my hors d'oeuvres. I took a step back, because legal documents never mean fun. They were a pungent reminder of Tony's legal adventures, although currently cloaked in Fresh Breeze scent.

She was right. I was nuts. This was bad. I had eight of my most hated people in the world coming to my apartment, and I needed to make sure they were completely blown away by my charm, poise, aesthetical ambience, and delicious food.

I must be a lunatic.

I glared at Maureen, pleading for help. "Can't you do that

tomorrow? I only need a couple of hours, and it's mainly moral support and guidance, although dusting would probably be good," I told her. Who else had guided her through the dark waters of her office politics? Who had been her friend when she was Fat Girl? Me. That's who. She owed me.

My ungrateful former friend barely spared me a glance, sitting down amidst the puddles of folders, picking up some legal documents. "Sorry. I've got to get back to work."

I almost walked out, almost let her desert me, but it wasn't self-dignity that commanded me to make a scene. I'd had it up to here. My stomach gurgled from lack of food, my abs ached from their recent abuse, and I was tired of being abused. Leah, bless her black heart, was right. After eighteen years, the dinner party was my kiss-off to all those memories that had noshed at my insides. I wasn't going to let Maureen, or anybody, for that matter, walk over me again.

I shoved the box to one side with my foot. It felt freeing. More than that, it felt right. "Look, Maureen. I'm asking for two hours. I need this. You *can't* sit here and go through this—this—*crap* that means nothing to you. Okay, I know it means something to you, but I'm your friend. I'm living, breathing flesh. I have feelings. I won't let you."

Impassively she stared up at me and then climbed to her feet. I thought I had scored a victory. I thought wrong. She walked into the back room and came out, handing me a plastic bag with pills in it.

That was it. My voice got unattractively screechy loud, but I didn't care. "You're giving me drugs? That's it, Maureen. Next time you need help with your job or somebody to listen to your whining, call Don Imus, because *I won't be picking up.*"

"It's Adderall. And you don't need to shout."

"I don't care. I don't need a pick-me-up. I need a friend," I said, but it was like talking to a wall.

"Take two of these. Trust me. You should really trust me. You'll have everything done in two hours."

I pushed them back into her hand. "No."

She pushed back. "It's not like speed or anything. Well, it's kinda like speed, but it's more streamlined. It's not addictive, and best of all, you can concentrate on anything." She pressed the bag into my hand.

"No."

She shrugged and sat back down on the floor. "Whatever sinks your boat, Elle. I'd take them, though. What can it hurt? It won't hurt anything. You get all the stuff done that you want, and get a personality boost as well."

I thought *personality boost* was overstating things. "I don't think so," I told her, but the bag sat there, calling me, like Circe to the rocks. If she hadn't lost those twenty pounds, and if my abs didn't ache, I think I would've been stronger, but instead I shoved the pills into my pockets and walked out the door.

Not that I needed them. I could show her. I could show everybody. I took the elevator downstairs, pepping myself up with words and inspirational quotes, the real motivators in life. I mean, who needs drugs when you can rely on the wisdom of Zig Ziglar?

I opened the door to my apartment, and my own wood-veneer life stared back at me. I had to find a place for my books. A set of dumbbells sat on my two barstools, laundry was spilling out of the hamper like tears, and the cereal bowls were piled three deep.

I put my hands on my hips, my mind ticking off the tasks in front of me. It was impossible.

My hand crept to the pocket of my jeans.

No.

I would be strong. I didn't need any magic powders to give me vim and vigor. I took a deep breath and tackled the dishes first, soaping, scrubbing, rinsing, and drying, only to realize that my cabinets were already stocked with dishes.

I had no space.

What was I gonna do? The pills were calling my name, but I held tough. I managed to resist them for a full three hours.

I talked myself into sorting through my collection of winter hats. I had them split up nicely into three piles. Give Away. Throw Away. Going to Wilmington. "Throwing Away" was leading "Going to Wilmington" by a big five to one, although if I decided to keep my mother's turquoise pillbox hat, not only would the scales of "Throw Away" shift to "Going with Me," but I'd also have a sentimental keepsake of the woman who birthed me but chose to abandon me in my time of need. The pills made me amazingly lucid and numb. There was none of the usual hurt I felt, and it was a truly marvelous experience. After the hats, I tackled the spring shoes, and I was in the middle of color-coding them by style and designer when the caterer showed up.

His name was Terrance Washington, and he resembled a gang-banger more than a chef. He wore a basketball jersey that hung off his thin shoulders, a backward baseball cap, and a chunky gold necklace that I could have traded for three years of rent. "You're the caterer?" I asked, not wanting to be as narrow-minded as to stereotype the poor kid, but he didn't look like a foodie.

"Yo," he said, popping his fist on mine. Then he looked around. "Where's the food?"

"I put most of it in my upstairs neighbor's apartment, but there's some in my refrigerator as well."

He strolled around the apartment (took less than thirty seconds), taking a mental inventory. I'd made a serious dent in the place since I'd taken the drugs an hour earlier, and it was all coming together nicely. In fact, I was rather proud.

"This place is too small. What's Ms. Weber wanting to hold her party here for?"

Small? I thought it looked intimate. And he said it as if it was all my fault. This wasn't my fault. Nothing was my fault.

"She had a freaking flood. I didn't arrange it. I don't want to have the party here, but all right, that's just the way it is. Time to pull on your big-girl panties, Terrance. Think you can deal?" As soon as the words were out of my mouth, I heard them echo in my head. Did I really say that? Jeez.

"Chill, bitch. Don't go slapping all that woman's metaphysical shit on me."

"I'm sorry," I said. "I'm not usually like this. The stress," I said, deciding that sounded better than "chemically induced bitch."

Terrance was much more forgiving than I. "Let's get to work. Got some tasty miracles to work. Bring down the food from up-stairs, and make it snappy."

He truly was a miracle worker. We bonded over crab canapés rolled in perfect symmetry, and the eggplant spread was to die for, and I wasn't even an eggplant fan. He taught me how to whip up a mean wasabi sauce, and this mango chutney that made my tastebuds sing. I was a lean, mean cooking machine.

And I hated to cook.

At one o'clock, I took my second dose, because I was Super-woman, I was Wonder Woman, I was the Queen of Clean. At T minus four hours, the second wave of invaders breached the apartment. Chloe the florist brought over several beautiful arrangements, although I only had table space for three. Barry, the other half of Terrance's catering firm, commanded a setup crew with split-second precision. In less than an hour, they were all gone, and my apartment was transformed. The scent of flow-ers drifted through the air, and my dingy furniture had been slipcovered into something new and shiny.

It looked marvelous.

The only piece of frumpiness in the apartment was me. I locked myself in the bedroom and completed an extra three hundred crunches in record time. When I tried on my size six dress, this time it fit. Maureen was right. Adderall was a freaking miracle.

Less than an hour later, I had cleaned and dusted my apartment, organized my closet, indexed my Rolodex (after four years), and turned my mattress. Adderall was an absolute freaking miracle. No longer was I discouraged by the mess in my apartment. Instead, it was like some Godzilla monster I needed to kill. And kill it I did. I washed, cleaned, packed, boxed, taped, filed, and trashed for the next three hours. I had never dreamed that I could accomplish all these things.

And with just two little pills? Who knew?

I called Tashondra at Citibank, and she patched me through to her boss, Grace. In less than fifteen minutes, I had not only convinced her I was the perfect customer service rep, but I also talked her into buying that cabin in the Poconos that she'd been eyeing. Grace needed a vacation/retirement home (nearly fifty, not too early to plan), interest rates were low, and with a couple of coats of paint, the interior could be perked right up.

After giving Grace my address, I hung up and stared at my fingernails. For forty-three seconds I analyzed why I chewed my nails but then decided it was a nervous condition I'd inherited from my grandmother, and there was nothing I could do about it.

I checked my watch. Only four P.M., and I still had lots of energy and no new projects left to tackle. The apartment was spotless. Terrance was happily singing and creating magical smells that drifted out of my kitchen. It seemed to me that this was the perfect time to go through my e-mail, sort the gazillion spam messages, and see if perhaps any actual clients had responded to the plug in *Community Living: The Jersey Shore Way*. After sorting through Nigerians who wanted to give me money, more Via8r* than you could shake a stick at, and eight thousand women named Julie who thought they could show me a good time, I found one nugget of gold. A woman, Jolie McGrath from Poughkeepsie, needed to find the courage to kick her freeloading sister out of her house and then tackle her credit-card debt. Perfect. Those were problems I could handle with my eyes closed. I dashed off a reply and gave her my phone number to call, and then sat and waited for her to call.

Adderall will do that.

By six o'clock, after six hours of hard labor, I was pretty wiped. I felt the lure of the Chivas calling my name, but I was strong. Instead, I popped two more tablets of Adderall. And thirty minutes later, I was zooming around so fast my own head was spinning. I laid out plates for Barry, brought up Italian sparkling mineral water for the crew, and sliced up strawberries with a surgical precision I never knew I had.

I started dressing with about forty-five minutes to spare. I made some quick sales-pitch notes on Good Vibrations, made up some heart-tugging stories about clients I'd helped. If I had really thought ahead, I'd have taken some pictures at our last session, but even on Adderall, I wasn't that thorough.

The doorbell rang, and my first guest had arrived.

Leah. The guest of honor.

She made her entrance and bobbed from tables brimming with food to huge sprays of fresh flowers, taking a breather to admire the silver-framed picture of myself with Caroline Kennedy (Photoshop is my friend).

"Elle, the place looks fab, fab, fab, and you"—she grabbed both my hands—"you look marvelous. Have you lost weight? You're just sparkling. It's enough to make me jealous. Almost." She gave me a kiss on the cheek. "We're going to knock 'em dead, Elle. I'll have them eating out of your advice-giving hands. Good times."

The doorbell rang, and she giggled, sending shivers of annoyance down my spine like tiny fingernails. Thank God, it was Alan. The charming man brought flowers, so I kissed him on the cheek and promised myself right then and there that before the night was out, I would service him better than he'd ever been serviced before. I didn't know the effects of Adderall on sex, but I suspected the Fourth of July would be tame in comparison.

The next couple was Mimi Hall and her husband, Jacob. I hadn't seen her in almost twenty years, and yes, she'd changed, too. She was a little hippier and wore her makeup a little heavier than my fluorescent lighting approved of. He had on an Elvis Presley tie. Not in the style of Elvis Presley, no. Those little boleros would have been preferable to the tiny Elvi that were scattered down the black silk. I hadn't met Jacob before, and the first thing Mimi explained was that he was a graduate of Princeton. I hugged him, simply because he was such a loser man, and I loved him for it.

I poured them a glass of wine and had Leah act as doorman. The guest list for the evening was as follows:

Mike and Tiffany Renteria. Yes, her name was actually Tiffany, and she completely lived up to it. She'd been Tiffany Morgan in high school, Leah's best friend, and it looked as if they were still pretty close. I had been to a party at her house once, gotten up close and personal with her toilet (American Standard), and the nightmares never left me. Mike had been a jock like Alan, only he had the sculpted-body look of a man who had one good plastic surgeon. Tiffany had been old money, and judging from the snappy attire, I suspected the old money was still being well taken care of. I made a mental note to myself to make nice-nice to both Tiffany and Mike.

Paul and Amber Obermann. Paul had been student body president, and I was pretty sure that his father had been somehow involved in city politics. Amber, who was about fourteen, had not attended St. Anthony's in my day or in the remaining two decades that followed. Can you say trophy wife? I knew you could. She wore a gold lamé sheath that clung to every visible skeletal cartilage in her body when she walked. Not only did she look fourteen, but she had the telltale shoulder blades of a woman with an eating disorder. Paul didn't seem to mind, and the way Mike's eyes would follow Amber around the room, I suspected he'd be willing to hold her head after dinner if she asked nicely enough.

Behave, Elle.

It would be a great time to note that bulimics make wonderful clients for a coach. I could put some meat on those bones in no time at all. I walked over and handed her a spinach cream puff.

The last to arrive was Sydney Moyer. I vaguely remembered Sydney, and when he started humming the tune from *Cabaret* with Mimi, it all came back to me. Drama. He was dressed in black, like a funereal wraith from *Les Mis,* and his hair was jet black as well. He held out a welcoming hand to me.

"Elle? Elle Shields! Look at you, darling! You are just the same."

"Hi, Syd," I said, while he spun me around the room.

"Syd-ney," he corrected. "I like the dress; it has that 'Take me, I'm yours' look."

"What are you doing these days, Sydney?"

"Directing, directing, directing. It's a mad, mad, mad world. One day, it's all cut the budget, cut the budget, cut the budget, and the next, it's Sydney, you're a genius. Schizophrenics. I'm surrounded by schizophrenics." He laughed. "I wouldn't trade it for the world."

Mimi came over, looking completely well adjusted and normal. That didn't do me any good. She air-kissed Sydney. "I saw you eating next to Keith Kelly at Michael's. What'd you have to do to get that four-star review, Sydney?"

"Get your mind out of the gutter, Mimi. I would never, ever compromise my artistic abilities with questionable moral practices." He clicked his tongue. "Gotcha."

"Mimi," I said, interrupting the love fest because tonight was all about hard-hitting life coach discussions. "What do you do now?"

"I work with the Susan Komen Foundation. Breast cancer. It's all about the pink."

"You always were the little do-gooder." I looked at Jacob, watching Elvis shake as he laughed. "He must be very proud of you," I said, and I truly meant it. In high school, Mimi had never been the enemy the way some of the kids were. She celebrated Earth Day by scheduling a march outside the DMV offices and petitioned the cafeteria to provide an organic alternative to the mystery burgers they served on Fridays.

"I can look at myself in the mirror, as long as I don't look too close," she said. She pressed a finger to her brow. "Botox injections. I just started. What do you think? Am I Plasta-Girl?"

"Do you have body image issues? You know, studies show that seventy percent of women are unhappy with their bodies. I know in my group, we take the time to develop—"

Leah interrupted. "Mimi!" Instantly there was hugging and kissing, and I had just wasted a good sales pitch. Oh, well, the night was young.

She held her by the shoulders. "Look at this dress! Who is it? You must tell me."

Mimi blushed. "I made it."

"Get out. Get out. You made this? Are you for hire? Could you design one for me?" Leah pulled at the hem. "And look at this line. It's so flattering to your shape. You have to make one for me." She wrapped an arm around her shoulder and led her away.

Sydney munched on a mini-quiche. "Are there really so many women ready to commit suicide because of their thighs? I don't know. Seems like a total waste of time to me. Life's too short," he said.

"Sydney, can I ask you a personal question? Are you happy with your life?"

"Gawd, Elle. This is a party! Lighten up."

"I'm sorry. I just think we don't take as much time to appreciate things as we should—"

"This is because of your father, isn't it? You're such a little trooper. Going along, making the best of things. Putting on a happy face, when inside you're dying, aren't you? Have you considered therapy? I have a great doctor. You should see him."

I rubbed at my temples, fighting to keep switching topics. *Why did everyone want to talk about other things?* "I'm a life coach, Sydney. I tell people how to achieve what they want in life."

"And good for you. Is that Scotch in Alan's glass? Do you have some stocked away? I'm really parched."

I forced myself into happy hostess mode. "I'll be right back."

I walked briskly, did not run, no, did not, did not, into the kitchen. But I could feel the little beetles of insecurities climbing right up my spine. I took a moment to polish the sink and noticed that a ceramic mug had a chip in it. Out in the trash that one went. I refilled the tray with the little breads and pimento cheese on it and took a moment to sample another puff. Delicious.

I ran into my bedroom and checked my pockets for more pills, but I'd taken them all. I called Maureen, got no answer, and decided that there was nothing left but the real me. *Oh, God.*

Of course, now the dress felt too tight again, so I smoothed the black fabric over my hips, trying to ignore the extra padding I'd carried since I hit thirty. I snuck back into the kitchen before anybody caught me.

"Elle?" It was Alan. He peeked into the doorway and then wrapped his arms around my waist, inhaling a good part of my neck. Delicious. "Mmmm, you smell marvelous. And all dressed up." He drew a finger down my cleavage, down, down, down . . .

Tell me, who really needs a bunny when you have a cleavage-drilling man right in your very own kitchen? I giggled like a little girl and then pushed him away. "Does everyone have enough to eat? I'm going to serve dinner in about an hour. Don't you think that's enough time? We could wait if it's too early."

He caught my hand. "Why are you so nervous? Everybody's having a good time. Relax." He pressed up against me. "I know I am."

"I can't screw this up, Alan."

"It's just a party, Elle."

Just a party. I wished. "I'm struggling, Alan."

His hands dropped to his sides. "With what?"

"My life coach business. I'm in trouble. I need clients, and I need them fast."

"But I thought Leah was going to help you."

"She did, in her little Leah way, and we're hoping to drum up some business tonight. Maybe you can help?"

He didn't look so enthusiastic. His face scrunched up more than usual. "Sure. Anything I can do."

"So here's the plan. First, we eat in about"—I checked my watch—"forty-three minutes. The mushrooms are ready, but I have to use Maureen's microwave to heat those up, and the salad only needs to be tossed and dressed."

His smile returned. "You really are nervous, aren't you? You know, a little tossing and undressing would do wonders for your nerves."

I patted him on the chest. "You keep thinking those thoughts. And remember, if you talk to anybody who has problems, or has friends who have problems, or has friends of friends who have—"

He shut me up with a kiss. Nice. Thorough. Long.

Oh, God. The mushrooms. I needed to get the rolls going. I pushed away, grabbed the dish of mushrooms, and flew out the door. "Entertain everybody while I'm gone. I'll be right back."

The air was getting too tight in there, and it had nothing to do with the extra five pounds I was sure I had just gained from looking at food, and most of all, Alan had the look of a man trying a little too hard. Takes one to know one. I ran out of my apartment, breathing in great gulps.

"Maureen?" I said, knocking at the door before I entered, in case she had the Lysol at the ready. There was no answer, and I used my key to go inside.

She really wasn't there this time, deserting me in my time of need (actually I was aching more for pills than insensitive human companionship). My head was starting to hurt, my stomach was returning to its normally distressed state, but the mushrooms cooked exactly as they were supposed to.

Not quite nine o'clock; dinner would be right on time. I slowed my heartbeat down to something that wouldn't give me a stroke (ancient Middle Eastern method, very useful in a crisis) and then dashed down the stairs, because the elevator was too slow. I was back in record time; if people missed me while I was gone, they sure didn't show it.

I came up to my next potential client. Amber. She was deep in conversation with Alan, so it was easy to sidle up next to him and butt right in. "Amber? I don't think we've met. I'm Elle Sheffield."

She looked confused. "I thought your name was Shields? Are you married?"

"Long story. Did you get something to eat? Have another puff." I grabbed the bowl and put it in front of her.

"No thanks."

Fine. "So, what do you do, Amber?"

"We're trying to have a baby, so I stay home all day and think positive thoughts," she said, patting her concave belly. Oh. Infertility? I could do infertility. I hadn't tried before, but beggars can't be choosers, and I had no desire to be a beggar.

Alan obviously didn't do infertility. He turned pale. "I need a Scotch. Call me when the baby talk is over."

I laughed, a graceful trill that I'd never done before, and turned to watch him go. "Isn't he the cutest? But enough about Alan. Let's talk about you and that baby of yours. What sort of training are you going through? Meditation? Medical treatments? Have you thought about in vitro? They're doing great things in science these days."

"Paul just got the idea in his head a few months ago. He wants a little Pauly to play catch with."

I looked over at Big Pauly, and thought that he didn't look like the Little League type, but what did I know? "And what about you? Are you excited, too?"

She sighed. "No."

Oh, crisis. Potential for marital conflict. *Excellent.* "So why are you letting him railroad your uterus into something you don't want?"

"It's not that I don't want a baby, exactly. But I want to travel, and go out late, dancing, partying. You don't have kids. You know how it is."

I nodded sympathetically. "Yeah, yeah. I do. Listen, I have some friends, a ladies' club. We go out once a week."

"Dancing? Do you go dancing?"

I could see that jogging in the park wasn't gonna cut it with Amber. "Yeah. Go, go, go. That's us."

Her eyes got way too big for her face. I pushed the cheese puff plate in her direction but was once again rebuffed. "It sounds great. And you have to keep the puffs away from me. I gained a pound last week. Next thing you know, you'll be rolling me out the door with a shovel."

"Are you dieting?"

She shoved a lock of long, flowing hair back over her shoulder. Very Lady Godiva. "I just watch what I eat."

I took a cheese puff and put it in my mouth. "Yeah, so do I. So you want to come with us next Monday?"

"Mondays? You go dancing on Monday nights? Isn't it, like, dead on Monday nights?"

Gotta hand it to that Amber. She's got stuff going on upstairs that I didn't even suspect. "Yeah. On Mondays we do lunch. It's Fridays that we go out dancing. You're welcome to do both."

"I go to the gym at noon. Pilates. Do you do Pilates?"

I remembered my elliptical era with the fondness of a woman who'd forgotten the pain of childbirth. "No."

"But I'd love to go on Friday." She handed me a card and made phone fingers. "Call me."

I nodded stupidly. "I will."

Dinner turned out better than I expected, and I was pleasantly surprised. It was probably the drugs, but I liked to think I had just turned up the juice for a crisis, and this time I was coming through with flying colors.

Leah pulled me into the bedroom while people were devouring dessert. I was holding on to the last of the cheese puffs like a starving man. "It's going beautifully, just like I knew it would. Didn't I tell you, Elle? A little social grooming, and poof, it's a miracle. I think I've got Mimi all signed up. This is so much fun. I've never done anything meaningful. And then along came a project to pull me right out of the doldrums of insignificance. And it's you! I don't know why we were never friends in school."

My face was gonna crack in two. "If you had treated me then like you're treating me now, who knows how I would've turned out?"

"Yeah, if only," she murmured.

"Very dangerous words," I told her. "We don't hear people say, 'If only I was dead.' Why is that? Because deep within us is the desire to have something better, to do something better, to be something better. When you say 'If only,' you're expecting a bolt of lightning to come down and zap you into something new. But you limit yourself when you stand idly by and wait for it to happen. You know what happens when you stand around in New York? You get whomped on your ass. That's what happens. You gotta move, Leah. You gotta be alive. You gotta find out what you want and then go for it. What do you want, Leah? What's your goal?"

She stared at me as if I was speaking a foreign language, and I thought maybe she'd either been drinking or had popped a perky pill, too. But then her smile wilted, and I realized she had heard me. "I want Harvey, Elle. I want my husband back. Can you help me fix that?"

At that moment, I think the last of the pills wore off completely. Now, I know I've given Leah a hard time here (she did deserve it early in life), but I now believed that in her twisted way, she was actually trying to help. I blinked a couple of times, trying to erase the very loud *no* that kept repeating in my head. I didn't know if it was the revenge talking or if it was something intrinsically appealing about Harvey that called to us both.

Out of all the people I knew or had ever met, Harvey was the only one who met the real Elle Shields and was intrigued. Not intrigued enough to stick around, but he was there when I needed someone to take care of me. No one had ever taken care of me before, and it had affected me way more than it should have.

I didn't want to be taken care of. I wanted to be the strong, invincible woman that Alan kept trying to see in me. But Alan didn't heat me up. Only Harvey did that.

I looked at Leah—the formerly-married-to-Harvey Leah—and I gave her credit because she saw the real Elle Shields, too. She knew I wanted Harvey, but unlike me, she was willing to fight for him.

"I'd be willing to hire you to help me," she said, her voice echoing in a long chamber. I felt this great poundage on my shoulders, and I would've been really happy to take me and my cheese puffs, go up onto the roof, and make everyone else go away.

"How much would you be willing to pay?" my ever-practical self asked, figuring that if I was on Leah's payroll, I *could* stay in New York. Maybe I could keep my business afloat, maybe I could make up for the mess I'd made in Barbara's marriage. It was a tantalizing proposal.

Her blue eyes looked at me, crystal-clear. She had a goal; she was going to do whatever it took to get it. I could learn something from Leah. I knew it.

"I'll pay you three thousand a month, with a bonus if you get him to attend social functions with me. Twenty-four months is the timeline."

Seventy-two thousand dollars. She was willing to pay me seventy-two thousand dollars. It wouldn't put me in a Ferrari, but it would pay the rent and give me a few extra bucks for advertising. The room became deathly quiet, all the niceties of social conversation stripped away. I knew I should take the money, for Barbara, for Leah, for my group, for me.

I even nodded my head and saw the flicker of relief in those blue, blue eyes.

"I don't do marriages," I said, and the room temp dropped several degrees.

"Why?" she asked.

I wasn't about to answer that question. I pushed the cheese puffs in her direction and ran out toward the kitchen. Right now, I really needed a drink.

When I got there, Tiffany was puttering around, snooping in the silverware drawers. "I was looking for a fork," she said.

"Why don't you tell the truth, Tiff? You're checking out my stuff, aren't you?"

She looked shocked. I've never been a mouthy person, but then I'd never taken Adderall, either. "I wasn't checking out your stuff, Elle. This junk? Puh-lease. I expected better from you."

She gave me a look, a superior, judgmental, "I'm better than you can ever be" look. I used to get them all the time in high school, but I was forty-two years old now. I was a mature, capable, successful adult. I knew exactly how to respond.

"Why the heck would you think that, Tiffany? I was never good enough. I wasn't skinny enough, I wasn't smart enough, I wasn't tough enough, either. You know something? I'm tough now."

"You've got the money, don't you? And now you want to just wave it in front of us, playing us all for fools, don't you, Elle?"

My head was threatening to split in two, and I remembered the night of her party, how she laughed, how everyone laughed. When I was seventeen, I never fought back, but I'd learned.

A crowd had started to gather in the kitchen, but crowds didn't bother me anymore. I shot her a smile. A confident, successful smile. "You've been tippling a bit, Tiff? You always were a lush in high school."

She gasped. The innocent.

Tiff raised a hand to her throat, as if I were choking her. *Right.* "Why are you doing this?"

"Because you deserve it, that's why. Or is that too complicated for you? You all treated me like garbage in school, Tiffany. I didn't deserve it."

Her perfectly shaped and lifted eyes narrowed. "Yes, you did. Do you know how much money your bastard of a father stole from us?"

"Oh, yeah, I can see you're really missing it." I waved a hand. "Look around you. Does this look like I'm rolling in the dough? It was twenty years ago. Get over it."

I felt Alan's hand on my arm. "Elle—"

I shook him off. "You people judged me because of something that wasn't even true."

"He was convicted," said Tiffany. "And you had that whole 'incident' after the trial."

"Just leave it alone, Tiffany. I don't want to rehash our old—and new—differences with you, but I will."

"What incident?" said Jacob, and I really didn't like him anymore.

Tiffany smiled, perfect white teeth, shark's teeth. "Let me tell you all about it."

I didn't listen. This time, I ran.

Eleven

There is a time for courage. Today is not it.

—Elle Sheffield

Alan found me on the roof. There were only so many places I could run to, and none of them seemed far enough away.

"Everybody's gone," he said quietly.

"Hope they had a good time," I said, not quietly at all.

"You shouldn't let her get to you, Elle. She's a bitch. She was a bitch in school, she was a bitch in college, and she'll be a bitch when she dies."

"Is that what you do, Alan? You just ignore them? Oh, sorry. You were never disrespected, were you? Never mind."

"You should come inside. It's starting to rain."

"I won't melt, but thank you for your concern."

"Come on, Elle. Let's go inside. We'll turn on some music and polish off the last of the Scotch."

"Is that your solution to everything, Alan? Get drunk?"

"I'm trying to help. I don't see anybody else up on this roof. Getting drenched, I might add. Why are you pissed at me?"

"Did they tell the story, Alan? Did you listen? Did you laugh?"

"I didn't laugh. I swear."

"But you didn't stop her, did you? Who laughed this time?"

"Mike. Paul. Amber thought you sounded cool."

"And Leah?"

He nodded. Just once, but I saw it.

"Did you say anything, Alan? Just a word to defend me?"

There was rain falling on his face. His dark hair was starting to get wet. "They're my friends, Elle. I need them for business."

I remembered Leah's business proposition, and although I had worried before whether I was stupid to turn down free money, now I knew for sure.

Yeah, I was stupid. Hell, seventy-two grand just to stay away from Harvey. I lifted my chin and caught a big raindrop on the nose. It didn't bother me. I had scruples, principles. I could look at myself in the mirror. I wasn't sure Alan would be so lucky. Even his comb-over was looking a little watered down.

"I think I'm going to stay up for a while," I told him. "Maybe watch the sunrise. I don't do that enough. Why don't you go?"

"I'm sorry. Let me make it up to you. We'll do dinner. Maybe we could head off to Cape May."

" 'Bye, Alan."

I heard the sound of crunching gravel as he left, and I wished that he'd been a braver man. I wanted someone with me, someone to stand up for me, someone to take care of me. Alan wasn't it.

I sat up there for a couple of hours. Mainly getting soaked. I thought about going to Maureen's, but it was two A.M., and she was probably brain-deep in legal documents. So where does a woman go when it's two A.M. and she doesn't want to be alone?

Where else but Harvey's?

I called him on my cell. Asked if I could come over. There was a moment of silence, and I thought Harvey was going to disappoint me, too. But then he said, "Sure," and gave me an address on the Upper West Side. With a view overlooking the park.

Jimmy Buffett had been holding out on me. Oh, well, we all have our secrets.

The doorman buzzed me up, and I wondered if Harvey had a steady stream of two A.M. callers. I didn't think so.

I knocked on the door. The bell seemed so impersonal, and I didn't want to be impersonal. I needed a person. Flesh and blood. I needed to be taken care of, and there was only one person I knew who could do that.

He led me inside, and I jumped him right then and there. He wore a pair of boxers and nothing else. Those were gone as soon as I touched him.

"Why are you here?" he asked.

"Do you care?" I answered.

"No," he said, and we didn't talk anymore for a long time.

"Why are you here?" he asked once more, and this time the clock said it was 5:47. Through the window you could see the sun was just starting to light the city, and I could hear noises outside. West Side noises. Even the trucks seemed quieter.

"Bad party. I needed a friend. Now I should go."

He looked as if he was thinking about saying something, but he didn't. My ego would have felt better, but I wasn't in the mood. Last night I had blown my second chance at making Good Vibrations work. Second chances don't grow on trees. Third chances are pretty much right up there with winning the lottery when you don't even buy a ticket.

I had bared my body with Harvey, and I was dying to bare my soul. I wanted to cry and scream and whine, but I didn't.

A long time ago, I realized that if you don't let people get too close, you miss out on a whole lot of bad crap. Today I was tempted to do just that. After all, this was a man who saw me through one of many less than stellar moments, and he hadn't judged, hadn't laughed, hadn't done anything but what I needed. Hell, he even tried to help. Here was a man I could love, here was a man who could break down my walls. I turned toward him, studying his face in the pale morning light. There were lines there. Marks of life that he didn't try to hide, but when the first streaks of sunlight hit my face, I turned away.

Here was also a man who had never asked me out on a date.

Morning is a wonderful time for clarity of vision.

He wanted to call me a cab, but I didn't have the change, and I wasn't going to ask him for money (ick), so I waved awkwardly, made a stupid comment about exercise, and cut through the park. I took off my heels at Third Avenue and got propositioned by a newspaper delivery boy at Seventy-third Street. Men don't usually proposition me. Of course, I don't usually look like a slut, either.

I wanted to stay in bed for the rest of my life, but Monday came like a hangover, and my conscience wouldn't let me desert the group. I dragged myself up and scheduled a lesson at the DSNY barge at Fifty-ninth Street. It wasn't a pretty place, but I told my girls to dress appropriately. I wasn't looking forward to this session, because I knew I was going to have to level with my girls about My Situation, and a garbage dump seemed poetic.

While staring at my bedroom ceiling, I had considered my options, not that I had many, but there comes a time when you have to give voice to the word *defeat*. It's usually at three A.M., when your eyes are wide open and you're staring sleeplessly at the ceiling, and all without the wonder of Adderall.

Today I would tell the girls I was heading west for Delaware, land of plastic conglomerates that lure unsuspecting clients into financial ruin. I knew of all the callings I'd answer, this was the one I was genetically engineered to succeed at.

I took a crosstown bus to the Hudson Department of Sanitation, where the stench was nearly overpowering. This time, I was the last one to show. They were waiting for me at the security fence when I arrived. I gave them all some Vicks VapoRub to put under their noses, and although Barbara balked, after she inhaled a couple of times, she decided to cooperate.

"Ladies, today we're talking trash," I said, as I led them down toward the dock where the big barges collected the nearly three thousand tons of garbage that gets hauled out of Manhattan on a daily basis. The big containers were overflowing with plastic bags, food remains, nonrecyclables, and the millions of Starbucks cups that people trashed every morning.

My heart wasn't in this one. I'd been stricken with a lethargy that I couldn't beat back. I took a good look at my girls and realized we all shared a common stench in our lives. We were all sinking in the garbage of life, but by God, we could all sink together.

I pulled out my rubber gloves and tongs and pointed to the bin. "This is garbage." Then I picked up an empty Krispy Kreme bag. "This is your brain on garbage. Today we're gonna tackle the negativity in our lives. First of all, I want each of you to verbalize the worst piece of negativity that you're currently dealing with. Joan, you go first."

"You have an extra pair of those gloves?" she asked.

I whipped them out, and she popped them on like a surgeon. "I can't handle all that dirt."

"What's bugging you, Joan?"

She gave me her confident smile. "I'm actually at a good place right now. Felix and I are getting married."

Barbara's mouth started working as if she was going to cry. She was such a soft touch sometimes. "Oh, he's a very lucky man."

"This seems rather sudden, don't you think?" I said, grateful to have something juicy to wrap my brain around. I dropped

234

the Krispy Kreme bag back into the pile, and Joan speared me with one of her looks.

"I've buried one husband, and I'm not getting any younger. At my age, you move and move fast."

"What does his family think?" I asked carefully.

"He doesn't have any relatives here. They're still back in Russia."

Tanja looked at her crosswise, rocking back and forth on her heels. "Make him sign a prenup. I bet he won't. I thought he was shifty. Nice, but shifty."

"Felix understands me. He takes care of me. That's what I need right now. The money isn't important."

Do you ever notice that? That the upper class doesn't really care about money? It'd be nice not to worry about paying the bills, having a ceiling over my head, or loading up on the packaged food at Big Lots. I gave Joan a smile. "It sounds like you're making the right decision. Now, let's get back to that negativity. You don't have any negativity in your life right now?" I said, raising my voice as a sanitation truck backed up to the docks.

"No. I'm alive. I'm here with my friends. What else matters?"

There were a lot of things that mattered. Nonexistent friends, uncooperative landlords, on-the-fence boyfriends who only jump off the fence in order to get something. Friendship didn't even rate.

"Okay, let's move on to Tanja. I bet you have tons of negativity in your life."

"Not today."

"Why's that?"

235

"Mr. Missed Connections took her out for coffee," answered Barbara.

"I like him, and he's not too nice," Tanja said.

"Why shouldn't he be nice?" I asked.

She flicked her hair nervously. "You know."

"No, I don't know."

"Because he won't like me if he's too nice."

Tanja had issues, but she shouldn't sell herself short. She had a good heart and deserved the best. I was ready to tell her just that when a dump truck pulled up behind us, the backup system beeping. Most of all, Tanja had the blessing of youth. She had the best years of her life ahead of her. We walked away from the noise and chaos, and I got myself right in Tanja's face. "You listen to me, right?"

She nodded.

"You think I'm a smart lady, right?"

Again with the nod.

I whapped her in the chest. "So why are you throwing yourself on the bargain table? Look at you. You're young, you're intelligent. You have your whole life ahead of you. Don't settle. Find someone who's going to treat you like you deserve."

"He did pay for the coffee."

"So what's wrong with the bozo?" asked Joan.

"He has a scar."

"What's wrong with that?" Barbara asked, scrubbing at the Vicks on her lip. I pulled her hand away.

"On his wrists," answered Tanja.

"Oh," I said, suddenly understanding. Suicide. It was one way out, but suicide was for the über-weak. "Is he better?"

"He's better. It was a long time ago, when he was messed up with drugs. He's clean now."

"So what's his name?"

"Nick. Nick Romero," she said, a nervous smile flickering on her face.

"Well, looks like we're all a happy bunch today," I said, a little punchier than necessary.

Of course, then Barbara, the meekest link, spoke up. "What about me?" she asked, almost defiantly.

It was a moment I'd been dreading and hoping not to face, because I wanted to be in Delaware, facing irate customers via the faceless anonymity of a headset. Instead, I was stuck looking at my friend, knowing the grenade she was about to launch.

"I think Larry is having an affair."

"Are you sure?" I asked, still hoping to avoid the thundercloud of certainty.

"A woman knows. He doesn't care what I cook for dinner anymore; sometimes he doesn't show up until after the late news is over. And this morning, I wore the pants that he hates, just to see if he'd notice. He ignored me."

She looked in my eyes, expecting me to make her feel better. Expecting me to tell her how to solve all her problems. These were problems that a financial windfall, a bottle of Chivas, or a couple of doses of Adderall couldn't fix. Sometimes I really hated myself.

I rubbed a hand over my eyes. "Maybe you're just borrowing trouble."

Joan shook her head. "My first husband had an affair in the '60s. I was a young girl then, in my mid-twenties. Such a long time ago."

"And you two worked it out?" I said with forced cheerfulness. I smiled at Barbara. "See. A good counselor, and everything can be fixed."

Joan pulled out a cigarette, ignoring the signs, and lit it. "Nah. It ruined the marriage. We stayed together another twenty years for financial reasons. I wasn't a dewy-eyed debutante anymore. I needed security. Edward gave me that."

Barbara's shoulders slumped, and I wished I could take away some of her pain. "I'm sorry, Barbara," I told her. Words that didn't do diddly. The story of my short-lived career in life coaching. "We're here for you. If you need a shoulder, a hit man, a cabana boy, not only are the rates reasonable, but we deliver as well."

That made her smile, and she wiped away an imaginary smudge on her cheek. "I'm trying to decide if I should ignore it and just pretend everything's normal, and I think I'd actually be happier, or should I be brave, and idiotic, and tell him that I know."

"Tell him? That'd be pretty rank," said Tanja. "You shouldn't tell him."

"I don't think I could anyway," answered Barbara with a sigh. She turned to me. "What should I do?"

I felt the walls of trash around me move in tighter, and even with the masking powers of eucalyptus, the smell was turning my stomach. "Don't make me make these decisions for you, Barbara."

"But you're my coach. If you don't, who will?"

A burly union type in coveralls came up and pointed to the dock. "We've got a boat coming in. No civilians allowed when we're loading or unloading." He tucked his thumbs in his pockets. "It's the law." He pointed at Joan. "No smoking, neither."

She smiled regally. "I'll put it out right away," she said, but didn't move a muscle. "Why don't you give us a few more minutes? She hasn't told us how to get rid of the trash."

He shook his head. "Sorry. Come back again."

We scurried up the stairs, back away from the stench of week-old refuse, and I looked at Joan when we got up to the top. "I think once is enough."

She winked at me. "Once is never enough."

Twelve

Men suck, except for Nick.

—JESSICA SIMPSON, BEFORE THE DIVORCE

On Friday I had my second and last date with Alan. I understood his type, marginalizing his principles, all the time understanding that he's marginalizing his principles (i.e., he has no backbone, and he knows it), and I felt sorry for him. He took me to a pizza place on Forty-eighth Street and Second, which was a long step down from Per Se. Somewhere along the line, I'd become cheap and easy, and I didn't even know it.

We ended up at a table in the back, next to a pack of Italian punks who conducted their business over panelle and fresh mozzarella pie.

"It's not Per Se," he said apologetically.

And it's not like I was a snob, either. "Carbs are good for the

240

soul. Besides, where I'm going, I'm not sure the pie will be as good," I said, taking a bite of coal-fired, oven-baked crust, the kind only found in New York City. There were several things I was going to miss about this place: my group, good pie, and the New York Yankees, not necessarily in that order. I shot Alan a fond smile. He was rich, he was handsome, and if there was justice in the world, we would fall in love and live happily ever after in his loft in SoHo.

"Where're you going?" he asked.

"Wilmington."

"Massachusetts?"

"Delaware."

At my answer, he frowned, and I noticed the lines around his eyes. Men wear age so nicely. He was hitting his prime, I was aged beef. I sighed.

"Delaware? Why?"

"Change of pace. I wanted someplace a little slower, a little less mercenary, a lot cheaper."

He laughed. "Yeah," he said, and covered my hand. "I'm sorry to see you go."

In my imagination, this was the part where he swears undying love, happily ever after, blah, blah, blah. Unfortunately, even if wishes were live horses, I suspected that after a few months I might reconsider my position, because as nice as Alan was, as rich as Alan was, as handsome as Alan was, Alan wasn't it.

"I'll miss you, too," I told him, which was as far as I was going to go on the emotional playing field.

"I've been thinking of clearing out of town, too."

"You're kidding," I said, unable to fathom why anyone who had a choice would leave.

"No."

"Why?"

"The business is slowing down. I've been living way up in the clouds, and it's time to face reality," he said, his words slow and quiet.

My mouth fell open. Gauche, ill mannered, that's me. But Alan had been my ideal for twenty years. How could he be a failure, too? "Oh, my God," I said, because I didn't understand why we were all getting smited. "Where are you going to go?"

"I've got some ideas. Nothing definite."

I perched my chin on my palm, wanting to know more. To me, it was like learning that Superman had taken steroids. "What do you want to do?" I asked.

"Something different. Something far away."

"There's always Alaska. I could see you in one of those red plaid shirts, chopping down trees, and then hoisting a beer at the end of the shift."

"A lumberjack?" He gave me a smile. "I never thought about that."

"If you're going to get away, you have to dream big. Go after the things you haven't done before," I lectured. I didn't know if it'd be easier for Alan than it would be for me, but I suspected so. He could spend the next thirty years basking in his own success. I wanted to be a basker, too.

He looked at me as if he was contemplating his dreams. I

liked the look of dreamers. When you hit a certain point in your life, the big asteroid crashes through the atmosphere, and dreams become extinct.

"What are you going to do? You should be a teacher or a personal assistant."

"I think I'm going to be in the finance industry," I stated, making it sound high-brow and exciting.

"You," he said, as if he couldn't contemplate me in my little cubicle, managing the dollars and cents of Middle America. He was a smart man, Alan was. However, I was, too. I wasn't going to influence as much as a piggy bank for Middle America. There were computer programs and elaborate algorithms that determined who we were and what we would achieve. Humanity had been replaced by spreadsheets.

Technology. Gotta love it.

I said my good-byes to Alan at my door, giving him a kiss on the cheek. He looked disappointed. Yeah, suck it up, bub.

There's a time in life to close doors as well. I was finally smart enough to close the door on St. Anthony's once and for all.

On Tuesday, Frank, my former financial wizard, showed up for work carrying a Macy's bag.

"I fired you," I told him, but I let him into my apartment anyway, because Frank was Frank, and he was irreplaceable.

"I came for my books," he said.

I kicked at the box next to my couch. The dust-gathering paperweight that served no functional purpose whatsoever. "I'd given up on you, Frank."

He cocked his head to one side and collapsed in the chair.

"Make yourself at home," I told him, and got uncomfortable on the sofa.

"How're you doing, Elle?" he asked, as if he cared. "Looks like you're almost packed up."

He was right. Seventeen boxes contained the sum of the parts of my life. It was humbling to realize that I couldn't even crack twenty. "Mostly," I said.

"When's moving day?"

"Weekend after next. Got my bus ticket and found a room for rent. Cheap."

"Cheap doesn't mean it's good."

"No, cheap sucks. But it's better than being homeless."

"You could stay with me," he offered.

I was touched. I had a small number of friends, but no one else had offered me a roof.

"You're a good man, Frank. I hope you find another one to appreciate it."

He shrugged. "I don't know, but I'm not dead yet."

I chewed on my lip, getting a sudden brain flash. "Do you like music?"

"As long as it's not Cher."

"I have a friend."

"Oh, God, not a fix-up."

"Hear me out, Frank. He's a Broadway director. He's funny and vibrant, and I think he would really appreciate meeting someone with your down-to-earth qualities."

"I'm not too"—he bent his head—"plain?"

I threw a cushion at him. "You're as plain as crème brûlée, my friend."

"Give him my number," he said, with the resigned acceptance of someone who has looked futility in the eye and blinked. Then he lifted a brown paper bag from within the Macy's brown paper bag. "A parting gift," he said.

I took the small bag in my hands. It didn't weigh much, so it wasn't a bottle of Chivas, and it was too small to contain cash of any substance.

"For me?" I asked.

"Just a little something," he answered. "Open it."

Inside was a white cardboard box, and I imagined that Frank had bought me a pencil holder. I peeked inside, and the bright pink eyes of my bunny peeked back at me. The ears looked to be a bit longer, and this one was cordless. After ten years, I suppose they had time to improve on the design. I looked at Frank, too beaten to be embarrassed. "You didn't have to," I murmured.

"The rose in your cheeks and the gleam in your eye are worth it."

"You're the devil, Frank. Couldn't you be hetero?"

"Couldn't you be a man?" he asked, and both of us sat there, contemplating impossibilities. However, I had a rabbit sitting in my lap, and the possibilities were endless.

He brought out two AA batteries. "In case all your batteries were packed."

"I think I'm going to cry," I said, "and I've become a noisy crier. You should probably go."

"Needing a little privacy, aye?" he said, his eyes fixed on the white box.

"Yeah," I joked. But I wasn't aching for some alone time with my bunny. It'd been too long, and my spirits had endured their own little hell. The little gesture of kindness in the face of everything else had restarted my heart, and I knew the waterworks weren't far behind. I wanted to throw myself on a pink-checked bedspread and cry my heart out, hoping and praying that everything would be okay. It hadn't worked when I was eighteen, and I sure as heck didn't think it was going to work when I was forty-two, but I wasn't born a woman for nothing. In the face of all else, tears were a requirement, and this time I didn't even lock the door.

I cried for a good two hours, yelled once or twice, too. I cried about men like Harvey and Alan who would never see me as anything more than a vagina that passes in the night. I cried for Leah, because if I had been someone else, we would have been friends. I cried for my ladies, who didn't need me as much as I needed them, and I cried for Frank, who had probably cried on a pink-checked bedspread in high school, too.

Unfortunately, tears dry up. The body isn't designed to unload water for hours on end. Dehydration sets in, and survival won't last. Biology is a very practical science. I got to my feet, lost in my small apartment, alone with seventeen boxes and eight pieces of furniture, and the phone rang.

It was Barbara.

"Elle, I know you don't make house calls, but I need your help. Please."

Barbara sounded shakier than usual, so I got her address and made my way to 820 Park Avenue. When I got to the door, the doorman was all over me because I obviously didn't fit their clientele. I told him I was the maid service, and *that* he believed, so he buzzed me up.

Their apartment was on the twentieth floor, and Barbara answered the door wearing a paint-splattered T-shirt and shorts.

It was so very un-Barbara that at first I didn't recognize her, but the quivering jaw was vintage Barbara.

"It's worse than an affair. Larry's got AIDS."

I nearly sagged against the wall, but she caught me before I got wet paint all over my back. "Why do you think that, Barbara?" I asked very carefully, even though I knew why she thought that, although why Maureen hadn't stuck to something more harmless, like genital herpes, I couldn't begin to guess.

"I heard him talking to the lab."

"And they said he had AIDS?"

"No, they just said it was a good idea for him to be tested. What's he doing? We've been married for twenty-seven years. I don't have AIDS. But what if I have AIDS?"

She needed me to be the strong, confident, lean-on-me group leader who could get her through anything. I wanted to be the weak, ulcer-ridden wreck who could barely make it to Delaware. But my training was good, and with only a small clutch of the gut, I was back to Elle Sheffield, life coach extraordinaire.

"Barbara, you're not sick. I swear. Sit down," I told her, and then realized all the furniture had plastic covering over it.

She moved like a zombie, following whatever orders I told her. "I've been painting the apartment. It's Peach Cloud. I thought maybe he would like it better than the white. He hates it."

"I'm sorry, Barbara."

"It's all right. I can repaint it. Lately I've been screwing up all over the place. The dinners aren't right. The clothes aren't right. The color isn't right." She buried her head in her hands. "I'm too old for this, Elle. I've been with him more years than I've been without him. What am I going to do? And if he really is sick?" She lifted her head. "What if I'm sick? What will I tell the women's club?"

"Barbara, you're not sick. Larry isn't sick. Doris isn't sick."

"You know about Doris?"

"I didn't mean it to turn out like this," I started. "No, I did mean for it to turn out like this, but I didn't realize it was you."

"What are you talking about?"

So much of me wanted to turn and run, turn the page on Barbara, too, which tells you how terrified I was. I didn't have many friends like Barbara. One, that was pretty much it. I sat down on her plastic-covered couch and searched for the right words to explain. Unfortunately there weren't any cute homilies, or homespun wisdom, or heart-soaring anecdotes that would cover it. I took a deep breath and settled on the truth.

"I was trying to help a friend. Maureen works in Larry's office, and Doris never gave her a chance to do any work. So we thought, so I thought, that if Doris got sidetracked from the Mancusi case, then Maureen would get some work thrown her way. I didn't know you were Larry's wife. I'm sorry."

"What did you do?"

I blurted the words out before I lost my courage altogether. "We sent Larry an e-mail and made him think that Doris was interested in him."

"You started this whole affair?"

"Yeah, but she's not sick. Larry's not sick. You're not sick."

"You made that up, too?"

"Yeah. I thought if Larry thought she had something—and I told Maureen to stop at genital herpes—he might back off."

Her eyes turned hard, her jaw firmed, and when she looked at me, this was somebody new. This wasn't the old Barbara. This wasn't a woman in need of a life coach at all. "You're fired."

"I understand. It's nothing more than I deserve." I got up, feeling like the lowest of the lowest. "I hope it works out, Barbara. I just want you to be happy. If there's anything I can do."

"Don't do any more."

"I understand. Barbara," I started, but there wasn't anything else for me to say, because sometimes your best just isn't good enough.

Thirteen

She wore far too much rouge last night and not quite enough clothes. That is always a sign of despair in a woman.

—OSCAR WILDE

When I was in the throes of deepest depression, I called Harvey. I told myself it was because I needed to tell him I was leaving town. It sure sounded good to me. Have you ever read the stories where when the heroine needs help most, a man appears out of the blue to help her through the darkest hours? Everybody who's ever had that happen, please let me know. We like to think our lives are neat and tidy, with solutions that are wrapped up with silver paper and a shiny pink bow. Inevitably, solutions never come. Instead, we have to struggle through the muck and mire simply to exist.

And if I was going to simply exist, I wanted company, and sadly, Mr. Bunny wasn't going to cut it anymore.

With everyone else, I felt like a failure, but with Harvey, I felt like a person—my own me. Odd, considering I'd spent my whole life trying to be somebody, but when I talked to Harvey, I *was* somebody.

He gave me a choice between dinner or seeing the Ashes and Snow exhibit at Pier 54. It wasn't difficult. Food was a high priority in my life. The kitchen was packed, and all I had left was microwavable noodles. I told him about a new seafood restaurant in Tribeca. I figured, this being our last date, no way was I going out on a slice.

One thing I liked about Harvey, he had made me feel as if it was okay to be rumpled in life. I felt as if he had trudged through muck and mire as well (I suspected marriage to Leah was majorly mucked up). Over dinner, the conversation went from baseball to Leah's new wood floors to the latest Lane-Broderick production on Broadway.

Since I was leaving, I finally brought up one of the things that I was dying to know: "Why did you marry Leah?"

Perhaps it was blunter than my usual style, but I was getting to where I didn't care. Adderall had taught me that lesson.

He sliced up his fish with razor precision, and I listened as the metal clinked against the glass plates.

"I didn't want to be alone. Leah was nice. We were married for nearly ten years."

"Why'd you divorce her?"

He studied me a minute, his mouth twisting back and forth while he thought. I was surprised that he didn't have an answer right away.

"You don't know why you divorced her?" I asked.

"One day she wanted me to go to some party. Leah always had parties to go to. I wanted to stay home and watch the baseball game, so I told her I wasn't going. She threw a fit." Then he shrugged, as if that was the end of the story.

Knowing Leah, I knew better. "So you just left?"

He gave me a half smile, a tired half smile. "It wasn't that easy, but it was something I had to do."

"What about Lindsey? How does she feel?"

"Lindsey doesn't care. She's into music and theater. Family doesn't enter into a teenage world."

"You'd be surprised," I said, because I knew that family was always a part of the teenage world.

"I don't think so. She's always been on a different path."

"Have you asked her?" I said, because I suspected Lindsey might tell a different story when asked.

"No," he said, staring at his plate, as if the grilled salmon contained the mysteries of the teenage mind. "Has Leah said something to you?"

I shook my head. "I was a teenage girl once. I know it's hard to believe, but I didn't talk to my father much. Didn't talk to my mother much, either. I had my own world, they weren't really a part of it, but I lost both of them, and it hurt more than I thought it should."

"What happened?"

"Leah didn't tell you?"

"No."

"My father was sent to prison at the end of my senior year,

and my mother moved to the Caribbean a year later. She couldn't hack all the media attention."

"What did he do?"

"Fraud. Money stuff."

"Sorry." He gave me a smile that I supposed was meant to cheer me up. "But you turned out okay."

See, this is why I liked being around Harvey. As someone who had tried to start over twice already—and failed both times—hearing "turned out okay" was like a deaf person hearing Beethoven's Fifth.

I looked at Harvey, and wanted so badly to stay around him and his rumpled life, but either I wasn't very good at sending signals or he was purposefully avoiding them, because I was currently on the fast track out of New York. There seemed to be no more room inside his rumpled life, and that made me sad.

However, I knew how to carry on—God knows I was getting really good at it—so I shot him a confident, successful, megawatt smile. "Enough about me. Let's talk about your career. Best picture?"

He thought for a second. "Lindsey at three."

Family counted more than he thought. It was there, floating in the air, transparent and sightless, but you knew when it was gone. "Second best picture."

"Crown Heights riot," he said, and there was an energy in his face that Jimmy Buffett didn't usually have in Margaritaville.

"Do you ever think of going back to news?"

"Sometimes. When things happen, I end up there. A habit. Maybe I take a few pictures," he said, shrugging it off.

But I knew. Some things aren't meant to be shrugged off.

"You should go back to it," I told him.

"Life interferes. The foundation settles, and it's really too late."

"You should try," I told him, sucker that I was, because I still believed.

"You think?" he said, his gray eyes lit up.

I nodded. "You gotta try, Harvey. Promise."

He shrugged casually, but the light in the gray eyes didn't dim. I only hoped I was steering him right. Chasing dreams wasn't for the faint of heart.

Trust me, I know.

We ended up at his place. I passed on dessert, because he mentioned some raspberry sorbet sitting at home in his freezer. I made short work of the sorbet, and he went right to work on me. "You know what I like about you?" he asked, his mouth exploring my shoulders.

"What?" I asked casually, but it wasn't casual. I needed to know. I needed to know why a comfortable, well-adjusted man would like me. In a city where dogs are treated better than average women, you learn to ignore the lack of attention. But when it does hit you, it packs a wallop.

"I don't know," he said. "I've tried to figure it out, tried to pinpoint exactly why I'm attracted to you, and I never come to one brilliant conclusion."

"Did you come to any small idiotic ones?"

"Not yet. I'm still working at it," he said, his lips nuzzling and talking and tickling all at the same time.

"You better work fast, 'cause I'm moving in about ten days."

That brought him off my shoulder. "Where're you going? Queens?"

"Delaware," I said, as if I was Christopher Columbus sailing off to discover the New World.

"You're really leaving?" he said, his brows drawing together.

There were thoughts going on in the grizzled mind, but I wasn't going to be privy to them.

He kissed me then, and maybe there was a little more heat than usual. Maybe I was just being hopeful. Don't know.

I woke the next morning, blinking as my eyes adjusted to the light. Harvey's bedroom had none of the clutter that you would expect from such a rumpled man. The walls were covered with photographs, some that I recognized as old New York, and some were the money shots. There were two different men who worked behind the lens, one a sentimental lug and the other a calculating businessman. There was no heart in the picture of a pearl necklace or the sports car posing on Wall Street. The picture of a butcher in his white apron, an air-conditioning unit from the second story dripping down on his head, that was nothing but heart. Or the little girl balancing her arms on the railing of the Empire State Building, gazing out on the city with big plans and hopes painted all over her face.

The sentimental shootist was lying next to me, fast asleep, one arm stretched out over the pillow, reaching for things that existed only in dreams.

I crept to the bathroom, deciding to be bold and adventur-

ous and actually use Harvey's shower. I wasn't sure if adventurous women lived in Wilmington, so I thought this might be my
last shot at pretending.

The bathroom was all I thought high-class bathrooms should
be. Black marble with lots of chrome. And shiny chrome, too.
The kind with no fingerprints. I had chrome in my old bathroom as well. It had fingerprints.

I loitered outside the medicine cabinet, thinking that I could
snoop, but first I was gonna lock the door. I reached for the
handle, but the door opened. I expected Harvey.

I shrieked, because it wasn't.

"Who are you?" she asked. She, in this case, being a teenager
who looked a lot like a younger version of Leah.

"Elle," I said, my hands in fig-leaf position, my breathing
starting to come in fast spurts. Every time I tried to inhale more,
it wouldn't work.

"Are you okay?" she said.

I nodded once and waved my hand in the direction of the
door. I needed to breathe, and right now I couldn't.

She didn't argue but fled out the door.

This time I locked it behind her and collapsed on the toilet,
waiting for oxygen to hit my brain.

Harvey pounded on the door. "Elle?"

"Go away," I said, as I felt consciousness start to return.

It was just like in the past. I grabbed a towel and wrapped it
around me, my hands securing it tightly.

I padded to the door and knocked softly.

"Harvey?"

"Yeah?"

"Can you pass me my clothes?" I whispered.

A few seconds later the knob turned. "You're gonna have to unlock the door, Elle."

"Right," I said, flipping the lock on the knob and then cracking the door open. I grabbed my stuff like the lifeline it was, and shut the door, locking it securely.

Much better.

I made myself exhale twice and then got dressed in record time.

I cracked open the door and heard voices. Loud voices. Loud, angry voices.

"You can't have a girlfriend. You're my dad."

I walked in, calming, ready to tell her that I wasn't her dad's girlfriend, but he beat me to it.

"She's not my girlfriend."

It was a clear statement. The exact same words I would have used, but I wasn't expecting the razor of pain that sheared through me. I knew where things stood between old Harv and me, but a woman always likes to think that she's wrong.

"You're too old for hooking up, Dad."

Harvey had lost some of his usual calm and cool demeanor. I went to pick up my bag, but I was slow, because I wanted to hear more of what Harvey-on-the-spot would say.

"She's not a hook-up."

I could see why he used a camera rather than a pen. Words weren't his forte.

"Then what is she, Dad?" asked the little Leah in training.

"A friend," said Harvey, his eyes asking me to understand.

I smiled as if I did. "Your father is helping me out of a jam. I'm about to move, and my bathroom and kitchen are all packed up."

"You're living here?" she yelled.

"No," said Harvey and I in unison.

"Clarify," she ordered in her mini-Leah tone. I held my breath, staring at the floor, because sometimes you see things you don't want to see, and you can never unsee them again.

"She's a friend, Lindsey."

"That you sleep with?" she asked, little-girl tension in the voice. She wanted her father to lie, she wanted a life that her family never gave her.

My eyes welled up with tears, because sometimes life wasn't fair, and I hated it.

"No," he lied, and Lindsey knew he lied, and I knew he lied, but the man had to choose between his family and the rumpled friend he never slept with.

I gave him another megawatt smile that said, "I understand completely."

"On that note, I think it's time for me to leave," I told him, as if my heart wasn't completely shot in two.

"Elle, wait." Harvey shot a moderately stern look at his daughter. "I'll be back. We'll finish."

He walked me out into the hallway, a fine place to share a tender good-bye moment.

"Thank you for helping me out in there."

I waved a hand. "Anytime. That's me, grace under pressure."

He gave me a kiss on the cheek. "Call me when you get to Wilmington."

"Of course," I lied.

I turned and walked away, closing another door.

I was on the phone, arguing with Dan's Moving Company, Reasonable Rates for All Your Moving Needs, when the buzzer sounded.

"Hang on a minute, Dan," I said.

Dan promptly hung up.

I swore.

"Who is it?"

"She says her name is Leah Weber, Miss Sheffield."

Why now? I pressed my thumbs into my eyes. "Tell her I'm not home."

The buzzer sounded again. "Don't think I don't know you're there, Elle Sheffield. We need to talk. Now."

I pushed the talk button. "Yeah. Whatever."

Two seconds later, she was banging on the door with all she was worth, which was quite a bit. I opened it before my neighbors complained. Like I cared anymore.

"What?" I snarled. Lack of sleep, emotional strip mining, and the general unfairness of the world were enough to make someone cranky. And contrary to what the rest of the world assumed, I was still a someone.

"You little slut," she said, charging through my door, immaculate in a blue suit, completely eclipsing my blue terry sweats that I got on sale at Century 21. "You haven't changed, have you? I thought you'd changed. I'm such a soft touch, but no, you're just determined to use, use, use. Stomp all over my heart, why don't you? I'm tired of being used by my so-called friends. Exhausted. Drained. It's just too much. Shoot me now."

I was ready to shoot her. She had everything, I had zilch, and if there was anybody who was gonna be whining today, by rights it would be me. "Excuse me. I'm not a user. And I was *never* the slut. I couldn't win the title from the reigning St. Anthony's Queen of Sleaze."

She slapped me, and it stung like hell.

I clutched at my cheek, the pain oddly sharp. I'd been going numb for so long that the feel of actual blood in my veins tingled through me, like a foot gone to sleep.

"I don't deserve this, Leah," I said, quietly dignified. I couldn't fight, but I wouldn't let her walk all over me. I'd learned that from my group.

The perky blue eyes sharpened to laser slits. "Don't deserve this? I tried to help you. How many people have tried to help you, Elle? I'm the only one, I know it. You're such an ungrateful little tramp. Sleeping with my husband is not the way to acknowledge your friends."

"Ex," I corrected, sitting down on a box that used to contain twelve-count paper towel rolls and now contained my winter clothes. I didn't have the energy to stand and face her. Not anymore.

"Ex. Smex. And Lindsey. I can't believe what you did to poor Lindsey. She's probably scarred for life. Seeing a naked woman with her father." Leah covered her eyes. "I get nightmares myself."

I pushed back my own nightmares, which seemed to pale next to everyone else's. "Come on, Leah. She's sixteen, not four."

"Fourteen," she corrected.

"She looks older," I said, partially because it was true but mostly because I wanted to hit Leah where it hurt. Right in the sagging solar plexus. Not that hers was sagging, but I knew she thought it was.

Her face wilted, and she pulled up the box next to me. "She hit puberty early. Just like her mother. God, please don't make me a grandmother at forty-five. I've tried to keep her from growing up so fast. You're lucky not to have kids."

By the age of forty-two, most single women are forced to come to terms with the knowledge they're not gonna reproduce. Although my parents weren't world-class, I always thought I could be. "I don't know. I always thought it'd be nice to have a family of my own," I said quietly.

"Don't get me wrong. I love Lindsey, and I'd do anything for her, but it's very hard, and I'm always doing something wrong, and it drives me crazy because I don't want to disappoint her. Once when she was seven, she wanted to see the Grand Canyon. I put my foot down because what seven-year-old needs to see that? Seven-year-olds should be at Disney World, or Disneyland Paris. Now, there's a trip for a seven-year-old. She and Harvey went without me."

"The Grand Canyon would be nice."

"How could you understand?"

"I was married. Once," I lied.

"You can drop the act, Elle. I never believed you were married."

"Why?" I said, because you'd think I could at least be good at lying.

"Your eyes start moving back and forth. Dead giveaway."

"Oh," I said, keeping my wayward eyes still.

"That's the problem, Elle. You don't have a daughter. Or a husband," she said, transitioning neatly from my failures to hers. As if my failures weren't big enough.

"Ex-husband," I corrected.

"Whatever. I just wanted to be the perfect wife, the perfect mother. I tried, but they weren't paying attention."

The tone I recognized. The doubts I knew. "You're a good mother, Leah," I told her, because she was forty-two, too.

Sadly, all the plastic surgery in the world couldn't hide the worry in her eyes. "I tried therapy, but I just can't get through it. I'm too internal. Do you really think I'm good enough? Why? Tell me, please, I need all the positive affirmations I can get."

"Because you love your daughter, and you're there for her." Leah had a lot of faults, but absenteeism wasn't one of them.

"They said your mother ran off with some Arabian oil sheik. Is that really what happened? I think that stinks. Damned Arabs. First it's the oil, next it's the women. Pretty soon the city will be overrun with foreigners. It's a crime."

At first I didn't answer; I didn't think Leah expected me to.

"Well? What happened?" she prodded.

I kept quiet.

"Come on, Ellie. Tell me. You need to unload these things."

Did I really need to unload anything? To Leah, of all people? And maybe that's why I wanted to tell her. I'd never been friends with the popular girl before. It felt good.

I took a deep breath. "She went to the Caribbean for a post-trial vacation. She said she was getting away from it all. She ended up opening a dive shop with the dive master."

After I was done, I took a look at the empty place on the wall where my parents' picture had been. Even though it was gone, I could still see it. I didn't hate her, but I didn't love her, either. Twenty years is too long to harbor strong feelings. In twenty years, we'd had four presidents, seven garbage strikes, and four blackouts. Over time, I had locked it in my closet, along with the size six cocktail dress that I needed drugs to fit into, the school yearbooks, and the coconut-scented sex gel I was never gonna use.

Leah patted my knee. I suppose she thought it would help. "A dive master? I think that's even worse than an oil sheik."

I gave her a tight smile. "I'm over it," I said. I didn't need Leah's pity. It was time for someone else to have "VICTIM" tattooed on their arm.

She stayed quiet, contemplating her own misery. I was quiet, too, but I was done with misery.

"You need to stay away from Harvey, Elle."

Of course, I wasn't done with pissed off. "You can drop the nice-nice act, Leah. In case you haven't noticed, I'm moving. Out of town."

She looked around, taking in the collection of mix-and-match liquor boxes, paper boxes, and fruit crates I'd scavenged from the stores on my block.

"This is it?" she said.

I spread my hands wide. "This is it."

She shook her head in disbelief. "Where're you going?"

"Wilmington."

"Massachusetts?"

"Delaware."

"Why? I mean, why would anyone leave Manhattan, unless you go to Connecticut, but the traffic on 95 is awful on the weekend. I went to a baby shower there once, took two hours to get back on a Sunday afternoon. I swore never again. Why would you subject yourself to such trauma?"

"New York is expensive, both fiscally and emotionally."

"But you're my friend. You can't leave me."

"Leah, you have lots of friends," I said automatically.

"Not like you."

"I'm just one of the special ones you call a slut."

"Oh, you know I didn't mean that. It's not like Harvey's gonna get serious with you, anyway."

"He might," I snapped.

"He could do worse," she finally admitted. "Do you think he still loves me?"

"I think he understands you and still wants to be around you," I said, which was as optimistic as I was gonna be.

"Why don't things turn out right?"

"Because we're too old for fairy tales, Leah. They tell you everything's going to work out when you're a kid, because if not, the suicide rates would be sky high in adolescence. A vibrator is pretty much all you can count on, and even that breaks after ten years."

She giggled. "And that's why you were at the sex shop. Ten years," she said, with a jealous sigh.

I nodded. "Ten good years."

"I'm sorry," she said, and I knew she meant it. Sometimes you never know where your friends will come from. But Leah understood. We'd both been through wars and lost. We weren't the greatest generation, we were just the survivors.

"I'm sorry about Harvey. Not the sleeping with him part, but the over part."

Her five-thousand-dollar bosom heaved with finality. "It is, isn't it?"

I nodded.

She broke down and started to cry. Perfect, perky tears, and I gave her a cautious pat on the back. She started to cry in earnest, and her new nose got splotchy, her mascara running down her cheeks.

I tried hard to savor the moment of seeing Leah down on the mat, pummeled by life, but I didn't have the stomach.

We survivors had to stick together.

Fourteen

Love is something external.

—VINCENT VAN GOGH,

TWO MONTHS BEFORE HE CUT OFF HIS EAR

M aureen had agreed to keep seventeen of my twenty-three boxes until I got settled in Wilmington. I had said my good-byes to some old friends in the building. Wrapping up my life in New York was both easier and harder than I thought. I sent my mother a change-of-address card—it seemed all that was necessary.

My final job interview was scheduled for Monday-week. Final. Such a final word. Then I'd be leaving New York for good.

Out of all the things I would miss, I would miss the buildings the most. After September 11, 2001, the skyscrapers came alive for me. You don't think about the death of buildings, only people. I had lost my grandmother when I was thirteen, and I never knew my other grandparents. And even though I spent most of my life absorbing the malodories of the East River, rather than the murky smells of Staten Island, I still felt the loss of two steel buildings as achingly as when my grandmother died.

After that day, I never took a building for granted again. I looked out of my tiny bedroom window and cherished my cheesy fifth-floor view. The memory of Icon Parking and the Great Wall of China would be burned on my brain forever. It wasn't pretty, but it was home. I hoisted up a box of bath towels and carried it to Maureen's apartment when she came home from work.

At two in the afternoon.

"I've been fired. Can you believe it? She fired me," she said, limping around in circles.

I dropped the box of towels in the middle of her floor. "She found out?"

"No, she says I'm not doing quality work. Screw that. I'm not doing quality work because I've been doing two jobs and sleeping three hours. Does she think she can do this to me? And my health insurance. Mother of God, I need my health insurance."

She sat down on one of my boxes and looked up at me. "What am I going to do?"

"Citibank is hiring, and I could use a roommate," I answered, because I had become very pragmatic about life. One foot in front of the other, one bill at a time. Do not stop and smell the roses, lest you get pricked by a bad batch of pesticide and die.

"Delaware? Get serious, Elle," she said. "For you, it's always a joke."

Actually, it hadn't been a joke, but I laughed. Ha-ha. "Sorry. Find another job, Maureen. You hated that job anyway."

She pushed back her hair, her mouth bee-stung with petulance rather than collagen. "Nobody will hire me."

"If they'll hire me, they'll hire anybody," I said, struggling to be optimistic and pragmatic at the same time.

"Have they hired you yet?" she asked, unplugging herself from her world.

"Not quite, but there's only one interview left, and Grace said it was only a formality. It's looking up," I told her, but even my good news didn't cheer her up. I pulled up another box and sat, because this looked to be a long session. "Do you know any other lawyers?" I asked.

"Tons. But nobody wants to hire a fat lawyer with health issues."

"Have you tried?" I asked.

She shook her head.

"Maureen, do me a favor, will ya? Don't get discouraged until *after* you lift a finger."

"You really think they'd hire me?" she said, as if I had all the answers in the universe. Why did they even bother?

I beamed at her. "Of course. You're a terrific lawyer. Look at how many times you've proved me wrong."

That cheered her up. "You really think?"

I nodded. "I really think. Still hitting the Adderall?" I asked.

"Why? You need some more?"

"Once was too much for me," I told her.

"Sorry about your party."

"Learn your lesson from me," I said, ready to shake a warning finger at her, but I was through doling out advice. Need advice? Call a psychic, not me.

"I'm cutting back," she said, and got up from the box. "See, the arthritis is back, and it hurts like hell." She limped around for me.

"Sorry about the pain," I said.

"S'all right. Everybody hurts. You hurt? 'Course you do. Everybody hurts."

"And that's why I'm heading for Delaware."

"How come you can't stay? You should stay. You could sleep on the couch."

"I need to leave, Maureen. I got to get away from this place."

"You're running."

"Darn tootin'."

"If you change your mind—" she started.

I interrupted because the last thing I wanted was more what-ifs. "Yes, that's just what Mr. Tierney needs, two deadbeat renters."

She stayed quiet for a minute. "It's weird being home at two in the afternoon. It's like I'm playing hooky or something. We should celebrate."

"You want to celebrate being fired?" I said, because I'd been fired. Twice. And God knows, I never felt like celebrating.

"Why not? Do you have a bottle of wine?"

"I'm on the wagon. Think I'm going to stay there for a while."

She thought for a minute more. "Me, too. I've got some Diet Cokes." She pulled a couple of cans out of the fridge. "Let's go on the roof."

I took a last look at her apartment, littered with the brown cardboard boxes that contained my life. I thought of the furniture I still had left to move.

"Yeah, sure. Hey, listen, do you want to buy a chair?"

Saturday turned out to be a beautiful spring day. Joan had booked an outdoor wedding at a castle in Tarrytown. No joke, there are actually castles within spitting distance of the city. I took the train up on Saturday afternoon, hoping the suburban MTA patrons would respect my best sundress.

I had major doubts about Joan's nuptials, but considering my track record, doubts were better than all-out failure. And it was hard to get antsy about a wedding party when the sun was sparkling on the Hudson and the roses were in high bloom.

Carefully I walked down the garden path, past the yellow and pink blossoms, the delicate scent calling me to inhale. But I was strong, so my nose remained breathless and unaffected.

The turnout was nice, about fifty people, of whom I knew about four.

I saw Barbara first, and I waited two beats to see what she

would do. She turned her back to me and grabbed another glass of champagne. I took the hint and found Tanja, with a glass of wine and a date on her arm (*a date!*). It was Mr. Curly Hair from Missed Connections. In my head I carried an impression of who would stoop to dating Tanja, and this tall, slightly gawkish, but still studly human being was not it.

"Elle, you've got to meet Nick."

I gave him a warm smile behind my shades and held out a hand.

"Very nice to meet you, Nick."

"Tanja's told me a lot about you."

"It's all a lie," I said with an easy smile. One of the nice things about divorcing yourself from your emotions is that things become much cleaner. I could smile and chat with Tanja and her new guy and not feel a single twinge of jealousy. Of course, I didn't feel happiness, either. But in the big scheme of things, I felt that was a small price to pay.

We spent some time talking about the impending subway rate hikes, whether the summer was gonna be killer hot or comfortably warm, and the curious allure of sports teams to Queens. I nodded like an idiot during the whole conversation, but Tanja was so blinded by love she never noticed.

Joan came over, gracious and elegant in a gray silk dress. Felix was to die for in a black tux. It was like stepping into the pages of a Neiman Marcus catalog, complete with the castle in the background. And that wasn't jealousy, only factual narration.

"Good afternoon, ladies. Stuff yourselves, please. I'm not

planning to take home the leftovers. Elle, there are some people I want to introduce you to."

She took me by the arm over to a gaggle of women who were standing there, balancing china and tea cups with the grace and ease afforded the upper class, who learn such tricks in the womb. The glare from the jewels was blinding, and I suspected somebody had jacked Tiffany's on the way over.

With lightning precision I was introduced to Meredith, Renee, Caroline, Anesia, and Rose. Gotta hand it to Joan, she's nothing if not efficient. "Did you bring your cards?" she whispered.

I shook my head, because I had burned my cards in the incinerator.

Joan slapped me on the arm, but it was a light tap, and I got the message. "I didn't know," I whispered back defensively. I had made up my mind. I was destined for mediocrity. I was destined for balancing on the bottom rung of the ladder. The falls were easier that way.

"Elle is a life coach. I'm assuming you've heard of a life coach, haven't you? They did a spread in *Vanity Fair* a few months back."

"You have a life coach?" asked the one known as Renee. "What did she help you with?"

"With Felix. I never would have had the balls to marry a younger man if not for Elle." The ladies tittered. "Isn't that right, Elle?"

"Of course," I said before she could elbow me in the ribs again. If I'd had any moral principles left, I would've objected. I would have told her friends that I had serious reservations about this alliance and suspected that Joan was being taken for a very expensive ride, but my moral principles had been dismembered and found floating in the East River.

"Joan didn't need much help. I was just there to give her encouragement."

"And yes, that's what a life coach is for. Encouragement to get over the hurdles in dealing with the stress we all have. Anyway," she said, looping an arm around my shoulders, "I just wanted to give her my stamp of approval."

It was the nicest thing anyone had ever said to me, if you didn't count Grandmother Shields telling me that I was the greatest granddaughter she'd ever had. She always laughed after that, because I was the only granddaughter she ever had, but I didn't mind. I laughed, too.

Zombielike, I nodded, did a very polite "Nice to meet all of you," and then departed for the safety of Tanja and Nick. My great wall of emotional reticence was starting to sprout a few leaks. I didn't want kindness, not from a woman who was about to make the biggest mistake of her life.

"What's up with Barbara?" asked Tanja.

"She fired me," I answered, seeing no shame since I was heading for the hills anyway.

"Why? I can't believe it. Barbara thought you were the greatest." Her eyes narrowed. "You must've really screwed up bigtime."

"Can we not discuss this on Joan's day of happiness?" I snapped.

"Come on, spill," said Tanja, hooking her arm through Nick's. "Barbara doesn't breathe unless Elle tells her to," she whispered to him, loudly enough that I could hear, of course.

"It's not my story to tell. And I don't think Barbara will say anything, either," I added, because I didn't want her bothering Barbara with it.

"Oh, yeah, that's fair. Some big secret, and nobody lets me in on it."

"Tanja, get a life of your own, will ya?" said Nick.

I waited for the inevitable blowup. The uncompromising "Shut up!" But she looked at him, then looked at me, and then frowned. "Fine." And that was it. End of Tanja tantrum.

Love truly does cure all. Assuming, of course, you can find it.

We all migrated to the food tables, where desserts were bountiful and free. I was helping myself to a piece of cheesecake when Barbara appeared.

"Joan wanted to talk to all of us," she said, by way of explanation, just in case I might actually believe that sharing my airspace was a personal choice. "She said to meet her inside at the bar."

Bar was an understatement. The place was a medieval dining hall loaded down with beer steins and suits of armor. Oak beams ran the length of the ceiling, and the towering stone walls made it seem chilly, even with the temperatures outside running hot. Joan had found a table in the back and was nursing a drink, no Felix in sight.

"Thank you for humoring a bride. I've got such a case of the jitters," she said, taking a healthy sip of martini. "Sit down." She motioned, and like the obedient subjects we were, we all sat.

I expected her to break the news that she'd come to her senses, that instead of a hunky twenty-something, she was settling for a sixty-something retiree who liked checkers.

After a round of drinks had been delivered, Joan filled us in on the truth.

"I wanted to share a story with you. It's about a woman who thought she was too old to enjoy life, to have love, and generally believed she was better off dead. And then one day, when the hacking cough became worse, she visited her doctor, who said her wish was about to be granted. I have to say that there's nothing like getting a death wish granted to turn it into a life-affirming event."

The air in the room turned cold, and when Barbara started wringing her hands, I didn't stop her. I didn't think I could move.

I took the glass of Chivas between my hands, rubbing back and forth, Aladdin desperately needing a genie from the bottle. When I realized no genie was forthcoming, I glanced at Joan. Not overt or anything, I didn't want to stare, but I needed to see. I wanted to see misery, anger, depression, any of the eight thousand little demons that were gnawing at my soul.

There wasn't any anger. She looked calm, well adjusted, even triumphant. I wanted to yell at her, but I wasn't even brave enough to do that.

She gave me a smile and continued.

"The first two weeks she spent sulking and cursing at God, alternating with the times she was convinced there was no God. Until finally, she developed a curious acceptance. Almost an out-of-body experience, and she decided to go out and do something marvelous. Unfortunately, she didn't have anything marvelous to do. So she joined up with a group of women who were all in search of their own marvelousness, and she watched, took notes, and learned a little bit about what she desired."

I pushed my drink away. I wasn't supposed to be tippling. I was supposed to be strong, cool, the woman who knew what's what.

"I'm sorry, Joan, but there are some holistic treatments you might want to consider," I said, trying to find my way back to standard life coach spiel.

"Elle, be quiet. Listen," she said, with a wave of her massive engagement ring, still the epitome of class and grace.

My stomach cramps reminded me exactly what a faker I was. I snuck a glance at Barbara and Tanja, who looked stunned.

"When her hairdresser started flirting with her, this time she didn't pat him on the head. This time she flirted back. I know what each of you thinks of my marriage to Felix, but he's a good man, and he's promised to stay with me until the end."

"When is that exactly?" asked Tanja.

"A year or two is the current prognosis. They're running bets in Vegas."

She was cracking jokes, laughing, hell, even getting married. I took a long sip of my drink, the alcohol eating away at my gut. Eventually I needed to say something. I wanted to think of something smart and teacherly.

"What about chemo?"

Joan shot me a patient look, a parent with a precocious child. "Too far along."

But I wasn't done trying.

"You could've hired a nurse," I put in, "or asked one of us for help."

"I'm fifty-eight years old, Elle. I need someone who's moldable. We've all been molded."

Barbara pushed her glass away and met Joan's eyes evenly. "You aren't scared?"

Joan laughed. "Scared to death. But I like plans. I like being in control. I'm in control."

I swallowed and looked at Joan square on, no flickering away. I lifted my glass. "L'chaim."

Tanja clinked mine. "To Joan. May you be an inspiration to us all."

Joan shook her head. "Don't worry about my life, worry about yours," she said, looking right at me.

I pretended I didn't understand, but I knew what she wanted. She wanted me to be like her, able to handle whatever life dealt me. I took another sip. Even in her late fifties, she had looks I would never have. And she had money to grease the tracks. No, there were vast differences between me and Joan.

"I have a little surprise," she said, and handed each of us a white envelope with "Tulliver's Travels" inscribed on the outside.

I ripped mine open to find a voucher from a travel agency.

"We're leaving next week," she said. "Two weeks on Paradise Island."

Promptly, Tanja had an issue. "I can't get off work."

"Then quit," I snapped. "When was the last vacation you took?"

"I haven't. Yet."

Joan pulled a cigarette from her case and lit it. Hair of the dog and all that. "It's time," she said. "Tell your boss you have the chance of a lifetime. If he doesn't let you go, you don't need to be working there."

Tanja frowned. "Maybe."

I handed Joan my envelope. "Have a great trip. I'll be in Delaware."

Tanja glared. "You can't leave. She's, like, dying, and you're all 'Gotta go.'"

I shot her a tolerant smile. "I don't belong."

Joan took a drag on her cigarette. "You can't move to Delaware, Elle."

"Why?"

"Because you have to learn to drive," she answered, all smug. If she hadn't been dying, I would have really hated her then.

"They have mass transit in Delaware."

"Why're you making this so hard?" asked Tanja, obviously missing the big picture.

But Barbara answered for me. "Because she hasn't learned one goddamned thing."

I tipped my glass to her, because that summed it up nicely.

Fifteen

Life sucks and then you die.

—SAID BY TOO MANY TO COUNT

After Joan's wedding, I came home and sat in my empty apartment. The neon "Park" sign flashed on and off, and for a time I watched it blink. I went over to the window, rested my hands on the sill, and watched the world move on without me. There was a silver spiderweb that ran from the ceiling to the window frame, the red neon catching in the strands and turning it scarlet. The spider had long deserted me, leaving only her mark on my apartment. My marks were all gone. A bottle of Chivas was calling to me from down the street at Larry's Wine & Spirits ("We Deliver"), but to be honest, I didn't need alcohol to numb me, I was already there.

So Joan was dying.

Yeah, we all have to go sometime.

Even me.

I was surrounded by people who'd left their mark on the world. Joan, Maureen, Tanja, Harvey, and Leah, who had Lindsey to carry on in her image. Even Tony Shields, who had achieved his own brand of immortality.

As for me, I was going to disappear to Delaware, a faded image that would start out as a vague memory and eventually burn off like the morning fog on the river.

The emptiness of my space was making me claustrophobic, so I took the elevator to the top floor and then took the stairs to the roof.

For a long time I stared out into the night, wondering what had happened to my life. When did I lose my youth? When did my dreams become foolish? It's not like one day you wake up and it's gone. Instead, it's a slow crawl down a long hill, and you never noticed that somewhere down the road, you had hit your knees because walking was too hard.

Life wasn't supposed to be hard. I opened my mouth and yelled. It wasn't anything specific, just a long, anguished, "*Aghhhhhhhhhhhh.*"

It was cathartic, emptying my cries into the night.

"Shut up, or I'll call the cops!"

I closed my mouth and trudged back downstairs, because I wasn't courageous enough to jump, and I wasn't even courageous enough to keep screaming.

Five empty days passed without event. Maureen was out every morning at nine A.M., pounding the beat, looking for work. Every afternoon she'd come back, frustrated, with wobbly legs and a soul-searing desire for alcohol. We were experimenting with sobriety, and so far things were wobbly and frustrated, too.

On Thursday afternoon, she came in with a happy face. That was a good sign.

"Guess what," she said, collapsing into my old favorite chair.

"What?"

I have two great pieces of news. First, I met L.T. for lunch. He wants me to take my old job back, because Doris quit."

"She quit? Why?"

"Apparently she was getting all sorts of looks from people. Rumors. Innuendos. And I suppose the double life was killing her. He said she freaked out in the office one day and went postal on the paralegals. She stalked out after that and never came back. Can you believe I missed it? Oh, to be a Post-it on the wall that day."

"Congrats, Maureen, you've ruined a life. You're taking your old job back, right?"

She shook her head. "Nope. I had a second interview yesterday with the DA's office, and today they called back. They want to hire me."

"Oh, *Law & Order*. Sounds like a huge promotion."

She shook her head again. "No. Less money. More hours."

"But?"

"No buts. I just want to try something different. I want to practice law instead of disorder."

"Okay, whatever you say," I told her, glad she'd gotten gainful employment, but I'd be lying to you if I didn't admit to having a twinge of jealousy. Sometimes there's a warm security in the old eight-to-five grind. Oh, yeah, I was headed for the old eight-to-five grind. One would think I would be happier, yes, one would think. "What's the second piece of news?" I asked.

"He wants to go back to Barbara."

Now, this news, *this* warmed the cockles of my heart. "Please tell me he's talked to her."

"No, he's too nervous to. He said he made all sorts of bad mistakes . . ."

Got that right.

"And that he wasn't sure if he deserved her. You have to do something, Elle."

It was my turn to shake my head. "I'm done with interfering, Maureen. I've learned my lesson, and trust me, being sent into exile to the icy wilderness of outer Delaware is more than enough to make me see the error of my ways." In the cold light of day, I could joke about things that kept my eyes toothpicked open at night.

"Elle, you have to." She shot me puppy-dog eyes. "Do it for Barbara."

"No."

"You're responsible for this. You have to fix it."

"No."

Maureen propped herself against one wall. "She needs you."

The words warmed me, brought me in from the cold. Being needed was my drug of choice. Oh, I'd experimented with many, but those three little words would have me salivating in a purely Pavlovian manner.

To be needed.

The words played inside my brain like the stupid song that won't let you go. "She fired me," I muttered.

"This is your chance."

I covered my eyes, seeking the quiet comfort of darkness. "No."

"All right," she said, and I heard her walk out the door. Heard her steps echoing, muted by the faded woolen carpet.

When the noise stopped, I raced to the doorway and opened it.

Maureen stood at the end of the hallway, arms folded across her chest. She grinned, her eyes sparkling with a particular sureness most often seen on gamblers at the track.

In the end, it was more difficult than Maureen had thought. Barbara wouldn't accept my call, and finally, by doing some serious arm twisting, Tanja called her and told her that Joan was having a dinner at Tribeca Grill at eight o'clock on Saturday. We made reservations for Saturday under Joan's name and told Larry to be there.

It was devious, underhanded, and terribly romantic.

On Saturday, I went at 7:45 and staked out the bar, determined to make sure that everything was perfect. Larry arrived precisely at 7:55 and ordered champagne for the table. As amends go, champagne is always a good way to start. Barbara showed up at 8:10, which was a huge shock, since Barbara is never late. And when she walked in, I immediately noticed the pearl necklace she wore like a white badge of courage.

There was a buzz in my blood, an extra hit of serotonin to the brain. It was comfortable, familiar. It made me happier than a drunk on Saturday night.

I watched from my little corner as she was led to the table, noticed Larry there, and then started explaining to the host that he had made a mistake. I had assumed that Barbara would never make a scene. I assumed wrong.

The Chihuahua had teeth.

Larry started getting a little flushed under the collar, and he took her arm, trying to get her to sit down.

I held my breath, willing her to sit down and listen.

Finally she did.

The host left them alone, and Larry started to talk.

And talk.

And talk.

I kept nodding my head, waiting to get to the good parts. For the first five minutes, Barbara listened politely. She was too well mannered to do otherwise. At seven minutes in, she checked her watch. I thought it was a great touch, and I was proud of her for learning to fight back.

The night was going great.

Then Barbara started to talk. She got more and more animated, picking up a fork and pointing it at him. He kept trying to keep her in line, looking around anxiously, but she didn't seem to care. Finally, after having been seated for no more than twelve minutes, she got up, lifted her purse, and walked out.

No!

I wasn't about to let her leave, not when her future happiness (which I had wrecked) was sitting at the table across from her. I took off after her, down Chambers and then up Hudson, shoving past two actress types who were handing out flyers. Eventually I cornered her before she could escape in a cab.

"You can't . . . just leave . . . like that," I said, struggling for breath.

"Elle?" she looked at me, her eyes surprised . . . and nervous.

I swallowed much-needed oxygen. God, I needed more exercise. "You don't understand. I set this up so you and Larry could talk," I said, because she needed to understand I didn't want to interfere. I just wanted to help.

"You did this?"

"Yeah," I answered cautiously.

She punched me with her bag. "Haven't you done enough?"

And there was my answer. "I thought you wanted to be back with Larry."

I scrubbed my face with my hands, because if there was a God, this would have turned out right. I'd earned this. Just once.

She pursed her lips, back and forth, collecting her thoughts. "No," she said finally.

"What do you mean, no?"

"I don't want to be back with Larry. Joan's taking control of her life, and so am I," she said, her mouth still and stubborn and final.

"What about everything you told me? What about the empty apartment? Isn't that more important than a few measly mistakes?"

She whacked me with her bag again, a show of violence previously unseen in my former client, but I suppose I produced violence in people. "He's a bastard. I'm better off without him."

"That would be correct, but you said Larry was your dream, your true love, your ideal." Actually, those weren't her words, those were mine, but she knew what I meant.

"Sometimes ideals change. And sometimes life changes us. For the better."

I kept struggling with this, trying to get through to her because, deep down, people couldn't change, people couldn't adapt. We were who we were, end of story. This was why my life coach business was such a scam. I couldn't change people. People couldn't even change themselves. Because if people could change, I could change.

No.

I was done trying, and I needed Barbara to quit trying, too. If she kept it up, she might put me back on the "Better yourself" track, too, and I was tired.

"Barbara, that's really nice and all, but what about on Saturday nights when you don't have anybody to see the new movie with? Or what about when the toilet leaks and floods the bathroom? What are you going do? Or the nights when you're just really lonely and want somebody to hold? You can't handle being alone," I told her.

But Barbara wasn't listening. "I can go to the movies by myself. Plumbers are found in the phone book. And as for the nights, I'd rather be alone. Why should I want to be with someone who doesn't put me first? I deserve better. Larry just wants a submissive. I'm tired of being a submissive. I want to live."

I stood there on the sidewalk in front of Nobu, while all the Saturday night partyers brushed past. I was really getting tired of everybody ignoring me.

My mouth opened, then closed, but there wasn't anything more I could say.

She noticed my lack of happiness and whacked me again, but this time in a nicer way. "You taught me this, Elle. It's what you've been telling all of us. Go after what we want. Sometimes what we want isn't really what we want, it's only what we think we want, and eventually we discover something else—something that's even better."

I glossed over the whole *want* thing and went right to the meat. "I taught you this?" Because, after all, that was the meat.

She beamed, and trust me when I say that Barbara isn't usually a beamer. "Yeah."

"Really?" I murmured to myself, still getting shoved, two middle-aged women having it out in Tribeca. But the night wasn't so dark anymore, and in the distance I swear I saw stars winking in the sky.

"When did I teach you all this?" I asked.

"You just had to listen between the lines, Elle. I did. Actually, Joan did first, but then I figured it out, too."

I mulled this over, letting the truth, or at least what Barbara assumed was the truth, resonate inside me. "So we're square?"

"Cubed, baby," she answered. "You were trying to help. In the end, it's the best thing that ever happened to me, and my entire apartment is now Peach Cloud. I knew it was over when Larry told me to paint it back in white. I'm done with white."

It was fascinating to see Barbara in General MacArthur mode. Part of me wanted to claim credit, but it was something she'd done all on her own.

"I'm really sorry," I said.

"Elle?"

"What?"

"Build a bridge."

My apartment was still empty, and I was sleeping on a torn white sheet in the middle of my living room. However, one thing had changed. I was going to Paradise Island with my ladies. A going-away present was what Joan said, and this time I didn't argue.

I still couldn't afford this city, and I had closed a lot of doors, but there was one that I hadn't closed yet, and it needed slamming shut.

I went to the prison on Monday first thing.

I sat down in the orange chair in the visiting room and waited for Tony Shields to appear.

"You're back!" he said, coming over to hug me.

I moved away. "Don't get excited. I'm here to say good-bye."

He frowned at me, the beetle brow forming one gray line on his forehead. "What?"

"I'm moving, Tony. I'm leaving the city."

"This is your home. I'll be out soon."

I smiled. "I know."

He covered his eyes with his hands. "I should have been a better father."

"You should have. You weren't. We move on."

"What about your friend from the *Times?*"

"You're not worth a mention in the *New York Times*. You don't rate."

"If they knew about the money, then I'd rate. Oh, well," he said, and then he smiled at me.

And I knew.

"You pig," I said quietly. I wasn't angry, because he didn't have that control over me anymore. See, Elle had learned something, too.

"Stay here, Ellie. Come and see me. I'm just a lonely old man, but I'll be out in another seven months. We can find a house in the Hamptons. Or maybe someplace on Park Avenue."

His eyes were off in Lala Land, dreaming dreams that had kept him going for twenty years. Sadly, I believed that Tony's dreams would come true. Money, all twenty mil of it, was a great way to make your reality better.

All those years, all that suffering, and he'd never let on. Never anything to ease my or Mom's pain. He'd always been the innocent victim. Ha.

I stared at the man whose DNA ran inside me, and I knew he owed me. Owed me big-time. Possibly twenty mil worth. After all, the apple doesn't fall far from the tree.

"I can't afford to stay, Daddy," I said, carefully looking down at my hands rather than into his eyes.

"Give me a pen and paper," he said. "Your old man's gonna take care of you."

I reached into my bag and pulled out a pen and paper and watched as he scribbled a bank and an account number on the Citibank notepad. It seemed appropriate.

"This is where the money is?" I asked.

He nodded and then looked around. "Keep it quiet. We'll draw a little at a time, but use what you need. There's almost forty million there. Interest," he said proudly.

I curled my palm over the paper and held on to it for dear life. Forty million dollars meant clothes, food, and rent for life. Hell, forty million meant liposuction and a personal trainer.

I gave him a hug just because he expected it, and then I zoomed out of the prison grounds as fast as I could. The guard called me a cab to get back to the train station, and I stared at the numbers written on the paper. It could have been a social security number, it could have been somebody's birth date, but instead it was the key to all my dreams.

I waited for the cab, the paper burning in my hand. I thought of Leah and all those St. Anthony's dweebs who had made the past twenty years such hell. And then I heaved a big sigh, because I was about to be stupid again. Twice I had my dreams in my hand, and twice I was gonna walk away.

Still, the sun kept on shining, and I suppose it was shining in Wilmington as well, I don't know. I only knew one thing. I gotta be me. Elle Shields. Rumpled, poor, forty-something Elle Shields. As much as I wanted to be Elle Sheffield, that wasn't who I was.

I pulled out my cell phone and dialed.

"Tracy? Elle Sheffield. How're you doing?"

I listened as she whined about the heat and her job assignment covering the firemen's fair at Monmouth Beach.

"Tracy, I've got a story for you. It's the story of a lifetime. Have you got a pen and paper? Take these numbers down . . ."

I'd talked to Leah the morning before we left for the Bahamas. Ever since the story about the money hit the *Times,* I'd gotten some respect from her. And we'd also hit every sex-toy shop in the city (only the high-class ones). She'd even bought me a very special present to take to the Bahamas. It was a thoughtful gesture, probably intended to keep me away from Harvey. She did promise to visit me in Delaware, and I believed her.

The group and I met at Terminal C at LaGuardia. It's not a great place for a party, but today we were celebrating life.

We commandeered a booth at a sports bar in the back and were just lifting a glass (ginger ale currently, but I was reserving the right to something pink and coconutty when we hit the beach). My phone rang, and I took the call outside the bar (the Yanks were beating the pants off the Diamondbacks, and the crowd noise was loud and proud).

"It's Harvey."

"Yes?"

"Where are you?" he asked.

"LaGuardia," I said, trying to be heard over a bad strike call.

"I need to talk to you."

"Why?" I asked, watching the business travelers walk with digital precision and families with wayward kids who curved their way through the crowds.

"There you are," he said, and then I saw him. Right next to the shoeshine stand.

I clicked off my phone.

"How did you know where I was?"

He shrugged. "Leah."

My eyes widened at the one word and all the implications behind it. She was a better friend than I knew.

However, Leah didn't occupy my thoughts the way Harvey did. "What do you want?" I asked carefully.

He took a step toward me, his ambling stride so out of place in New York. "I've been thinking," he said slowly, and then stopped. While the world stopped turning, he ran a hand through his already rumpled hair, which made me love him even more.

I waited, holding my tongue, holding my hopes tightly in check.

"I took some shots the other day."

"And?" I said finally because the suspense was killing me.

"The chief said they were good. Some of my best." He took a visible breath. "I'm going back to the hard stuff. Rekindle some of the magic. I used to love my job."

And then he went silent.

I waited, but he didn't seem ready to say more. So yes, here we were, a life coach affirmation moment, but for once, it wasn't the life coach affirmation I wanted. I wanted something much more personal.

"That's very nice," I told him. "I'm glad you found your dreams."

"I don't want you to move to Delaware. I want you to stay in New York."

I took a step back.

"Don't run, Elle," he said, taking a step closer. "Stay."

I took another step back, running into the free-standing Budweiser sign that displayed the Yankees season schedule.

There he was, dangling my dreams—new and improved dreams—in front of me. I struggled to retain my hold on reality.

"Everything costs too much in this city. I'm tired of living on the edge. I need security, and I think Wilmington is the perfect place for me. I'm quitting. I'm going to work for Citibank."

He took my hand, and his own was rough and callused. I swear I heard my heart sigh. "You need to tell people what to do. Sometimes it doesn't work out, sometimes it does, but people need you, Elle."

"Everyone will be fine," I told him patiently, because I had to believe they were better off without me.

"I need you, Elle."

Oh.

I closed my eyes and counted to ten, because it was time for Elle to kick the habit. It didn't matter if people needed me, I thought to myself. It was a huge lie, and I knew it, but the first step in modifying behaviors is to state your desired state of being out loud.

"You don't need me, Harvey. You can't even call on a weekly basis. You like the idea of needing me, but you're in a good place in your life. Now's not the time for you to start over."

"No, but maybe I want to start over, and we're good together."

As soon as he said it, the words hit something deep and dark inside me. A primitive response that made me want to launch myself into his arms and forgive him for all the crap that he and everyone else had put me through.

We women are really whacked, yeah?

But this time, I was taking control. I was going to pull all the strings. I had my hand on the trigger, and it was time to squeeze.

I picked up my purse, dug through until I found what I was looking for. No more Ms. Nicey-Nice.

I pulled out the box and opened it, waving it like a Saturday night special, and I noticed a few people ducking in their seats.

"This is the Wahl 7-in-1, the most powerful electric vibrator in the world. Six and a half inches of pure clitoral stimulation and no head games involved. One hundred watts of pure orgasmic delight. It doesn't stand you up, it's always there when you need it, and best of all, it has seven handy attachments depending on your mood. Beats a man, hands down. You think you're going to get lucky, Harvey? Do you?"

I saw a cop coming toward me, but I didn't care. I was making a point, and this particular point was important. If Joan could do it, if even Tanja could do it, hell, if Barbara could do it, then so could I.

Harvey cracked a smile. I really wish he hadn't, because it made walking away that much harder. "I deserve that. I'm sorry."

I crossed my arms across my chest, Wahl well in hand. "For what?" I asked, because it was important that he understood how he had hurt me.

"I should have told Lindsey the truth. She's old enough, and I took the easy way out. I'm sorry."

"I can't stay in New York. I don't have a choice."

"Yeah, you do. You could move in with me. I wouldn't even charge you rent."

My fingers were losing the grip on my vibrator. I could feel Harvey snipping away at the umbilical cord that bound me to my toys. He made it sound so easy. So possible. "Big of you," was all I said, still not ready to walk over the line.

"Sometimes I can be sensitive. It doesn't happen very often, as you've figured out by now."

I didn't know what to say. I didn't quite trust him. To be perfectly frank, I wasn't ready to trust anybody yet, but Harvey made me think about it. Made me think about it hard.

He took the Wahl and tucked it into my purse. "You take your little friend on vacation. Bring it back. But I'm going to find you. I don't care if you're in Delaware. Don't care if you're in Timbuktu. This isn't over. Not by a long shot. You need someone to take care of you, Elle. You need someone to listen to your problems. You need someone to hold your head when you drink too much."

"I gave up alcohol," I said stubbornly.

"I can't give you up," he countered.

"I wear a size ten," I told him, because I was sure once he knew the down and dirty on Elle Shields, he wouldn't be so intrigued.

"I don't care," he said, with a light in those wise, gray eyes. Each time he gave me that look, oxygen was sucked out of my brain. I was getting lightheaded and dizzy, and we weren't even in the high altitudes yet.

"My senior year, I passed out on the toilet in Tiffany's bathroom. The door was unlocked. Pictures were taken. Now, this was long before the Internet age, so it's likely they aren't floating around in cyberspace." His thumb began a slow drag on my palm. Parts of me melted that hadn't melted in years. The human touch is a magical thing.

"Do you want me to beat her up for you?"

"You'd really beat a woman?"

"No, but I'd make sure she doesn't hurt you again."

"What about Lindsey?" I asked, moving from my scars to his baggage. This time I was leaving no stone unturned.

"She's fourteen. She'll grow to love you. Just like I did."

I gulped. "And Leah."

"She'll get over it. You can be her life coach. She needs new goals," he said.

"It won't be easy," I answered, because I thought he was being way too optimistic.

He shrugged. "I've had easy. It's overrated."

Then he kissed me. A slow, comfortable, rumpled kiss, and

right then, it didn't matter that I was a size ten with a father who was a (now poor) convict. It's amazing what a little love can do for you.

"I'll be here when you get back." Then he lifted my hand to his lips, pressed a kiss into the palm, and closed my fingers around it. My knees buckled.

"Think about it," he said, and walked away. The easy strides of a man who knew who he was and was okay with that.

I watched until he disappeared and then made it back to our table in the bar, slightly dazed and confused.

Barbara's mouth was working, so I knew she wanted to say something.

"Just spit it out," I told her.

"Can I see that?" she asked.

I brought out my vibrator, and we took a good ten minutes to examine the finer points of American craftsmanship.

For a woman who had once been mortified by passing out on a toilet with the door unlocked, this was a sweet victory indeed.

Tanja wasn't interested in vibrators. Ah, the young. That'd come in time. "You can't go to Delaware."

It was nice. All these people pleading with me to stay. It was how it was supposed to be. "I already gave up my apartment."

Joan waved a hand, her new rock from Felix gracing it nicely. "We can take care of that. The important thing is that you have to be here on July 17."

"Why?"

Barbara put down the vibrator. "We're scheduled to speak in

front of the New York Women's Society fund-raiser at the Met. I told Sheryl my story, and she told me I had to speak. You know I can't get up in front of all those people, so we're going to have to do it together. And then you're booked on *The View*."

"Why?"

"We have an interview scheduled. All of us," said Barbara, as if I was a moron.

"How did you do this?"

"I picked up the phone and dialed, silly. You know, life coaches are very hot right now. The producer told me that after the article in *Vanity Fair* . . ."

There was a buzz inside me, a thing I believe is called happiness. My life wasn't perfect; it never was going to be perfect. But I've got perspective now, I've got my friends, I've got Harvey, and best of all, I've got me.

Up Close and Personal With the Author

DOES YOUR MOTHER KNOW THAT YOU'VE WRITTEN A BOOK ABOUT VIBRATORS?

No. My mother thinks Mr. Goodbunny is a heartwarming story about a woman's search for a long-lost stuffed toy. I'd like to keep it that way, so please don't tell her.

DO YOU ACTUALLY KNOW SOMEONE WHO BURIED THEIR VIBRATOR?

Heh-heh-heh. For six-figures, I might consider talking. Rumor has it it's buried in a vacant lot in Queens, right next to Jimmy Hoffa.

THE GROUP DYNAMIC WAS RATHER INTERESTING. HAVE YOU EVER BEEN INVOLVED IN GROUP THERAPY?

No, but I have a group of good friends, which for me has functioned the same way.

DO YOU THINK THAT FORTY-TWO YEARS OLD IS TOO OLD TO START OVER?

God, I hope not.

DO YOU THINK ELLE IS DESTINED FOR SUCCESS?

I think Elle is destined for survival, which in many ways is much sweeter.

IS IT EVER TOO LATE TO CHASE YOUR DREAMS?

No, if you look at the people who have started achieving success late in life, and I mean, *really* late in life, you can see that whether you're twenty, forty-two, or seventy, it's never too late to try.

DO YOU HAVE DREAMS OF YOUR OWN?

My dreams are just like clouds. They change, they evolve, they poof away, but then they reappear, sometimes bigger, sometimes smaller, and sometimes completely different. Dreams are very important.

DID YOU ACTUALLY RESEARCH THE LIFE COACH BUSINESS?

Yes. I talked to a very nice life coach named Carla Birnberg, who was much more of a professional than Elle, and I read a ton of life coaching, self-improvement books. The books didn't propel the story much, but I did fix a lot of problems that had been nagging me in my own life. Amazing, that.

LIKE WHAT?

My favorite technique is to take an hour, sit down, and make a list of all the little undone tasks that annoy you when you notice them. These are usually the small things, the "Gee, I need to buy another sauce pan because that handle is about to fall off," or "Gosh, the tile under the sink looks like a bacterial fungus; I should clean that before someone dies." Once you make your list, you take an entire day (the next day is usually best) and you go through it. One by one, you check off the list everyday annoyances. When I was done, I realized they were all relatively easy. After that, I began to notice when I passed something that annoyed me, and rather than put it on the mental to-do list, I simply stopped whatever I was doing and tackled it right then and there. I'm much happier, my house is much cleaner, but I'm behind on a deadline. Oh, well.

Want it ALL?

Want to **read books about stuff *you* care about**?
Want to **meet authors**?
Heck, want to write stuff you care about,
want to *be* **an author**?

Want to **dish the dirt**? Sound off? Spread love?
Punk your boss? Out your mate?

Want to **know what's hot**? Want to *be* **what's hot**?
Want **free stuff**?
Want to do it **all at once, all in one place**?

18-34 year olds, there's only one stop… one spot.

SimonSaysTheSPOT.com

Visit us at http://www.simonsaysTheSPOT.com